289 Friends

JO CLYNES

First published in January 2025 by Amazon KDP Print Edition

Copyright © Jo Clynes 2025

The moral right of Jo Clynes to be identified as the author of this work has been asserted in accordance with the Copyright, Designs and Patents Act of 1988.

This book is a work of fiction. All characters and events in this publication, other than those clearly in the public domain, or historical fact, are fictitious. Any resemblance to real people, living or dead, is purely coincidental, or used fictitiously, unless permitted by the relevant person. No identification with actual persons, places, buildings or products is intended or should be inferred.

All rights reserved. No part of this publication may be reproduced, distributed, stored in a retrieval system, or transmitted in any form or by any means, without the prior written permission of the copyright owner and publisher. For permission requests, please contact the author.

ISBN 9798304117968

Cover by Victoria Heath Silk
Images © Shutterstock
Typeset by BB eBooks

www.joclynes.com

For Charlie

xx

Chapter 1

Christmas Eve, 2017

Tilly Jenkins had 289 friends. She knew this because her phone had told her so that very morning, along with the fact that she'd been a member of Facebook for exactly 10 years and had posted 326 times. She wondered if that was more or less than most people, and then instantly felt cross that she was comparing herself to the findings of a computer algorithm that knew nothing about her at all, really.

She leant towards the large tub of Quality Street on the sofa next to her, and rummaged amongst the shiny plastic wrappers, making them squeak as they jostled against each other. Selecting a strawberry cream, she gently pulled the ends apart so that the wrapper opened, and the contents revealed themselves. The scent of synthetic but strangely enticing strawberry wafted towards her, and she felt her mouth water before she stopped staring at the slightly nobbled top of the milk chocolate and just ate it instead.

Tilly was sure they'd got smaller over the years. Not just the tins, which had morphed into ugly plastic tubs, but the sweets themselves. And she also wondered why there were so many toffee fingers, which always ended up in the bin by January.

Flicking through the TV channels, Tilly channel hopped past the usual Christmas Eve re-runs of films she'd already seen or comedies that she didn't particularly like, and the evening stretched ahead of her like a slow-motion countdown to enforced global joviality. Leaning forward to slide her mobile phone off the coffee table, she tapped the familiar blue logo of her most frequently visited app and scrolled through the recent posts of her friends. Picture after picture of happy smiley people filled the screen. Huge Christmas trees sat proudly above piles of neatly wrapped presents. Shiny festive greetings wished her "seasonal joy" from perfect families, each one bigger, better, glossier than the last. Photo after photo boasted of limitless decadence. My God, didn't these people have anything better to do?

She clicked on one of her friend's posts. A woman she knew who was run off her feet with a full-time job, two kids, three dogs, and a caffeine addiction. Tilly thought that if she spent as much time with her poor children as she did editing, cropping and posting photos on Facebook, they might all be a bit happier. A picture of raised

Champagne glasses filled the screen, and she wondered what was so desperately important that it justified having to be announced on Facebook so urgently.

"Quick, take a photo before we drink our Champagne!"

She flicked the cover shut and tossed her phone back onto the coffee table. It annoyed her so much, this relentless pursuit of the perfect image. When did everyone get so competitive? Uncurling her legs from under her, she stood up stiffly from the sofa and walked through to the kitchen. Food. That was what she needed. Opening the fridge door, she perused the contents of the shelves before shutting it again and pulling a family bag of Kettle Chips out of the cupboard instead.

Tilly returned to the sitting room with a bowl of crisps and a large glass of red wine, and scrolled through the saved films on the TV. There it was. Top Gun. Her default feel-good movie. If she had to guess, Tilly thought she must have watched it about forty times, but it never lost its appeal. The delectable Tom Cruise, endless LA sunshine, and a stirring soundtrack whisked her away from her dull life in Kent every time.

Settling back into a cosy corner of the sofa, she pulled her favourite pink throw from the armrest and tucked it over her legs.

"Oh my God, you're such an old lady," she said

aloud, and then laughed at the sheer fact that she was talking to herself. That was one of the things she loved about being single. You could watch trashy '80s films over and over again without anyone moaning, and have crisps, wine and chocolate for dinner as often as you liked. And talk to yourself, even if you were only 37 years old.

By the time the credits rolled Tilly had finished the whole bag of crisps, most of the wine, and another eight chocolates. She turned the television off and glanced at the clock, counting backwards to work out what time it was in Florida. Two hours of American accents and sandy beaches had made Tilly think about phoning her parents. Gloria and Bob Jenkins had emigrated a few years previously, figuring that now both their daughters were in their thirties they had done their job as parents, and could head off and have some fun of their own. One daughter was married, the other had a good career, and both had bought nice houses thanks to healthy deposits from the bank of Mum and Dad. So with parental duties completed, they had sold the family home, bought a villa in a fabulous complex on the Gulf Coast of Florida, and to Tilly's complete surprise, had literally just upped and gone.

Her mother's parting shot had been to warn Tilly that if she didn't meet someone soon, she'd end up a lonely old spinster, and her words of advice had cut Tilly to the core. Was that all her mother thought about? That her life was incomplete until she got married and had a baby or two? But as the years had gone by, and all of Tilly's friends had done exactly that, she began to wonder if maybe her mother had been right after all. She looked sideways at the empty sofa and wondered why she didn't have a boyfriend sitting there, sharing her Christmas Eve with her. Where was he, her Mr Right?

It wasn't that she chose NOT to have a boyfriend, she just hadn't met anyone that she liked since she'd broken up with Ethan seven years ago. Never met anyone full stop really, other than the girls she knew from school and her colleagues at work. A neighbour who waved from across the street, and the man who checked her ticket at the train station every weekday morning didn't exactly count as potential dating material.

And of course her sister had done everything the right way round. Perfect Mimi had married a man she'd met at university, had a couple of kids, and now lived in a gorgeous house on a tree lined street in Berkshire, with no need to work thanks to her "something in IT" husband. She had a fancy gym membership, a cleaner who came in twice a week, and a very nice car that was replaced every few years. It was alright for some. Tilly had been glad when her mother had gone to Florida if for no other reason than the reduction in the number of times she'd have to listen to the line "Why can't you be more like your sister?"

Maybe she wouldn't phone her parents after all. She didn't want to listen to yet another lecture about why she *still* wasn't married, and she'd almost certainly talk to them the following day anyway from her sister's house. Mimi always made sure the children phoned their grandparents on Christmas Day to say thank you for their presents, whilst Tilly hovered nervously in the background waiting for her turn to speak. It made her feel like a child again, the phone being passed around quickly, her father's voice echoing down the line half-jokingly reprimanding her for chatting for so long.

"It is SO expensive for you to phone America darling, and anyway we're meeting friends shortly so we really must dash!"

That seemed to be their normal day to day life now, and they absolutely loved it. Their villa was on a large golf complex with a clubhouse, spa, and several restaurants, and by all accounts their lives were now simply some sort of never ending party. Every day there was a round of golf with the boys, a girls' lunch or sunset drinks – Tilly knew her parents were living the dream. They loved the endless sunshine, and her Mum enjoyed dressing to impress for the numerous social functions; Gloria was the life and soul of the party, and *"Baaaarb"* (as the locals called him) frequently entertained everyone with tales from his Met Police career. The Americans loved hearing his stories, even though the English cops weren't a patch on the rather intimidating American ones Tilly had seen when she'd once flown over for a visit.

Gathering the evidence of her evening's snacking, she shoved her phone in the back pocket of her jeans, turned the sitting room light off with her elbow and walked through to the kitchen. Sighing, she dropped the rubbish into the bin and put her wine-stained glass in the sink. It was probably still too early to go to bed, and she wished she had a handsome boyfriend to chase her up the stairs as an excuse to have an early night. Filling a glass with water, she took it with her as she unlocked the door to the garden and stood on the back step. Her phone pinged. Pulling it out of her pocket, Tilly swiped the screen open. It was a message from her sister, finally replying to a text she'd sent hours ago.

Hey Tills, sorry, only just seen this. What are you doing in on xmas eve? Thought you'd be living it up at some party! Honestly, you really should get out there and have some fun. Life's too short you know… Love you, see you tmrw xx

Laughter drifted through the cold air from someone else's garden. Tilly shut her phone and looked up at the sky. Her sister was right, she should be out. Why wasn't she out? Why did no one invite her to their Christmas Eve gathering? She never went out anymore it seemed, never got invited to parties. Smug marrieds in their thirties only invited other couples round, not lonely singletons who they thought would have plans already, or might actually come along and flirt with their husbands. It was ages since she'd even been to a dinner party, let alone had one. Maybe if she had a boyfriend she might be more inclined to invite people round, but it wasn't much fun doing everything yourself and watching couples all night before waving them off, clearing up and going to bed on your own. Again.

Oh well, maybe next year, she thought, as she went back into the relative warmth of the kitchen and rummaged unsuccessfully in the tub of Quality Street for another strawberry cream.

AS SHE CLIMBED under the duvet later that night, Tilly thought about the last time she'd hung a stocking on the end of the bed on Christmas Eve. She'd actually hung two, one for her and one for Ethan. A stash of small festively wrapped gifts had been under the bed, ready to be stuffed into the large red socks at some point during the night. Unbeknown to her, he had done the same, and Christmas morning in their bed had been a happy mess of colour as they'd peeled away the paper and laughed their heads off at the number of times they'd bought each other almost identical items. They were so similar, and she'd just presumed they'd be together forever. Which is why him leaving so suddenly had hurt so much.

Tilly turned out the light and squished her head into the pillow. That was a long time ago, she thought. Too long. Maybe next year would be different. Maybe 2018 would be her year. An article she'd read in one of the Sunday supplements sprang to mind, about three women who had started the previous year determined to turn their lives around. They'd all done it. One had started her own business, another had written a book, and the third had adopted a baby. The thing they all had in common was that they had made these things happen *themselves*. They had decided what it was that they wanted, gone out, and got it. It made her think, what did she want? Tilly chewed her bottom lip in the darkness and tried to sum up the whole of her disappointment in a few bullet points.

She wanted to be popular. She wanted a boyfriend who loved her. And she wanted a house full of people. Her eyes sprung open, the faint glow of streetlights illuminating the outline of her bedroom furniture. That was it, that's what she'd do. She would have her own party! Sitting up quickly and turning the bedside light on again, Tilly reached for her phone and swiped the screen open. Who could she invite?

Opening the Facebook app she scrolled through her list of friends. In alphabetical order, they were a right old mixed bunch. School friends, work colleagues, a couple of neighbours she'd befriended during the infamous wheelie bin saga, even her hairdresser was on there. As she ran through the list of names it dawned on her how many of them didn't even know each other. But they were all *her* friends, weren't they?

A thought came into her mind like a bulb lighting up. What if she just invited all of them? Every single one of her 289 Facebook friends? How many of them would come?

Some of them didn't even live in the country anymore, so of course not everybody would, but she was pretty sure she'd get a decent number of people. She felt a bit sick as she imagined every single one of them all turning up and the house being trashed, but instantly quashed the thought. They were her friends, weren't they? They wouldn't do that. And anyway, she could do an RSVP so she knew exactly how many people would come. Tilly fizzed with excitement, her mind filling with all the things she'd need to think about. Wine, beer, glassware. Invites, nibbles, music. The more she thought, the more she realised how much there was to do. This would definitely justify a new notebook.

As soon as Christmas was over she'd do it. Start making her plan for a new life in 2018. For a sociable Tilly. For a boyfriend. And for the best party anyone had ever been to.

Chapter 2
Christmas Day

THERE MAY NOT have been a bulging stocking at the end of her bed the following morning, but Tilly's head was overflowing with plans and ideas when she woke up on Christmas Day. She had slept soundly, and when she reached for the alarm clock, Tilly was surprised to see that it was almost half past eight. Her body clock was so used to waking up at six in the morning, five days a week, in order to catch the train into London for work, and it was frustrating when she woke up at silly o'clock at the weekend too, so this morning's lie in was a bonus.

Rolling onto her back, Tilly smiled to herself as she remembered the decision she'd made the previous evening. Planning one event, albeit a pretty big one, was only one element of the new Tilly. The old her would've woken up and instantly changed her mind, but not now. 2017 was on its way out, and the looming arrival of the New Year was inspiring her to shake things up.

There were some elements of her life she had no

intention of changing, like where she lived or how she earnt a living. Tilly loved her home. It was a nice house, on a good street, in a popular Kent market town, or so the estate agent had told her anyway. It had turned out to be a good investment, but more importantly, Tilly was really happy living there. She had decorated it simply, with pale walls and cosy furnishings. The kitchen and bathrooms were clean and modern, and her neighbours were polite and well behaved.

She also loved her job. Mortgages might not be the most exciting thing in the world for some people, but Tilly had been promoted up through the ranks over the years, and she now held a relatively senior position in the company. She loved the methodical nature of her work, and now had the added bonus of managing a large team of administrators and brokers, which she didn't get paid too badly for either.

But the main thing that was lacking from Tilly's world was a social life. Her commute meant that she didn't get home from work until almost eight o'clock in the evening, by which time she was generally exhausted. She subsequently spent most evenings on the sofa in her pyjamas with a bowl of pasta and East Enders or Holby City for company, before laying her clothes out for the next day and falling into bed. At the weekend she bought food, cleaned the house, and wondered why she'd bought a house with three bathrooms when she was the only person who lived there. She drank half a bottle of wine on Friday night, the other half on Saturday, and before she knew it, it was Monday again and the whole thing started over once more.

If she was honest, Tilly didn't *really* mind the monotony of her weekly routine. Sometimes she would go to her sister's for Sunday lunch and a change of scenery. Occasionally she'd go and stay with one of her old school friends on a Saturday night and immerse herself in familiar faces and their busy family lives. But when she returned home to her silent empty house, Tilly often wondered why *she* didn't have a husband, kids, a house full of happy noise too. She was in her mid-thirties, wasn't she supposed to be a grown-up by now?

But things were going to change. Excitement tingled under her skin as she thought about the next steps. As soon as Christmas was over she was going to make a plan of action. An actual list of all the things she could do that might kick start her boring life. She could join a gym, which was something she often thought about but invariably couldn't be bothered with. Or join a sailing club, she'd always fancied having a go in one of those little training boats. Surely that would be a great way to meet people. Or maybe she could even follow her parents' lead and learn to play golf. Her mother was one of the most sociable people she knew so there must be something in it.

And if she was really brave, she might even think about joining a dating site. However you did that, these days.

Pushing back the duvet and climbing out of bed, Tilly unhooked her dressing gown from the back of the bedroom door and went downstairs to make a cup of tea. Whilst the kettle boiled she picked up her phone for a quick glance at Facebook, to see what exciting things people were up to. Posts showing piles of presents seemed to be the main theme that morning, each one battling to be the biggest and best. Scrolling through the images made Tilly feel a bit sick at the scale of lavishness. How did any child need that many presents? It was never like that when she was little. Pouring boiling water into a mug, she left the tea to brew whilst continuing to scroll. One of her friends appeared to have actually colour-coded her entire wrapping, and Tilly wondered if she'd had to secretly remove anything from the piles under the tree that hadn't matched her perfect arrangement. It made Tilly's own artificial Christmas tree look a bit pathetic – she definitely wouldn't be posting a picture of *that* online today. Realising that her tea was now beginning to stew, and that she was standing staring at things that weren't benefitting her in any way whatsoever, Tilly fished out the teabag, added a splash of milk, and quickly typed a text message to her sister wishing her a Happy Christmas and confirming that she'd be with her by midday.

As she walked from room to room with her mug of tea, opening the curtains as she went, Tilly realised that she genuinely meant for this life change to happen. Something in her had shifted, and deep down in the pit of her stomach she knew that she had crossed a line. She was fed up of looking at other people's perfect lives, their full diaries captured by social media for all to see, yet simultaneously letting her own life just drift along without very much excitement at all.

Talking of which, time was drifting along pretty quickly that morning, and although she had been organised and already wrapped all the presents and placed them in named gift bags, *and* packed her overnight bag, she still needed a shower and something to eat before heading off around the M25 to her sister's house. Time to start moving and stop day dreaming. Start how she meant to go on.

"AUNTIE TILLY! AUNTIE Tilly's here!" a chorus of small voices called through the front door excitedly.

Tilly smiled. She loved how much her niece and nephew adored her. Pure unbridled love, no expectation and no judgement. The door opened and they bundled into her, almost knocking her flying, packages and all.

"Hey kiddies! Happy Christmas my little munchkins," she smiled, as she wrapped her arms around them and planted a kiss on the top of each one's head.

Mimi laughed behind them. "Come on you two, let your Auntie in out of the cold. It's freezing out there."

They jostled in through the door, and Tilly embraced her sister, pleased to be finally out of the car.

"How was the journey?"

"Hideous. I thought the roads would be empty, I mean who drives on Christmas Day?"

Mimi chuckled. "You said that last year! Anyway, you're here now, put your bag in the spare room and I'll get you a cup of tea." She glanced at her watch. "Or a glass of Champagne?"

"Oooh yes please," Tilly nodded. "Champagne would be lovely. It is Christmas!"

"Do you want me to help you Auntie Tilly?" asked a small voice.

"Oh yes please Oscar, why don't you take the presents and put them under the Christmas tree for me, and I'll be back in a minute and you can tell me all about what Father Christmas got you."

Tilly took her overnight bag up the stairs and plonked it on the bed in the spare room. Her sister had made it look so beautiful, with a small Christmas tree in the corner of the room, a garland above the bed, and a soft tartan blanket covering the red checked bedding. As she walked back across the hallway Tilly spotted her brother-in-law, Andrew, in the master bedroom. He was standing at the end of the bed, half turned away from the door, phone in hand, typing something with his thumbs.

"Merry Christmas, Andrew!" she called through the half open door. He turned quickly, slipping the phone into his back pocket, and smiled broadly.

"Hey, I didn't see you there, Happy Christmas!" he said as he walked out into the hallway, leaning in and kissing her on the cheek. "How are you? Good journey?"

They walked down the stairs together and into the large sitting room, where Mimi was peeling the foil from the top of a bottle of Veuve Clicquot. Three glasses were on the square coffee table waiting to be filled, and Oscar and Rosie were loitering with intent by the large bowl of crisps next to them. The fire had been lit and the sound of Christmas music wafted in from the kitchen across the hall.

The cork popped out excitedly, and Mimi topped each glass to the brim before passing one to Tilly.

"Happy Christmas, my lovely sister," she smiled, chinking glasses before they both turned to Andrew and did the same.

"Me, me!" cried Rosie, raising her plastic beaker up towards the grown-ups, and they all turned and bent down and gently tapped each other's drinks until Tilly was taken away by her niece and nephew to see what Father Christmas had delivered down the chimney.

LATER THAT NIGHT, when Tilly had eaten more food than she could possibly have imagined, she made her way up the staircase to a very welcome bed. It had been such a wonderful day, full of laughter, gifts, and games. They had all stopped what they were doing at three o'clock and watched the Queen make her Christmas Day speech, and then stood to attention for the National Anthem, just like Tilly's parents had made her and her sister do when they were little. Oscar had saluted at the end and marched like a little soldier out of the sitting room which had been adorable and made all of them melt with his cuteness.

After mugs of hot chocolate by the fire, Mimi and Tilly had carried the children up to bed and taken it in turns to tell each one a bedtime story. Tilly tucked Rosie's duvet around her and knelt on the carpet beside the bed. As she read carefully through the pages Rosie stared at her, eyes wide in the gentle glow of the bedside lamp.

"Auntie Tilly, will you have a baby one day? I think you would be a really lovely Mummy," she said quietly.

Tilly put the book down and looked at her niece.

"Yes, I think I probably will Rosie," she nodded. "And when I do I hope she is just as lovely as you are."

Rosie smiled and snuggled down deeper into her bed. "Can you finish the story now please?"

Tilly kissed her sleepy niece on the forehead and smoothed her hair. "Of course I will darling."

She opened the book where she had left off and continued to read. As she turned the page, she glanced down to see that the little girl's eyes were half closed already, and she lowered her voice until it was almost a whisper. When she was sure Rosie was fast asleep, she stood up slowly and turned out the bedside light, before pulling the door to and creeping back down the stairs.

Andrew was lolling on the sofa playing with his phone and Mimi was still upstairs with Oscar, so Tilly went into the kitchen to tidy up a bit. The dishwasher was on but there were an extraordinary number of glasses on the side that needed hand washing. How had three adults and two small children created so much mess? She filled the sink with hot water and bubbles and made a start, carefully washing each one before rinsing with hot water and placing it upside down on the draining board. Just as she was pulling the plug out Andrew walked into the kitchen.

"Oh Tills, don't worry about that, we'll do it later," he said. "Fancy some port and cheese?"

He opened the cupboard and pulled out a box of oatcakes. A selection of cheese was already breathing on a vast platter at the centre of the kitchen table, and as he emptied the packet into a basket Mimi appeared through the kitchen door.

"Both kids now finally asleep," she yawned. "Oh, look at you two, you've washed up and everything. What superstars!"

Tilly was far too diplomatic to point out that she'd actually done most of the work herself, and that all Andrew had done was open a box of crackers. She knew from conversations with her sister that he wasn't the most helpful person in the world when it came to keeping the house tidy, so she suspected that Mimi knew she'd done most of the tidying up anyway. Andrew very much considered housework a women's job. After all, he was out all day earning money, and the last thing he thought he should be doing when he got home from a long day in the office was more work. Tilly sometimes thought that Andrew had rather outdated views, but she would never have criticised her sister's husband out loud.

As she sunk back into the fat pillows Tilly wondered if she'd still be on her own in the spare room the following Christmas. She hoped not. She'd had a lovely day but she didn't want to be the lonely spinster Aunt forever. Rosie's comment had struck a chord with her – even a four-year-old had questioned why she didn't have any children. But then she remembered her plan. The Party. And all the other things she was going to do over the next 12 months. She hiccupped loudly and hoped that no-one had heard her. Maybe that third glass of port was not such a good idea after all.

Turning out the light, she tucked the duvet under her arm and snuggled down. Tomorrow was a new day, and the new year was only a week away. A Boxing Day walk with her sister, brother-in-law, and kids in the morning would blow the cobwebs away and set her up for the exciting things to come. She hiccupped again.

Turning the bedside light back on, Tilly looked around for her glass of water. Not seeing it anywhere in the room, she realised that she must have left it downstairs. Opening the bedroom door slowly so as to not make a noise, Tilly tip-toed down the stairs and into the kitchen. Spotting a large tumbler by the bread bin she went over to pick it up. As she did so a mobile phone on the charger gently vibrated and glowed as a text message was delivered. That was strange, so late at night. She found herself glancing at the screen, purely out of habit, even though the phone wasn't hers.

**P mob*
Night. Miss you x

Instantly reprimanding herself for being so nosy, Tilly took her water and headed upstairs. But as she shut the door and climbed back into bed she found that she was still wondering who would send a text message so late at night, who P was, and who's phone it even was. That was a bit weird. Wasn't it?

Telling herself to stop being so suspicious, Tilly snuggled down and closed her eyes, ready for sleep to take over. And as she did, she realised that her hiccups had finally gone.

Chapter 3

January 2018

THE NEW YEAR was always a busy time at work for Tilly. Things tended to grind to a halt over Christmas; lenders seemed to disappear into a land of tinsel and staff parties, and unless you chased individual cases yourself, nothing much got done. So by the time everyone was back at their desks at the start of the month there was a mountain of work piled up and everything was labelled URGENT.

Tilly relished times like this. She remembered being a newbie in the office, daunted by the mountain of folders in her in-tray that never seemed to get smaller. But now it seemed to supercharge her, set her off on a mission to work twice as hard and twice as fast. It didn't matter that she barely saw daylight, arriving at work when the sun had not yet risen high enough to make a difference, and leaving when it had long set. The tally on the office board would climb higher each day, new customers, completed mortgages, targets reached. Sometimes she wished she could put a camp bed under her desk just so that she didn't have to waste time commuting each day, but even she could see that that was possibly a bit sad.

Her first full week back in the office flew by and before she knew it she was on the packed Friday night train heading out of London with several hundred other weary thirty somethings. As the buildings receded and the sky opened up, Tilly looked at the faces of her fellow travellers, wondering where they were going, who was waiting for them. She imagined the girl opposite her arriving back home, pushing her key into the front door and turning it, a cheery "Hi honey, how was your day?" greeting her from the kitchen. Or maybe the man sitting across from her, walking back into a warm house, kids running to hug him and a waggy tailed dog in the background.

She missed that, someone to share the day with when she got home. Someone to make you a cup of tea or hand you a glass of wine on a Friday night. It was lonely going back to an empty house day after day, month after month. Her mind cast back to Ethan, remembering him cooking in the kitchen, radio blaring and pans covering every surface. She smiled at the memory. It used to make her mad, how much mess he created when he was cooking. Funny how you can suddenly miss something that used to irritate you so much.

THE SKY WAS grey when Tilly woke up on Saturday morning, but that didn't dampen her spirit a jot. Pulling on navy tracksuit bottoms and a baggy grey sweatshirt, she made herself a mug of tea and picked up a brand new notebook from her desk. Rummaging in the pen pot for her favourite biro, she pulled her diary from her bag and put everything on the kitchen table. Dropping the last two slices of bread into the toaster, she took butter and apricot jam from the fridge and stared at the toaster whilst she pondered on what to do first. When the toast popped she spread both with butter, one with jam, sliced them neatly into triangles and sat down at the table to make a plan whilst she ate.

"2018 To Do List" she wrote in firm letters at the top of page one.

1. Plan party. Pick date.
2. Send a save the date invite!
3. Join dating site.
4. Lose weight.
5. Go to after works drinks. At least once.
6. Sign up for golf lessons.
7. Visit sailing club.
8.

She couldn't think of an "8" so left it blank and turned to her new diary. Slowly flicking through the weeks, Tilly wondered when the best time of year would be for the party. Easter? No, that was family time. Spring? No. The pages fanned through her fingers as she skimmed past her birthday (too much pressure), Halloween (too much aggravation with fancy dress), and ended up at the last month of the year. December. Christmas. Tilly chewed her bottom lip. That was ages away. But it was a definite option. It would give her plenty of time to plan things, or back out, if she changed her mind. But it would also be a great time of year to hold a party – at least being in December she wouldn't have to plan for indoors or outdoors, it was always going to be inside. And she realised that there was something quite satisfying about holding it in, effectively, a year's time. What a difference a year could make. She'd have plenty of time to tick off all the other projects on her list, and who knows, she might even have a boyfriend by then to share it with, if things went the way she was hoping.

The Saturday before Christmas was December 22nd. Tilly wondered if she should hold her party the week before instead, leaving the "prime" night of the year free for other people's parties. Taking a bite of toast she sat up straighter as she chewed. No. Why should she? This was her party and she wanted it to be fabulous. And that meant it should absolutely be the weekend right before Christmas. Saturday 22nd December it was then.

Turning to a fresh page of her notebook, Tilly

moved on to start writing some ideas for the "Save The Date" post. It was harder than she thought. Some sounded too desperate, some just plain dull. She picked up her mobile and opened the Facebook app, looking for inspiration.

Beaming faces shone out at her from the news feed, eyes covered with reflective goggles and bodies padded with the latest skiwear. "Best ski *ever*!" one of her friends told her. Good to know.

She scrolled down, the constant stream of her friends' latest photos whizzing by. When they stopped, the screen landed on a pristine white sandy beach. "Back at our favourite New Year's escape," it bragged. "Life doesn't get much better than this!"

Yeah, thanks for that, thought Tilly, pulling her sleeves down over her wrists and wishing it was a bit warmer than it was.

She put the phone down, picked up her pen, and started to write.

> *SAVE THE DATE! OK, so I know it's only January, but I've set myself a New Year's resolution and I'm going to stick to it. I'm having a party, a big one, and I would like to invite every single one of my Facebook friends along! This is a personal invite though, so please don't forward it to anyone else! More details to follow nearer the time, but for now, just put Saturday 22nd December 2018 in your diary! Love, Tilly x*

She read it out aloud and in her head about sixteen times, making several alterations as she did, then picked up her phone and opened her profile page. Typing the message in carefully, she read it twice more to check for spelling mistakes, took a deep breath, and pressed POST.

Her phone pinged to inform her that the message had been posted, and she swiped the notification away and shut the cover. No point watching and waiting. She was sure she'd get a few messages in return, but a watched kettle never boiled so she left her phone on the table and went to find her trainers. She needed more bread, a newspaper, and a bit of fresh air.

WHEN SHE GOT back, Tilly dropped the bloomer into the bread bin, flicked the kettle on, and picked up her phone.

"Oh my God," she said aloud, as she saw the amount of notifications on the screen. It appeared that most of the people she knew were actually on Facebook that morning, because so many of them had liked or commented on her Save The Date post. She scrolled through the list of names.

Work colleagues old and new, school friends, a girl from her old riding stables, even the man who serviced her burglar alarm, had all responded.

How exciting! Can't wait!

Wow, go girl! I'll be there!

Not sure if you're mad or brave but count me in!

She had 89 likes from that post alone. In less than an hour.

Tilly suddenly felt a bit sick, wondering what on earth she had done and if it was too late to change her mind. Still scrolling through the replies, she shook her head at the incredible response. She hadn't expected anything like that. A couple of comments maybe, but certainly nothing like the tidal wave of excitement that was spilling out at her from her Facebook page.

Oh my God, what if all these people actually turn up at my house?

The landline rang shrilly, startling her out of her stupor. Tilly knew it would be her sister, as Mimi was the only person who ever called her on the landline.

"Helloooooo!" she answered, hoping it actually was her sister, not the doctor's surgery or something, who would then have thought that she was a bit loopy.

"Tilly Jenkins. I have just seen your post on Facebook. What on *earth* were you thinking, are you mad?" her sister chuckled.

"Oh don't," Tilly closed her eyes. "I actually feel a bit sick now, I had no idea that it would get such a ridiculous response. What am I going to do?!"

"Well either get planning or hope they all forget about it," laughed Mimi. "Honestly Tills, you do make me smile. When you said you wanted a better social life I thought you meant a few nights out at the pub, not inviting the whole flipping world round to your house for Christmas!"

Her phone pinged again from where she had left it on the kitchen table.

"Oh no, it's going again, that's probably another attendee! What have I done?!"

BY THE END of the weekend Tilly had almost 200 likes to her post. If it hadn't been for the fact that the date for the proposed party was over 11 months away she probably would have been running for the hills, but the vast distance made her feel slightly more secure, a giant buffer zone in which to come up with a get out clause should it be required. But equally, there was a small part of Tilly that actually felt quite chuffed with the reaction. Nearly 200 people wanted to come to her house and eat crisps with her. That could only be a good thing. And that was nearly 200 people who could lead her out of her monotonous life and into something potentially way more exciting.

Chapter 4
February

POINT 3 OF Tilly's To Do List (Join Dating Site) filled her with dread. She had never been on a dating app in her life. In fact her only experience of them so far was listening to the younger girls in the office laughing as they regaled tales of disastrous dates and photos of men with massive fish. Tilly didn't actually know if that was a euphemism or not, in fact she didn't know what was worse, men posing online with fish or men posing with, well, the alternative.

A brief search of "internet dating" opened her eyes to the almost unbelievable discovery of just how many different options there were. Not feeling inclined at this stage to commit financially, Tilly then tried "free dating sites" and discovered that the best, or at least the most popular, was an app that you simply downloaded to your phone, added a picture and a few words about who you were, and then simply swiped left or right depending on whether you liked the look of the person you saw or not. How complicated could that be?

Tilly downloaded the app and scrolled through the photos on her phone looking for something suitable to add to her profile. There were quite a few from Christmas, but none of them were right. Most pictures of Tilly had Oscar and Rosie in them too, or involved someone pulling a silly face in the background. In many of them she donned a green paper hat, and there was a particularly fetching one of her reclined on the sofa with her mouth hanging open, when she'd drifted off somewhere between the Queen's speech and the cheeseboard.

Eventually Tilly found a photograph she approved of, taken 18 months before in Florida. Her mother had insisted on taking "A nice picture of my lovely daughter," which she had then forwarded to Tilly, and although she'd hated being made to pose on the beach en-route to dinner at the time, she was most grateful to her mother today.

Adding the photo to her profile, she pondered on what to say in the comments section. What the hell did people write here? She'd already ticked the "interested in men" box so she couldn't see what other women had written, so she settled on playing it cool. Less is more and all that.

Hi, I'm Tilly, I am 37 and live in Kent.

Was that it? Would that do? Exasperated, she sighed loudly and wondered how much she was supposed to reveal at this point.

She back cursored and deleted what she had written.

Normal 30 something from Kent looking for similar.

Yep, that would be fine for now. She could always update it once she'd got the hang of things. Pressing enter, Tilly was relieved to see that she had done everything she had to and could now concentrate on looking at her potential matches, which instantly flooded the screen.

An over tanned face called Tom, 64, grinned at her from the screen.

64? He was almost as old as her father! She swiped it away, feeling a twinge of guilt that she had rejected him so brutally. Five minutes later however she realised that she was going to have to reject many, many more, and the guilt lessened somewhat.

Tristan, 18. Oh for God's sake, she was old enough to be his mother. The penny dropped as Tilly realised that she hadn't set the age filter properly, so she adjusted it to a suitable two years younger, five years older, and clicked on the "matches" page again.

A selection of men she definitely did not find attractive sprung on to her phone, one after another. Delete, delete, delete. And then Tariq, 39 popped into view.

Tilly stopped. She recognised something about him. Switching apps, she flicked over to her Facebook page. She was sure that he was one of her neighbours, the same one who had written to the council on her and the street's behalf after the whole wheelie bin saga. They'd swapped names somewhere along the line and he had sent her a friend request which she'd accepted and then promptly forgotten about. And who now would also have received the group invite to her party.

Scrolling through his profile page she realised how little she knew about him, despite having lived just across the road from each other for several years. There were various photographs of him with different family members, including several beautiful women who she presumed, in light of the dating app, were siblings rather than girlfriends. Or hoped, anyway. He really was actually rather good looking, and she wondered how on earth she hadn't noticed this before. Most times when she saw him he was either heading off for work or coming back from a run, and if there was any contact between them at all it had been just a nod or a quick wave, nothing more.

Tilly clicked on his personal information. According to Facebook he was a lawyer, had been with the same company for eight years, and had checked in at Oblix at The Shard, The Serras Hotel in Barcelona, and a Gordon Ramsay Cookery

Masterclass. Wow. She didn't even know you could do that.

His likes included a local running group, a Kent cheese producer, and some obscure French film that Tilly had never heard of, but was about to Google before suddenly realising that she was acting a little bit like a stalker.

Flicking back to the dating app she wondered if it was a bit weird to "like" someone who lived in your street. What if he liked her too and they went on a date and he was really boring? Or even worse, if she thought he was gorgeous and he found *her* really boring?!

Leaning back into the sofa Tilly perused the ceiling whilst she considered her options. God, she hated Artex.

Picking up her phone again she decided to take positive action and swipe YES before she changed her mind. If he didn't swipe her in return then he'd never know she had liked him in the first place, and if he did, well, who knows!

Her finger hovered over the screen very briefly before she quickly swiped his picture.

"Noooooooo…."

The wrong way.

"Shit." Staring at the screen she frantically tried to work out how to undo her last action.

Too late. Gone.

This option is only available to premium members, the

automatic message told her.

"Oh for fuck's sake," she said out loud, before throwing her phone onto the sofa and stomping out of the sitting room.

"Morning Tilly," said a voice behind her.

Tilly turned around in the queue and clocked the girl standing next to her, neat and tidy in a camel coat.

"Oh, morning Karen, how are you?"

"Fine thank you, tired, need a coffee to perk me up."

Tilly smiled. Karen had never struck her as the sort of person who needed caffeine to get her going in the morning. She was always so efficient. She was never late, looked immaculate every day of the week whatever the weather, and was frequently the last one to leave the office, conscientiously finishing up when everyone else had hot footed it to the tube or the wine bar down the road.

"Yes Miss, what can I get you?"

"Oooh, sorry, please can I have a skinny cappuccino, extra shot, no chocolate." She twisted her head around awkwardly. "Can I get you a coffee?"

"Oh no, thank you, I'm going to order my lunch too. Saves a bit of time later. But thanks anyway."

Tilly paid for her drink and loitered as Karen took her place at the front of the queue. It was warm in the little Italian café, and the delicious smell of pastries, coffee and almonds was making her tummy rumble. She glanced at the display of brioche and biscotti and wished she'd ordered something sweet to go with her coffee, before reminding herself that A, she'd already had breakfast, and B, she wanted to lose a few pounds anyway.

"OK, all done, let's go," said Karen, interrupting Tilly's thoughts of almond croissants dipped in hot chocolate.

The two girls walked side by side along the wide pavement of High Holborn, Karen's pristine heels clip clopping on the stone slabs.

"How was your weekend? Do anything nice?" asked Tilly, realising that she didn't know much about what was going on in the life of someone she sat eight feet away from most of the working week.

"Quiet, met a friend for lunch yesterday, just the usual, you know. How about you? What did you get up to?"

"Oh God, don't," she said, shaking her head. "For some ridiculous reason I decided to go on a dating app this weekend, and I've woken up to about 20 messages from highly unsuitable men this morning."

Karen turned to look at her, eyes wide. "You did not. Oh my goodness you're so brave! Are any of them any good?"

Tilly shook her head. "Nope. Not so far. Well, there was one, but I swiped him the wrong way."

"Oh dear," she laughed. "Well, maybe your perfect match just hasn't logged on yet."

"Yeah maybe. Honestly, where are all the nice men? Apparently, most people meet their other half at work, but just my luck, I work in an office where the only attractive men my age are either married or gay!"

She stopped talking, her cheeks reddening as she realised how rude that sounded. She hadn't meant it to be – she wasn't homophobic by any stretch of the imagination, but Tilly didn't know Karen well enough to be making such potentially outlandish statements, and certainly never meant to be offensive.

"I mean, well, just that there's no-one suitable at work really."

Karen nodded. "Well, there's a few good-uns in the office. A few lovely ones actually! And you never know, a new advisor could be waiting for the lift as we speak, and he could be your perfect man."

They turned the corner into Great Queen Street and Tilly breathed a sigh of relief. She was glad Karen hadn't taken her comments the wrong way, although she was now intrigued as to who her colleague classed as "lovely". As they approached the glass doors of the office one of the senior mortgage advisors overtook them on the pavement.

"Good morning, ladies. Here, let me get that for you."

They slowed as Alan pulled the heavy door open and waved them through into the warmth.

"Why thank you Sir," said Tilly.

"Good morning Alan," smiled Karen. She cocked her head. "See, I told you there were some gentlemen here."

Chapter 5

March

TILLY HAD DISCARDED most of the unsuitable men from the dating app early on, having quickly got over her feelings of guilt every time she deleted someone. She certainly wasn't brave enough to contact a man first, and if they messaged her with some overly forward comment or semi naked photo they'd go straight into the little black bin too. It did feel rather ruthless, but she figured that if there was someone nice out there, someone *right* for her, they'd contact her first, respond to her reply, and not be too keen or too absent.

Harsh maybe, but Tilly was approaching this online dating malarkey with the same way she approached anything serious in her life. Swiftly, efficiently, and methodically. She allowed herself to look at her messages on the train to and from work, and again after dinner, but no more frequently than that. She didn't want to end up glued to her phone like some lovesick teenager, wondering if "Chris, 38" had read her message yet.

Or at least this was the plan until she matched with "Steven, 35".

Handsome, tall, and with a thick head of hair, Steven looked like just the sort of man she'd imagined herself meeting. His profile said he was single (although surely that was a pre-requisite), never married, no kids, ran his own business and liked good food and fine wine.

Hiding her amusement over the expression "fine wine," Tilly replied to his message about three minutes after she received it. He looked so normal, which was a relief after the number of strange men in jogging bottoms she'd seen leaning against someone else's Lamborghini.

They'd ended up messaging each other all night, until Tilly had made her excuses and gone to bed with a smile on her face. The following morning she was chuffed to see notification of a new message from Steven, until she opened it whilst the kettle was boiling and discovered that he was asking if she'd like to go for a drink the following weekend.

Tilly gulped. Suddenly it all felt a bit real, venturing from the safety of the internet to the vulnerability of the big wide world. And pretty damn quickly too.

When she got to the train station she walked right to the end of the platform, pulled out her phone and clicked on her contacts list. Jemima or Becky? Both of her best friends would be able to advise her, but two decades of friendship had proved that they would have very different advice. The three of them were a perfect triangle, a balanced mix of reliability, naughtiness and wisdom.

Tapping on Becky's face, she waited as the phone rang. She knew Becky would be either waiting for, or on the morning train already, and when she answered with a whisper, Tilly knew it was the latter.

"Hey Tills, you OK? I'm on the train."

"Morning! I'm fine, I just need some advice, you got a minute?"

"Anytime my lovely, what can I do for you?"

Tilly filled her in on the dating app and current situation with "Steven, 35", aware that her friend's response might be somewhat guarded considering she was on the train. Jemima wouldn't have cared, she was so loud and would've positively rejoiced in entertaining the entire carriage with tales of her friend's love life, but Becky was a little more discreet.

"So what do think, should I say yes? Meet him for a drink?"

"Oh God, I dunno, it's so scary! I don't envy you." She sucked the air in between her teeth. "But yes, I think you probably should, because you'll have to take the plunge at some point, and he does sound nice."

Tilly nodded to herself. "Oh Bex, what am I

doing, why did I start this?"

"Because you're on your own, and that's how people date these days, and in a way it's no different to meeting someone in a bar and swapping numbers. Like we did in the olden days."

"I know, you're right."

"But listen, you need to give me all the details of where you're going and who he is, you can't just go off on your own and not tell anyone, OK?"

"I will, I promise, thank you my darling."

"Listen, I've got to go, I'll ring you tonight so we can talk properly, yeah?"

"Yep, cool speak later, bye babe."

Tilly ended the call and breathed in the cold frosty air. It was still dark and she looked down the platform at the familiar shapes of her regular commuters. Most were staring at their phones, their faces illuminated in the gloom by news sites, emails or Facebook.

God, when did we become so obsessed with technology? thought Tilly, as she stuffed her phone back into her bag and rummaged for her gloves. Everything was done online these days, even flipping dating. She preferred the old way, meeting people in real life, and she thought back to the first time she'd met Ethan, in a queue for the loo at a music festival. They were so young, carefree, drunk of course, but that had just made it easier for them to chat. They'd bumped into each other again later that day in the beer tent and Ethan had bought her a plastic pint of not very cold beer as the Stereophonics blew the audience away on a sweltering summer's evening.

By the time Coldplay had taken to the stage they had decided that they were soul mates, and the rest was, well, history.

A whoosh of air pulled Tilly from her memories as the 7.08am finally arrived, still very fast as it rushed past where Tilly was standing on the platform. She usually stood somewhere in the middle, near the café for warmth, so was pleasantly surprised when she boarded the end carriage to find that it wasn't completely full.

Tucking herself into a window seat, Tilly decided to seize the moment and retrieved her phone from the depths of her handbag, tapping out a reply before she changed her mind.

> *That would be nice, thank you, Saturday evening is good for me.*

THEY'D ARRANGED TO meet at a wine bar in Sevenoaks, which Steven had suggested and Tilly had been happy to go along with. It was a public place, only a 10 minute train journey away, and an area that she knew well. To be honest, Tilly was happy to meet in an adjacent town. Meeting in Tonbridge would have felt a bit too close for comfort. What if she'd bumped into someone she knew, or if he turned out to be a weirdo and followed her home? Nope, a quick hop on the train was fine for Tilly, close but not too close.

The night was bitterly cold but thankfully dry, so Tilly wrapped up in her super warm fake fur. Not only did it look pretty awesome, it also had a big inside pocket for her house key, phone and credit card, which meant that she didn't have to worry about attempting to find a coordinating bag. Plus what do you do with your bag if you sit at a bar? Hold it? Perch it on your knee? It was all just a bit too awkward – a coat with good pockets was so much easier.

She'd decided to wear her skinny black jeans and a shimmery batwing top, and checking herself in the full length mirror before she set off, Tilly was pleased with what she saw. Glam but not tarty, just confident and stylish. Her reflection totally betrayed the nerves that were beginning to swirl around in her tummy, and she wished she'd had a glass of wine whilst getting ready.

The train journey did nothing to ease her increasing panic. What if she didn't recognise him? She was a bit short sighted at the best of times but would never wear glasses on a first date, so now she had visions of walking into the wine bar and smiling at the wrong man. She pulled out her phone to check the screenshot of him she'd saved. Good, still the same as she remembered.

Tilly took a deep breath in through her nose to calm her down, and exhaled in the stuffy carriage. A group of girls, younger than her, were giggling together a few seats away, and she envied them their carefree laughter. Life was so much simpler when you were in your twenties. Everything was so much more optimistic, until you hit your thirties and it all started to get a bit serious.

The train slowed as it approached Sevenoaks, and Tilly stood up and swayed as the train banked around the bend. The girls looked up at her briefly before resuming their heated debate about whether Ryan was better looking than Oliver, and she wondered what she looked like to a 20 something year old. Glancing down at her shimmery top, the phrase "mutton dressed as lamb" crossed her mind, before the doors of the train opened and she stepped out into the cold night.

The wine bar was only a short walk from the station, and Tilly glanced at her watch. Quarter to seven. She was a bit early, and wondered if she should walk around a bit before she went in. No, that was silly, he might be there already, and anyway, even if he wasn't, she'd always quite liked the idea of perching at the bar and waiting for someone. The confident side of Tilly took charge and she made her way towards the warm lights of the wine bar.

As she pushed open the door, a babble of voices and friendly banter greeted her. A waiter glanced over and smiled, and she made her way towards the quieter bar area. Most of the other customers were sitting at tables in groups of two or four, there was no-one sitting alone, so unless he was in the toilet or had brought a friend, Steven wasn't here yet.

"Good evening Madam, what can I get you?" smiled a handsome young bartender, clearly well trained in making his customers feel at ease.

"Oh, I'm actually waiting for someone, is it OK if I sit here and have a look at the wine list?"

"Of course it is, here we go," he said, passing Tilly a small red embossed folder.

"Thank you," she replied, smiling politely and settling herself onto one of the high backed bar stools. She looked around the room before sliding her coat off and hooking it over the back of the chair, thankful that there were enough people in the bar to create a bit of ambience.

Once she'd read the wine list cover to cover, and decided what she was going to drink, Tilly pulled out her phone in case there was anything from Steven. There were no messages so she decided to send him a brief text.

Hi, I'm here, perched at the bar! No rush, just thought I'd let you know :)

She set her phone down on the counter and

flicked open the wine list again before it pinged quietly, and she picked it up.

Sorry, slow train, be there in about 10 mins!

Tilly sighed. Oh well, she might as well order a drink. Catching the barman's eye, she ordered a glass of Rioja and put her phone away whilst he poured it.

"There we are Madam, one glass of Rioja." He slid it across to her. "Would you like to start a tab?"

"Er, yes OK, do you need a card now?" she asked. Typical. First date money awkwardness and her date wasn't even here yet.

"No, no need, you don't look like the sort of person who'd leave without paying," he smiled, winking at her.

Tilly took a sip of wine and looked around. She was perfectly positioned to see the door when it opened, and felt relieved at the sense of control her being early had given her.

Shit. She'd totally forgotten to text Becky, who'd insisted she let her know when she arrived, and when she left the bar. Her heart rate increased and she pulled her phone back out, hoping to get the text sent before Steven arrived.

She was just sliding it back into her coat pocket when the door clicked open and a group of three men walked in. Not him then. She turned back to her drink and was just taking another sip when she heard her name.

"Tilly?"

Jerking her head around as she quickly swallowed her mouthful of wine was never going to be the cool first impression she'd envisaged, and she coughed loudly into the back of her hand as Steven stood smiling at her.

"Oh my God, I'm so sorry, I didn't see you," she laughed, blushing deeply as she tried to compose herself.

"No no, it was my fault, I shouldn't have startled you." He stood up straight and pulled his shoulders back. "Steven Coldwell. Pleased to meet you," he said firmly, thrusting his hand out to shake hers. "And I hope you can accept my sincere apologies for being so late. Not the first impression I was hoping to make!"

Tilly shook his hand and gestured to the empty bar stool next to her, thankful that her coughing had finally stopped.

"Oooh I see you've got a drink already, my sort of girl!" he continued in his rather plummy voice. "What are you drinking? No, hold on, let me guess. Merlot?"

Blimey, this man can talk, thought Tilly. No need to worry about awkward silences, she'd be lucky to get a word in edgeways at this rate. And also, actually, how rude. She'd only ordered a drink because he was late.

"No, Rioja actually, it's….."

"Oh, Rioja," he said, pronouncing the J with a guttural roll from the back of his throat. "A superb wine. Excellent choice Tilly. Now let me see. What other decent wines do they have on this list then?"

He picked up the menu and scanned the reds.

"Ah ha. A cheeky little Malbec. That'll do." He signalled to the barman and ordered, before turning back to Tilly and continuing.

"Now did you know, and this is a rarely known fact, that Malbec is not actually from Argentina like everyone thinks. Nope, it's actually from…. you'll be surprised…. Ta da….France!" he announced with a flourish, before educating Tilly about how viticulturists (she hadn't even known that was a word) took a Malbec vine to Argentina in the 1800s in the hope that the weather would improve the grapes.

Tilly listened to Steven talk. And talk. The man clearly loved the sound of his own voice, and although he was entertaining, after a while it definitely began to feel like a bit of a one way date.

By the second glass of wine Tilly had discovered that Steven bought and sold rare vintage wines via an online platform, which didn't really sound like a proper job at all. And by the time they'd ordered a third glass (Steven had insisted on one more round, despite Tilly having contemplated wrapping up the evening after the second), she was discovering that maybe he wasn't quite the independent business owner she'd initially been led to believe.

"So Tilly, Tonbridge, what's that like then? Do you rent or did you buy? I hear it's a pretty nice part of the woods, if you like that sort of thing. It's a commuter town isn't it?"

Trying to ignore the slight slur that Tilly hoped wasn't meant to be as rude as it had sounded, she started to answer the first of his several questions.

"Yes, I bought a house there a few years ago, it's...."

"Oh you *bought*, well done Tilly! Wow, a little homeowner. Good girl!"

Tilly winced at his patronising comment.

"How about you, where abouts in South London are you?"

"Well Tilly, I'm in between things right now. I'm concentrating on the business side of life so I'm at my folks at the mo in Pett's Wood. *Goooorgeous* house though and masses of space so we just rattle around together," he laughed. "Plus Mummy's a marvellous cook and an absolute saint when it comes to laundry and so on, so really, what's not to like! Means I can concentrate on the business and when the right place comes on the market I'll make a move."

"So have you recently sold somewhere then?"

"Well you see Tilly, it's all about being in the

right place at the right time. The market can't really keep going in the direction that it is, so I'm just biding my time for the mo and I'm ready to swoop in there when the market crashes. Which it will, believe me!"

Tilly had met people like Steven before. She wasn't born yesterday and could quite clearly spot a chancer when she met one. It definitely took a certain type of person to answer a question without actually managing to answer it. Her initial optimism had by now given way to her inner voice, which was shouting at her to see the light and let Steven prance back to his Mummy's house before bedtime.

"Can I get you anything else?" asked the barman, glancing at Tilly with a knowing look in his eye.

"No actually, I really must be going, I've got an early start tomorrow," she lied, pushing up her sleeve to look at her watch. It was only half past nine, and she hoped he didn't enquire as to what she had to get up for so early on a Sunday. "Could we just get the bill please?" she asked.

The barman nodded, and turned away to the till.

"I'm just going to pop to the little boy's room," announced Steven, before sliding off his stool and walking confidently to the customer toilets.

Oh my God. Was he actually trying to get out of

paying the bill? Clearly she wasn't the only one who thought that, for the barman raised his eyebrows as he slid the padded folder across the bar.

"I'll wait til he comes back," he nodded, noting that at least he'd left his jacket on the chair so almost certainly *was* coming back.

After what felt like a very long time indeed, Steven walked slowly back to the bar and looked from the bill to Tilly.

"So…. you treating me tonight then Tilly?" he guffawed, completely oblivious to the expression on her face. "You modern women, love a bit of equality don't you!"

The barman returned. "So, are we splitting this or are you treating the lady, Sir?"

Despite the young man's very clever intervention, Tilly had no plans to see Steven again any time soon, so she took her credit card out of her phone case.

"No, half and half is fine," she said, watching Steven pull a few crumpled 10 pound notes out of his pocket. The barman stood patiently as Steven counted out the exact number of pound coins extracted from the other pocket, before thanking them both and smiling sympathetically at Tilly.

"You guys have a great evening," he said, as they made their way towards the door.

OUTSIDE, THE NIGHT air had got even colder, and Tilly pulled her coat tightly around her. A slight mist had begun to descend and despite Steven's rather obnoxious nature, Tilly didn't consider him a threat in the slightest, and was actually quite grateful of the company for the short walk to the train station. There were a few people around regardless of the freezing weather, and in a weird way Tilly enjoyed the thought that to a stranger, she just looked like another normal girl out with her boyfriend. Even though she had absolutely no intention of him being her boyfriend. Ever.

Steven talked all the way to the station, about business opportunities coming his way despite the disastrous Brexit ruling, and Tilly simply nodded and "mmmm-d" in the right places. Before she knew it they were there, and to her absolute joy the tannoy was announcing the northbound train arriving on the opposite side of the track in two minutes time.

"Ooh that's me, I'd better dash, don't want to miss my train. It's been a joy meeting you Tilly, let's do it again. I'll text you!" he gushed.

Steven leant forward and air kissed the right hand side of her face, before pulling up the collar of his coat and walking briskly in the opposite direction, hands plunged into his pockets, and whistling loudly to himself.

Tilly took a deep breath and turned in the opposite direction, her exhalation creating a small cloud in the cold air. He was exhausting! She was surprised he'd even managed to get through three glasses of wine; his mouth had barely stopped talking long enough to breathe let alone drink.

She pulled her phone out and leant against the wall as she waited for her train. There was a message from Bex.

How's it going?! xx

She quickly typed out a reply, her fingers cold and keen to return to her coat pockets.

Just left. OMG he did not stop talking! Think I can safely say I won't be seeing him again though. Call you tomorrow xx

When the train arrived Tilly slid into a window seat far from the door, grateful that at least the train company had the heating set to a decent level. Leaning her head against the window, she sighed as she wondered if she'd ever meet anyone normal. Her previous correspondence with Steven had seemed so promising, and yet here she was, heading home early after a disappointing date.

The worst thing about it was that on paper, Steven had seemed like the best out there. Handsome, normal, single, businessman. To be fair, he hadn't written anything that wasn't true, it was just that her perception of the whole story had been somewhat different to the reality.

A bit like all social media, she thought. People post the image that they want to portray, not the whole truth and nothing but the truth. How was that even allowed? Rarely were the gritty undesirable aspects posted, except when they were there to draw attention to some cause or other. No-one was interested in the day to day boring bits. Imagine if Steven had written the truth under his profile pic.

> *"Loud, confident freeloader seeks attractive lady to pay the bill. Live with my parents and have no guaranteed income. Never run out of things to say. Apply here."*

Dating apps were just as bad as social media, she thought. So fake. So disappointing.

As Tilly walked along the pavement back home, a very light drizzle began to fall. Great, now her hair was going to go frizzy too. Oh well, at least it was the end of the evening not the start. A car slowed down somewhere behind her, and she glanced over her shoulder nervously. The foggy night was making her feel more vulnerable than she normally did, and she was relieved when she saw the car pulling into a space and parking a couple of houses further along on the other side of the road. It was obviously a resident, no-one to worry about.

As she reached her house, the driver climbed out

of the car and turned to look in her direction. Tilly squinted a bit until she realised that the man raising his arm to wave at her was Tariq, and she quickly waved back as she pushed open the little gate in front of her house. Turning the key to open the front door she mentally kicked herself for not saying hello, then instantly chided herself for being so presumptuous. Why would he care if she said hello or not? She shut the door firmly behind her and felt grateful to be safely back at home. In her empty, silent, lonely house. Turning on the hallway light, she slipped off her shoes and sighing, walked through to the kitchen to put the kettle on.

What she didn't know was that across the street, Tariq was doing exactly the same thing.

Chapter 6

April

Tilly turned left into High Holborn and looked down at her watch. She still had time to pop into her favourite Italian deli en-route to the office, as long as the queue was short and Gianni didn't chat for too long. Weaving her way between the monochrome sea of opposite direction suits and coats, she made her way along the busy pavement, eyes scanning the shopfronts she knew so well. Aveda, where she'd had her hair done for her sister's wedding. Rymans, where she bought far more stationary than she ever needed.

The neon sign of Gianni's came into view, and she wondered if she should order a cappuccino or a flat white today. Her tummy rumbled; breakfast felt like a long time ago.

"Tilly!"

A voice broke into her daydreams and she turned her head sideways, looking for the source. Her eyes scanned the sea of faces and she heard it again, closer this time, as she simultaneously felt a hand tap lightly on her shoulder. She stopped and turned around, disrupting the uniform flow of commuters from their well-trodden paths. A man tutted loudly before the stream of bodies found a new route around the inconvenient obstruction in their midst.

"Ethan!" Tilly took a sharp intake of breath, her face flushing from the bottom up as her heart beat faster. "What a surprise! What.... what are you doing here?"

All those years. All the times she'd imagined bumping into him. The hours she'd spent perfecting the cool, calm and collected speech that she'd planned to deliver. And now here he was, the handsome face that she knew every inch of. Standing right in front of her. His hair looked thinner, shorter maybe. His skin was thicker, his expression older and wiser with age. Maybe. A hint of stubble was visible; she knew, without touching, exactly what it would feel like under her fingers. And the twinkle in his blue eyes that had not diminished with the passing of time.

He was talking, saying something about an interview in Great Queen Street, but although she could hear the sound, she wasn't listening to a word he was saying. She was remembering him standing in their bedroom, packing books in boxes and clothes in a case. Visualising him carrying half their house down the stairs and into his car. Her tears, his reasoning. And then the silence, when he was gone, and she was all on her own.

Ethan must have finished what he was saying, because he was staring at her, smiling, a slightly bemused look on his face.

"Tilly? You OK?"

"Yes yes, oh I'm sorry, I'm just a million miles away this morning!" she laughed, nervously wafting her hands in front of her face. "It's such a shock to see you. You look so well."

You look so well? Oh for God's sake, what was she, 60?!

He looked at his watch.

"Listen, I've got to dash, I can't be late for this interview, but do you take a lunch break, do you fancy meeting for a coffee?"

"Yes, OK, I can do that, where do you want to meet?"

He looked around. "I don't really know anything around here anymore, do you know anywhere decent?"

"Umm yes, there's a deli just up there that does really good coffee," she said, turning and pointing up the street. "Gianni's."

"OK, perfect." Ethan put his hand out and gently touched her arm. She felt the still familiar shape of his hand through her coat, and the prickle of goosebumps as they spread up her spine. "12 o'clock, is that OK?"

"Yes, perfect, 12 is great, thank you. See you there."

"Will do, right, got to dash, see you later Tills."

And then he was gone, swallowed up by the morning commuters making their way purposefully along High Holborn, just another brown haired man in a suit, on the way to an office, a meeting, an interview.

And Tilly took a step forward, and another, until she caught up with the pace of the jostling bodies around her, and remembered everything about Ethan that she knew made him so much more than just another man in a suit.

At 11.45 Tilly closed the file she was working on and picked her coat off the coat stand. Karen looked up at her from her desk and glanced at the clock on the wall.

"You OK Tills? Bit of an early lunch for you isn't it?"

"No, I'm meeting someone, I'll be back in an hour," she said, buttoning up her coat.

Karen raised her eyebrows, a smile playing on her lips.

"OK, see you later. Have fun."

Tilly made her way out of the office and for the first time since she'd arrived at work that morning, allowed herself to properly think about what she was doing.

What *was* she doing? So much time had passed since she'd seen Ethan, and she had no idea why she was meeting him or what she was going to say. He had left her so abruptly with no real explanation as to why he'd gone, he'd just left her with a broken heart and a list of unanswered questions. When she'd thought over the years about meeting him and maybe getting some closure, it was over a bottle of wine somewhere private, not a cardboard cup of coffee in a busy London café.

As she approached Gianni's she could see him standing in front of the steamed up window of the little deli, staring up at the buildings opposite. God, he was handsome. As if reading her mind, he turned to look at her as she approached, and smiled at her with that ridiculous smile that still had the power to make her insides flip.

"Tills, you came, I thought you might stand me up," he winked, confident in the knowledge that she would never not have come. He pushed open the door and ushered her through.

Tilly chose a table to one side of the busy café, and Ethan went to the counter to order their coffees. She'd turned down an offer of a sandwich, but he returned with a plate on which a large almond croissant sat.

"They're going to bring over our drinks, and I got this for you, I hope you still like them," he said, setting it down in front of Tilly.

"I do, thank you," she replied, touched by his gesture. "We can share it."

"No you're OK, I've got a panini coming. I'm starving, it's been a pretty full on morning."

"Oh God yes, how was your interview? What was it for?"

Ethan was an estate agent, although not your average run of the mill smarmy estate agent who didn't like buyers or sellers and just did the job out of necessity. No, Ethan was property obsessed. His mother had once told her that when he was a little boy, the only reason he liked going to other people's homes was so that he could nose around and see what their house was like compared to his.

"Well, do you remember how I always wanted to work for Baxter and Rhinehart?"

Tilly nodded. It had been his ultimate ambition since before she'd even met him.

"Well today I finally had an interview with them. They've got a vacancy for a Senior Consultant in their Clapham branch, so I applied, and, well, we'll just have to wait and see!"

"Oh wow, that's amazing Ethan. I'm sure you'll be fine. You were always brilliant at your job."

The waitress arrived at their table with two coffees and a huge panini oozing with cheese which instantly made Tilly regret not having ordered one.

"Thank you," he said, before returning to face

her. "So anyway, how about you? I presume you're still working at the same place then?"

"Yep, I'm the Head of Department now, still love it there."

"And are you still in the same house in Tonbridge?" he said, taking a bite of his sandwich.

"I am yes," she laughed. "Nothing's really changed since the last time I saw you. How about you? Are you married?"

"God no," he said, wiping his fingers on a paper napkin and glancing at her left hand. "Too busy with work. So why aren't you shacked up with a husband and a couple of kids under your arm then?"

Tilly swallowed. *Because you broke my heart and I've never met anyone I loved like I loved you,* she thought.

"Oh you know, high standards and all that," she laughed, picking up her cup and staring into the froth as she took a sip.

Ethan looked at her intently.

"Tills, I know what I did was awful, things ending the way they did, but I just want to say that I'm sorry, I'm sorry about how I handled things back then."

She looked at him, glad of the noise and chatter around them to absorb some of the enormity of what he was saying.

"I just panicked. About where things were heading, and I've thought many times over the years about how I should have done things differently. I'm sorry I hurt you."

Tears welled in her eyes and she swallowed hard.

"Thank you," she said, mortified that her body was reacting the way it was, and hoping desperately that he wouldn't say anything else.

He pulled a folded napkin from the dispenser on the table and handed it to her.

"Sorry, I didn't mean to upset you."

She blew her nose loudly and attempted a smile.

"Yes, you bugger, I only came in for a coffee, I didn't think I'd have to reapply my make up before I went back to the office!"

"You look absolutely fine, no-one will notice. In fact you look lovely."

Tilly's heart beat a little faster in her chest and she tucked the napkin up her sleeve.

"Right, come on then, eat that croissant up and tell me what else is going on. How's that crazy friend of yours, Jemima, does she still hate me?!"

"YOU DID *WHAT*?" exclaimed Jemima. "No, hold on, we need another bottle of wine before you fill us in." She gesticulated wildly at the waiter, smiling sweetly to make up for her demanding body language.

Tilly, Becky and Jemima were having a doesn't-happen-often-enough Friday night after work drink, and Tilly had been loath to admit that she'd seen Ethan for fear of exactly this reaction. Jemima had never liked him, and hadn't held back in making her feelings known, both when they were together, and even more so after he'd left her. But the three of them were best friends, had been for 25 years, and if you couldn't talk to your besties, then who could you talk to?

"Jems, go easy on her, can you at least listen to what she has to say before launching into one?" laughed Becky.

Tilly explained how she'd bumped into Ethan on the way to work, had met him for a coffee later that day, and was now contemplating replying to his text asking if she'd like to go for a drink the following week.

"Whoa... that's massive. What are you going to do?" asked Becky.

"I don't know, I'm so torn. Half of me hates his guts for disappearing the way he did, but the other half of me thinks... well, what's the worst that can happen?"

"Er... that he picks you up and drops you all over again... which he will, because that's just the sort of man he is," said Jemima. "I didn't trust him last time, and I don't trust him now. And I'm only being honest because I love you and I don't want to see you getting hurt again my darling. You're worth so much more than that."

Becky looked across the table at her best friend. She knew how much Tilly had loved Ethan, and that sort of love never goes away, it just files itself in a secret place until you open the door and remind yourself how good it was. No-one ever remembers the shit bits as much as the good stuff, she knew that better than anyone.

"I know, but I've been on my own for so long now, and I swear, there are just NO decent men out there. You two are so lucky, happily married to gorgeous men…"

Jemima scoffed into her wine glass. "Yeah right…"

"Honestly, you don't know how good you've got it. It's not fun out here in no man's land in your late thirties. Maybe I should stick with what I know."

"Oh yes, talking of which, heard anything more from mummy's boy Steven?"

"No, thank God. I think he got the message eventually. I did try to let him down gently, but to be honest he's so thick-skinned I really don't think it would've bothered him anyway."

"You gonna have another go?"

"What, on the dating app?"

"Yep."

"No, in fact I think I might just delete it. I keep

getting messages from 65-year-old taxi drivers and unemployed artists."

Jemima guffawed. "Bloody hell. Hugo might not be the most perfect husband in the world but I think I might hang on to him for a bit longer."

Tilly looked at Jemima.

"You two are OK aren't you?"

"Oh God yeah, of course we are doll, he's just a pain in the arse sometimes. You know what he's like."

"Uh oh... not up to his old tricks again is he?" asked Becky.

Jemima shot her a look. "No of course not. He knows which side his bread is buttered on. And he also knows that I wouldn't let him get away with it again." She raised her eyebrows and took a large gulp of wine.

Tilly flashed a look across the table at Becky, who she knew would be thinking exactly the same as her, before swiftly changing the subject.

"Anyway, more importantly, I hope as my two best friends in the whole wide world, you're both coming to my party?"

"Absobloodylutely!" said Jemima. "I wouldn't miss it for the world!"

"Me too," said Becky, "I've already roped my mum in to babysit! How's that for forward planning?" she laughed.

"Oh fab, I knew I could rely on you two, thank

God for that. Just the other 287 I've got to worry about then."

"I tell you what Tills, I've gotta hand it to you, you've got balls!" said Jemima. "I wouldn't do that in a million years. Although I imagine your mortgage buddies are a civilised lot really."

"Oh no, they're not all work people. In fact I'm probably only Facebook friends with about a dozen or so from work."

"Who have you invited then?"

"Well, quite a lot from school, ex-colleagues, some family, a few people I've picked up along the way."

"Aren't you scared?"

"Petrified!" she pulled her mouth into a grimace. "But I can't back down now, I've sent the invite, made the decision, I'm not backing out! Anyway, now I know I'll have you two to help me, I'm not worried anymore. And if no-one else turns up we'll just have a lovely evening together!"

"Oh I don't think you need to worry about that, in fact I reckon you should be more worried about how you're going to fit them in if they do all turn up. And even scarier, how long the queue for the loo will be. Bet you're glad you've got three bathrooms now!" laughed Jemima.

When the second bottle of wine was empty they

paid the bill and headed off together towards their respective trains home.

"So Tills, what are you going to do about Ethan?" asked Becky gently as they arrived at the station.

Tilly sighed. "I don't know Bex, my heart says go but my head says don't." She raised her eyebrows and shrugged her shoulders.

"And your bestie says bog off and leave my friend alone," slurred Jemima, who had been drinking at twice the speed of them both and was clearly a little the worse for wear.

"Look whatever you do, just be careful. We love you and want you to be happy, that's all."

"I know, thank you, my lovely," said Tilly, hugging her friend, before being extravagantly embraced by Jemima.

The three of them diverged across the vast station concourse, each lost in their own thoughts. But the one thing they were all thinking was that when it came to romance, Tilly always, always, followed her heart.

Chapter 7

Tilly turned the car's engine off and pulled her phone from her bag. She was a bit early, and her sister had a tendency to be a bit late, especially when she had the kids in tow, but there was always the joy of a scroll through Facebook to entertain you whilst you waited for the train, the kettle to boil, or your sister to turn up.

A memory flashed up from a couple of years previously, a gorgeous beach shot from the last time she'd been to Florida. Her parents were so lucky, living in endless sunshine, and she peered through the windscreen at the grey murk that was framing the trees and wished she was there and not here.

She scrolled slowly through the news feed, spotting a post from her book group about the latest must-read novel, and then a heartfelt "If you care about the future of these unwanted pets please repost and share this message." Oh God. Of course she cared about them, but the modern-day equivalent of chain letters that now filled a good percentage of her social media messages did get a little tedious after a while.

A picture of an old school friend who'd apparently *just* given birth to twins flashed up. She looked serenely beautiful, smooth hair and a fresh complexion, two little bundles of joy wrapped in pink and blue blankets held perfectly in her arms. Tilly smirked, she could bet her bottom dollar that she hadn't looked like that in the moments after they'd popped out into the world. Knowing Tamara she'd have had her hairdresser on hand and a filter on the shot before she posted the expertly chosen image that she wanted to share with the world.

A crunch of gravel alerted her to the arrival of another vehicle in the small car park, and Tilly looked up to see her sister's BMW pulling into the space next to her. She looked at the rear window to see Oscar waving excitedly and Rosie fast asleep in her car seat, head lolling and mouth hanging open. *Just like her Auntie*, thought Tilly with a smile.

"Helloooo!" she said, greeting her sister with a huge hug before opening the back door and unclipping her nephew.

"Auntie Tilly, guess what, Mummy brought snacks with her. *Lots* of snacks. But we're only allowed them when we've done some good walking," he told her seriously.

"Oh well that's good Oscar, because I really do like a snack when I'm in the woods," she smiled, lifting him out of the car. He wrapped his little arms around her neck and snuggled into her.

"Ooooh you're so warm Oscar, toastie toastie!" she teased, planting a kiss on his slightly damp cheek.

Mimi shut the door with her hip and walked around the back of the car to join them, a sleepy Rosie hiding in the folds of her Mummy's coat, until she saw Auntie Tilly, and a smile crept onto her face.

"There's my favourite girl!" Tilly smiled, leaning forward to kiss her forehead, Oscar still hanging around her neck like a baby monkey.

"Ha, you wouldn't have said that if you'd seen the meltdown she had as we tried to leave the house this morning," laughed Mimi. "This coat, those shoes, no coat, oh my God, I swear Tills, I nearly left her behind," she joked. "Didn't I, my little princess!" she said, looking questioningly at Rosie.

"I love you Mummy," came the response, eliciting instant forgiveness and adoration.

Mimi rolled her eyes and set the little girl down on her feet. "Right, come on then you two, let's see how many interesting things we can find today, and maybe your Auntie and I might actually manage to have a bit of a catch up along the way."

Tilly slipped her arm into her big sister's and they set off down the well-trodden track. These woods were a great place to meet. Halfway between their respective houses, and a perfect circular child-friendly walk that the kids loved.

Mimi took a deep breath in through her nose, and exhaled loudly.

"You OK?" asked Tilly.

"Oh, I'm fine, I'm just knackered. The kids seem to take it in turns to wake me up throughout the night, Andrew of course *never* hears them…" she rolled her eyes. "And I feel like I don't ever, *ever* get any time to myself. Roll on September, that's what I say."

Tilly turned to look at her sister inquisitively.

"When Rosie starts school."

"Oh of course, wow, that's come round quick."

"Not quickly enough if you ask me. She is *so* ready for school, it will do her the world of good, and I cannot *wait* to finally get some time alone." She groaned.

"Oh Mims, it's not that bad is it? A lot of women would cut their arm off to live the life you do."

Mimi sighed. "I know, and I don't mean to sound ungrateful, but sometimes I just feel like I'm on a treadmill, going round and round like a flaming hamster. Andrew's never at home, he works such long hours these days, and when he is he just flakes out in front of the telly and still expects me to do bloody everything."

If she was honest, Tilly did think her sister sounded a little bit ungrateful. Andrew worked his socks off for his family and provided an amazing life for them all. Mimi never had to ask for anything, and she always seemed to manage to fit in visits to the hairdresser and beauty salon without any problem at all.

"What about the health club? Are you still a member?"

"Oh now yes, that is one place I can go and actually get some me-time," she laughed. "They have an amazing crèche where you can just drop your kids for an hour or so and go and do a class, or have a swim, or sometimes even just go and sit in the bar and have a coffee. It is so nice."

"Well there we go, that's something isn't it?"

"Yeah, I guess so, and do you remember my old personal trainer, Pete?"

Tilly shook her head.

"Well he's working there a few days a week too now, although I don't know how he manages to fit it all in, he's so busy with his private clients. Honestly, if I hadn't have met him when I did I'd be on a looong waiting list!"

"Mummy, Mummy, Oscar's being mean to me," cried Rosie, running towards them.

Tilly watched as her sister refereed the sibling fall-out, wiping tears away and fishing conciliatory cartons of juice from her bag. She was an amazing Mum despite her earlier rant, and Tilly wondered where this outpouring had come from. It wasn't often that they got time to talk properly, without

Andrew or the children within earshot, and she wondered if there was more to the story than was apparent.

They continued walking along the path, the children flitting in and out of the trees in front of them, prohibiting any inquisitive questions from Tilly.

"So anyway, tell me about this date, how was it? What was his name, Steven?"

"Oh don't, it was awful," she said, wondering if she should admit to having ditched the dating app and agreeing to go for a drink with Ethan instead.

Tilly had pondered the Ethan thing on the journey there, and had decided that as much as she loved her sister, she didn't feel ready to tell her that she was in touch with her ex again. Mimi had seen first-hand how broken-hearted she'd been after Ethan had left her, and would always resolutely protect her little sister from further harm. She also remembered his somewhat jealous tendencies, which Tilly had brushed aside but her sister had considered a little bit over the top.

She filled Mimi in on the disappointing date with Steven, making her laugh at the audacity of his attempt to get out of paying the bill.

"Blimey, I'm so glad I'm not single, even if I do feel like a single parent sometimes," she laughed. "Do you know, twice in the last month I've had to order a takeaway for *one* on Friday night when

Andrew's had to take clients out at late notice. I mean really, how sad is that?"

"Sounds a bit like my life," snorted Tilly.

"Yeah but you don't then get an inebriated man crawling into your bed in the early hours stinking of booze and snoring his head off all night."

"Wow, some clients! Who's he taking out? My lot aren't like that! We're done way before last orders. And Friday night? Who takes clients out on a Friday? I thought that's what Thursdays were for," she laughed.

"Ha ha, God knows, your guess is as good as mine… Oh Oscar, stop that!" she cried, running towards the doggy poo bin that he was trying desperately to prise open with a stick.

Rosie headed towards her Auntie with her fingers delicately holding her little nose shut.

"Pooo-eeeeey, that stinks," she said.

"I know. Little boys are horrible," said Tilly. "Come on, why don't we go and have a look over there. I think that's the secret path to The Look Out," she said.

Rosie nodded.

"Mims, we're going down here," she called, getting eye contact with her sister before she disappeared into the trees.

"OK, be there in a bit," Mimi replied, pulling wet wipes from a packet and holding Oscar's hand well away from her cashmere jumper.

Tilly chuckled to herself and took Rosie's hand in hers. *Yep, boys could be horrid sometimes,* she thought. You just had to look for the nice ones, and hopefully find them before someone else did.

Chapter 8
May

It was now four months since Tilly had sent her "Save The Date" invitation to all 289 of her Facebook friends, and the blooming spring days reminded her that the year was passing by at a pretty swift pace. Although it was probably another four of five months until she was going to send out the *proper* invite, Tilly Jenkins was not one to leave anything unplanned, and so had earmarked the May Bank Holiday weekend for some serious party planning.

She'd purchased a beautiful spiral bound notebook from Paperchase especially for the occasion, and had devised an all-singing all-dancing Excel spreadsheet for the list of attendees. Even for somebody who absolutely adored a good list, there was no way on earth she was going to handwrite nearly 300 names in her notebook.

However, when she attempted to copy and paste her list of friends directly onto the spreadsheet, she realised that it was not possible to do that, so ended up having to prop her iPad next to her laptop, and type every single one of them in by hand after all. Which ended up being a rather interestingly distracting exercise in itself, and somewhat of a time-consuming event. Tilly was amazed at some of the people she was still friends with – there were even a few of her parent's friends on the list, which was a bit weird, and also vaguely terrifying. For all she knew, some of them might not even be alive anymore. It did make her wonder how and why she was still linked to these people, and if it hadn't been for the fact that she'd invited them all to a party, it would've been a great time for a serious cull of her contacts.

As she dug a little deeper into the social media minefield, Tilly discovered that most of her contacts had a similar numbers of friends to her, although somewhat shockingly a few of her acquaintances had over a thousand. She wondered if it were actually possible to know that many people, or if they'd simply sent a friend request to anyone they met, however loose the connection. It was almost impossible to tell just from looking at their pages, unless you went full on detective and clicked through to every single person, and that was one step too far even for Tilly's inquisitive nature.

But what the process did make her realise, was just how random the mix of people she had invited to her home were. There were lots of school friends, work colleagues old and new, ex-boyfriends, friends of ex-boyfriends, siblings of friends, and friends of friends.... There were people she'd met on holiday once and never seen since. Her old ballet teacher, her dentist, and her hairdresser, various people who had serviced her boiler/ painted her sitting room... her parent's golf friends, husbands and wives of loads of different people, some girls she'd done a course with many moons ago, a bunch of relatives, and even a couple of semi-famous people she'd followed over the years – a cookery writer, a novelist, and an artist.

Tilly sat back in her office chair.

Wow, it would be cool if they turned up, she thought.

Tilly tried to imagine her house stuffed to the rafters with such an eclectic mix of people. Old and young, rich or not, from every walk of life. It suddenly felt like some crazy social experiment, which it sort of was, but it was happening to her, in real life. She gulped, and started to draw up her spreadsheet, in a vague attempt to take control of the situation.

Five columns: NAME – RSVP'd? – YES – NO – MAYBE.

It was that last column that she really hated. If she didn't know, then she couldn't plan, and in Tilly's world, if you knew what was coming, you could handle anything.

Turning back to the calm of her aesthetically pleasing notebook, she started to make lists of food and drink, with the assistance of some party planning websites suggesting food ideas for feeding a large crowd. There was no way Tilly wanted to spend all night in the kitchen, or walking around topping up people's drinks, so she decided to make it as simple as possible.

One suggestion she found was inspirational. "Set up a DIY bar area so that guests can help themselves" it offered. That was a great idea. If she put a large drinks table at the front of the sitting room she could shepherd people through the hallway and they could help themselves. The website showed an image of a huge expensive looking silver punch bowl, filled with crushed ice and bottles of Champagne, which looked brilliant. Tilly's budget wasn't going to stretch to Champagne, but it was a great idea for white wine and prosecco. Then bottles of red wine on the other side of the table, and a mixture of wine and Champagne glasses in the space between.

She turned to a new page and wrote "Things to do – hire wine glasses". That was easy, so long as she remembered to do it in good time. Otherwise it was going to be a last minute trip to Ikea and another thing to add to the bill.

Turning to food, Tilly searched for canapé ideas. One web page suggested eight savoury and three sweet canapés per person. She pulled her calculator from the desk drawer and totted up the numbers. That was over 3,000 in total! Staring at the wall above the computer she bit her bottom lip and hoped silently that most people couldn't make it that night. Without even knowing how much it would come to, the bleak realisation dawned on her that this party could cost her an absolute fortune. Well, she should have thought about that before she invited all and sundry round for drinks and nibbles.

Tilly closed her eyes and imagined being in a crowded house, with a buffet table at the end of the room. Walking towards it in her mind she pictured what she'd like to see on it if she was a guest at that party. Easy. Cheese, chorizo, and something sweet and chocolatey.

That was it! She could do a few huge cheese-boards, some charcuterie plates, and a beautiful mountain of gooey chocolatey brownie bites. Add some bread, crackers, and grapes, plus a plate of bitesize Christmas cakes and a *lot* of crisps, and she'd be sorted.

Scribbling it all down before she forgot, Tilly felt a buzz of excitement. For the first time since she'd had the crazy party idea she was excited about it. Properly excited. Chewing the end of her pen, she pushed back her chair and walked around the ground floor of her house, imagining it full of people, Christmas tunes in the background and a massive sparkly Christmas tree in the sitting room.

Tilly shrugged her shoulders and smiled to herself. She would make sure that this was the best party *ever*.

Chapter 9
June

TILLY HAD EVENTUALLY given in to Ethan's multiple persuasive text messages and agreed to meet him for a drink. Which had led to more drinks a week later, and then a curry the following weekend.

The first time they'd met up had felt like a first date all over again. Tilly had spent ages fretting over what to wear that day, wanting to create the perfect mix of a slightly older and more mature Tilly, yet gorgeous and carefree at the same time. They'd met at a bar on the south bank after work one Thursday evening, and the afternoon leading up to it had seemed to slow down inextricably. Each time she looked at the clock Tilly then had to check the numbers on the bottom of her computer screen in case the wall clock had stopped working for some reason. She was like a child on the last day of term, desperately watching the big hand drag itself around the clock face and willing it to go faster.

Finally the hands reached home time, and Tilly stacked her files up neatly, turned off the computer, and stood up.

"Oh Tills, before you go, can I just ask you to cast your eyes over this for me please?" asked a voice from across the office.

Tilly inhaled sharply and pasted a smile on her face. "Of course." She walked over to Karen's desk.

"Are you OK? You've been a bit distracted today."

"Yes, I'm fine, sorry, was it that obvious?" She pulled over a wheelie chair and wedged herself halfway between the partition and Karen's neat desk. "I'm going for a drink with my ex-boyfriend," she confessed, safe in the knowledge that Karen was not one to gossip.

"Aaah... I wondered how the dating was going. Not very well then if you're thinking about getting back with your ex!"

"No, it was a disaster, but that's a story for another time. No, I bumped into my... well, you remember Ethan, a few weeks ago, and we're having a drink together tonight."

Karen raised her eyebrows. "And how do you feel about that. Is it OK? If I remember rightly you were pretty cut up about him for a while."

"Yeah, I'm fine, sort of better the devil you know, if you know what I mean."

Karen nodded. "Absolutely. Well, you'd better

get going then, don't want to keep him waiting!"

"Didn't you want to show me something?"

"Ah, no, don't worry about it, it can wait til tomorrow, you go. Have fun."

Tilly smiled as she stood up. "Thank you my lovely, see you in the morning." She pushed the wheelie chair back to its original position, and strode past the rows of consultant's desks, nodding or smiling as she went, at the few that weren't in a meeting or at the pub already.

ETHAN WAS ALREADY there when she arrived, perched on a high bar stool facing the river, a bottle of Champagne sticking out from a Veuve Clicquot ice bucket and two glasses waiting to be filled. Tilly had actually been fantasising about a nice glass of rosé all the way there, but as soon as she saw the familiar yellow logo she knew that she could be easily convinced otherwise. And also, how romantic of him to order Champagne on a normal Thursday evening, that was a really sweet thing for him to do.

Ethan stood up as she approached and kissed her on both cheeks, before pulling out the adjacent chair for Tilly, and pouring two glasses of deliciously cold bubbly.

"Well, this is nice, thank you!" she said, raising her glass towards Ethan's.

"Well, we've got something to celebrate!" he

said, chinking his glass gently against Tilly's.

She smiled back at him, chuffed that he was being so lovely about their meeting up again, and she blushed with the extravagance of his gesture. Maybe he really had changed after all. Maybe he wanted this to work. He was clearly trying to impress her.

"I agree," she said coyly, nodding her head and taking a sip of her drink.

"I got the job! At Baxter and Rhinehart!"

Tilly swallowed quickly. *Oh God, the job. Of course.*

"Oh wow! Congratulations, that's amazing!" she gushed, hoping that her face wasn't giving away her emotions and showing her disappointment that this wasn't the romantic gesture she'd thought.

Ethan was obviously over the moon; she'd known for years how much he wanted to work for the most reputable estate agency in London. And now his dream had finally come true. As he babbled away she wondered what they looked like to an outsider. Colleagues? No, colleagues probably wouldn't order Champagne. Husband and wife on a rare night out? Doubtful so early in the evening in work clothes. Actually, she thought they probably just looked like most of the other couples scattered around her. Partners, boyfriend and girlfriend, whatever you wanted to call them. But she quite liked that, it had been so long since she'd been out, just normally, with a man. With Ethan. She missed being a team. The partnership. The day-to-day banter about normal office stuff and what they should cook for dinner that night. About whether or not they could justify getting a cleaner so they didn't have to spend half a day of their precious weekend cleaning the house. And about how they were going to spend the rest of their lives together.

But this evening Ethan was telling her everything she could possibly want to know and more about his new job, and before she knew it they'd finished the bottle of Champagne. Tilly had been listening for most of the rather one-sided conversation, and therefore drinking faster than Ethan had, whilst fantasising about ordering a big bowl of chips like the ones she'd seen delivered to a neighbouring table. Lunch seemed a very long time ago, and she wondered what Ethan was doing about dinner. Maybe he would suggest they go on for something to eat.

"Well, this was nice," said Ethan, waving his credit card at a passing waiter. "We should do it again sometime."

Maybe not then.

By the time they were on their way to the tube station, Tilly's stomach was grumbling very angrily at her indeed.

"I'll text you Tills, let's fit something in next week, yeah?" He kissed her on both cheeks again as they parted to their respective tube lines.

"Yes, great, let's do it," said Tilly, smiling hungrily and trying to ignore the Burger King billboard that she could see over his shoulder, and the gnawing feeling of disappointment that this had not turned into a longer, more romantic evening.

And then she watched as he disappeared through the ticket barrier, and she turned towards hers, kept walking past it – went up the stairs, back onto the street, and straight to the nearest McDonalds.

A FEW DAYS later Ethan had texted again suggesting another post work drink, and then the following Friday they'd arranged to go for a curry at their old favourite haunt in Tonbridge. Ethan was going to get the train out of London after work, and although they hadn't discussed him getting the last train back, Tilly was presuming he would be.

Just in case though, she'd spent the night before cleaning the house even more thoroughly than usual, changed the bed sheets in case she had a change of heart and invited him back, and put a bottle of wine in the fridge. Three times in as many weeks felt like a bit of a habit was developing, but Tilly wasn't really sure what was going on, or even what Ethan was thinking. There hadn't been any talk of them getting back together and he had kissed her on the cheek when they'd parted the last time they'd met, as if they were just old friends. What she did know though, was that the evenings were so lovely and light these days, and the urge to rush home and hunker down was long gone, so it was satisfying to know that there was someone only a text away who might just be up for a drink after work if the desire arose.

When her mother had phoned a couple of days earlier and asked what she had been up to recently, Tilly didn't disclose the fact that she was back in touch with Ethan. Her parents had liked him, and when they'd broken up they'd seemed almost embarrassed that their youngest daughter was on her own again, as if there was something wrong with her. All their friend's children had got married and settled down, as Gloria never stopped telling Tilly, and she presumed that her mother would encourage her to get back with Ethan just so that she didn't have the apparent shame of a spinster daughter. But Tilly didn't want to do anything because it was expected of her, and thought it best to leave Ethan out of the conversation for now.

She had however talked to her mother about the party. Gloria and Bob were avid Facebook users, they had been since they'd moved to Florida so that they could not only keep in touch with their friends in the UK, but also so that they could join the many golf groups, local resident's forums, and charity pages that they were involved in. So obviously, as "friends" of their daughter as it were, they had been invited to save the date for her Christmas Party.

"Now darling, about this silly party idea of yours."

"It's not silly Mum, it's fun," she said, wondering why her mother was always so negative about everything she did.

"It is silly, Tilly. You're a grown woman, you can't just go inviting hundreds of people to your house for a party. That's what teenagers do for goodness' sake."

Tilly sighed, and wished she'd worked out how to exclude certain people from the invite. She knew her parents wouldn't be coming back to England in December, it was one of the most sociable months in the calendar for Gloria and Bob and their golfing buddies. But the idea had been to invite ALL of her Facebook friends so leaving them off the list would've defeated the object of the game somewhat.

"And what's all this about a dating app? Your sister told me you'd been on a date. With a stranger? You need to be more careful, you don't know who these people are."

Tilly felt like she couldn't win. One minute her

mother wanted her to get married, the next she was frowning on her attempts to even get a boyfriend.

"It's what people do these days Mum, no-one meets anyone in the pub like they used to. It's not like your day, it's different now. Anyway, I'm not seeing him again so you needn't worry."

"Oh that's a shame, another one down the drain…" sighed her mother.

At that point Tilly had given up and changed the subject, turning the conversation around to what her parents had been doing, thus sending Gloria off on a convoluted story about the new hurricane watch group they'd set up at the resident's association. It was actually quite an interesting subject – Tilly was well aware how those big storms could sweep in from the Gulf of Mexico, but her mother's earlier negative comments had ground her down and she just listened and uh huh-ed and waited for the call to end so that she could go to bed.

AS SHE GOT ready for her date (if it was a date) with Ethan she wondered what her mother really would say if she knew Tilly was seeing him tonight. She looked down at her linen shift dress and wondered if she was smart enough, remembering how much effort her mother always made when she went out.

Accessories – that was what she needed. She

rummaged in her jewellery box and dug out a long silver necklace with a star on the end, her Tiffany sweetie bracelet, and a gorgeous aquamarine ring that Ethan had given her a long time ago. But which had *not* been an engagement ring, much to her mother's disappointment.

THE RESTAURANT WAS buzzing when Tilly and Ethan arrived, and the waiter led them through the busy restaurant to a booth at the back.

"Oh dear, you can tell we're not regulars anymore," said Ethan once they'd been given their menus and left alone. "Stuck at the back out of eyeshot."

"It'll be fine," said Tilly, "we're not in a rush are we?"

"No, we're not, and it's lovely to have you completely to myself. Now, what shall we eat? I'm starving!"

Tilly had forgotten until that moment just how carried away Ethan got in Indian restaurants. The waiter brought poppadums and chutneys along with their gin and tonics, which were devoured by them both in no time at all. Once they'd ordered their respective curries (neither of them particularly liked to share their main course), they ordered a large rice, and then Ethan added a peshwari naan, some dhal, and a side dish of saag aloo too.

"Oh, and a couple of onion bhajis whilst we're waiting please mate," he added, winking at Tilly, who cringed internally at his attempt to get pally with the staff.

A different waiter appeared with a bottle of white wine, which he opened and poured quickly before dashing off to serve another table.

"So Tilly, what else have you been up to, what's new with you?"

Nothing was ever really *new* with Tilly, but she didn't want to appear dull. She still hadn't got round to joining the gym, the sailing school, or the golf club, and she realised with a jolt that the only interesting thing in her life was the one thing he didn't know about, seeing as how she'd unfriended him on Facebook after they'd broken up.

"Well, it might sound a bit weird, but I'm having a party at Christmas, so that's taken up a fair bit of time recently."

"Christmas? But it's only June. How come you're thinking about it now?"

"Well, I've invited quite a lot of people. In fact, you should come if you're free. If you'd like?"

"Well, I might just do that, thank you. Who have you invited then?"

As Tilly explained how she had invited almost 300 people to her normal-sized house, had no idea who was coming, or how she would fit them all in, she realised just how preposterous it actually sounded. Ethan stared across the white tablecloth at her in awe.

"Whoa Tills, you've changed. That is very brave, if not a little bit crazy, I must say!"

"Yeah, I know, but now I've done it I can't back down. I guess… well… I just wanted to liven up my life a bit to be honest. Get back in touch with some old faces. See what people were up to rather than view them through the snapshots of their lives."

"Well, good for you. Sounds like you might need me there to help you out though."

Tilly was just imagining being at her Christmas party with Ethan by her side, proud to have such a handsome boyfriend, when a waiter appeared next to the table.

"Onion bhajis?"

"Oh yeah, great, just in the middle… Thanks mate."

Ethan gestured to Tilly to help herself, and she took one from the plate along with a large dollop of raita. The smell of the food woke her stomach up to the fact that she was absolutely ravenous, and she started eating before Ethan had even picked up his cutlery.

"Oops sorry," she mumbled, covering her mouth with her hand.

In between bhajis, which were deliciously crispy

and juicy at the same time, Ethan updated Tilly on the latest developments regarding his new contract at Baxter and Rhinehart. He was so excited about it, which she thought was rather sweet. He did have a tendency to be a little unemotional at times, so to see him gushing so enthusiastically about something important to him made Tilly very happy indeed.

A trolley appeared next to the table followed by the same waiter who had brought their wine, and seemingly endless dishes were piled onto food warmers that had been laid out on the table. It looked amazing, and the two of them met each other's eyes across the food in mutual appreciation of their choices.

BY THE TIME they'd finished Tilly thought she would never eat again, and realised that the flat-ish stomach she'd had at the start of the day would definitely not look the same anymore. Although she always wished that she was half a stone lighter than she was, Tilly was generally in pretty good shape, and had the amazing capacity to pretty much regain her figure overnight even after a massive blow out.

But a post-curry figure was not the look she had imagined when she was changing the sheets on her bed last night, so when Ethan leant across the table and took her hands in his, she instantly regretted that second helping of biryani.

"So, Tills, what's going on here then?" He stared into her eyes in a way that made Tilly want to laugh. "What are we doing, I mean, what do you want to do?"

Tilly blinked and squirmed a bit in her seat, not entirely sure if he meant it in a romantic way, or just whether they should order another bottle or go to the pub.

"I mean, it's been great seeing you again," he continued, "and I didn't realise how much I'd missed you til we bumped into each other, so I guess, we're both single, and, well, what do you think, fancy giving things another go?"

Even though Tilly had thought about this moment a lot in the previous few weeks, and in fact somewhat obsessively over the last few years, the moment he said it out loud the bubble seemed to burst and the image of her falling into his arms and living happily ever after simply drifted off into the distance. This was not how she'd imagined things. She wanted romance, gestures, and bunches of flowers. More apologies, endless reassurances, a weekend away somewhere gorgeous and long walks on the beach, hand in hand.

Not an Indian restaurant down the road with a half empty bowl of dahl in front of her.

Realising that he was expecting her to say something, she opened her mouth to speak only to find that words failed her. Thankfully the waiter then arrived to clear their plates, so Ethan let go of her hands and they sat back in their chairs.

"You like ice cream? Dessert menu?" he asked, stacking up the empty dishes on the trolley beside him.

Ethan looked at Tilly. "I won't, but you have something if you want, Tills."

"No, no I'm fine, thank you."

"OK, good, some more wine?"

"No, I think we're OK for the moment, thanks mate," said Ethan, smiling at the waiter.

When the table had been cleared and the debris scraped onto a saucer with a little metal scrapy thing (which Tilly loved watching, for some weird reason), he finally retreated and left them alone to finish their wine.

"So, Miss Jenkins, you didn't answer my question. What do you say. Fancy hanging out a bit? Seeing how things go?"

"Yeah, OK then, I guess so!" she said. It wasn't exactly the positive reaction she imagined he was hoping for, but then he hadn't exactly sold the idea to her in the most attractive way either.

"Excellent!" Ethan picked up his wine glass and raised it towards her. Here's to you and I then."

"Cheers," she said, chinking her glass against his and taking a large sip of her wine. It was no longer cold and made the edges of her tongue retract with its sharpness. Funny how the end of the second glass isn't a patch on the start of the first.

ETHAN PAID THE bill and handed the last chocolate mint to Tilly.

"So do you fancy a drink in the pub? Or something?"

Tilly was pretty certain she knew what he was angling for. An invite back to her house for a drink and then you know what, probably. But although it had been a long time since she'd had any romance in her life, she did still have some standards, and if he thought his proposition after dinner this evening meant a quickie tonight, he had another thing coming. All the "Make Him Want You" articles and "How To Get What You Want" books Tilly had read over the years came flooding back to her. He needed to work a bit harder if he wanted an invite to her house, that was for sure.

"Yeah, let's get one more in the pub, if you've got time before your train?" she said confidently, pleased with herself for having taken control of the situation. And also making sure it was absolutely clear that he was going home later.

The evening was still warm, and they set off to an old pub that Tilly had been to before and that she knew had a lovely outside seating area, all scatter cushions and twinkly lights.

"I'll get these," said Tilly, as they approached the bar. "You go and find us a nice table outside."

She watched as he walked through the pub towards the back door. A couple of girls followed him with their eyes as he walked past, and Tilly looked away quickly before they noticed her watching them. He was undoubtedly a very attractive man, but for some reason Tilly's stomach just didn't flip like it used to when she looked at him.

How had things changed so quickly? She was so confused. For years she'd thought about him, missed him, hated him, loved him, all at the same time. And when she'd bumped into him again on High Holborn a couple of months ago it was as if the world had temporarily stopped spinning. But now…? She couldn't put her finger on it but something had shifted. They got on so well together, it was almost like nothing had changed sometimes. And yes, it had been lovely to have someone to walk along the Thames with after work and share a drink with before heading home, and she was definitely enjoying the novelty of having something in her diary most weeks, but what if she was doing the wrong thing getting back with Ethan so quickly? He had broken her heart, and as she paid for the drinks she realised what the problem was.

When Ethan left her, he had shattered the trust

that she'd invested in him, and one brief apology wasn't enough. He needed to prove to her that he wasn't going to waltz off into the sunset again. That this wasn't just a fling. But Tilly knew that words don't always work on their own in situations like this. Maybe time was what they needed. Time together to prove that this was what he wanted, what they both wanted, before they could even begin to think about moving forward.

Tilly carried their drinks through the pub and out into the garden. She spotted Ethan straight away and walked over to the table, setting the drinks down and sliding onto the bench seat next to him. Leaning back against the cushions she breathed in the evening air, and caught a waft of his aftershave. The one he always used to wear.

"Penny for them, Miss Jenkins," he smiled, taking her hand in his.

"Sorry, I was miles away." She smiled, a flicker in the pit of her stomach as he stroked the back of her hand.

"Tonight's been really nice Tills, I love spending time with you, and I just wanted to say that I hope you know I'm not going to hurt you again," he said quietly.

She nodded, wondering if he'd actually been reading her mind.

"I wouldn't be here if I was just after one thing, I know I hurt you, and I'm so sorry. I promise I won't do it again." He lifted his arm and wrapped it around her shoulder, turning his head to kiss her on the forehead.

"I know. But thank you for saying so." Tilly snuggled into his shoulder, savouring the feeling of being held, and not wanting to move for a very long time.

Chapter 10

IT WAS A tradition in Tilly's office that every year on the Summer Solstice as many people as possible went out for after work drinks, to make the most of the longest day of the year and celebrate accordingly. Which basically was an excuse to drink as much as was humanly possible before ending up in a curry house, or falling into a taxi.

This year June 21st fell on a Thursday, and after a spectacular first six months of the year, business-wise, the department was in high spirits. They'd hired the basement of one of their favourite local wine bars, and the MD had put a good amount of money behind the bar to kick things off.

Tilly and Karen walked the short distance to Bailey's together, about half an hour behind the rest of the team. Both of them were in their mid-thirties, and neither had the stamina that they'd had a decade earlier, like the more junior members of the team did these days. And although seniority certainly didn't have any impact on how sensible anyone was on work nights out, Karen liked to take on a more motherly, pastoral role with the younger girls, making sure they weren't being bothered by anyone, and that they got in a black cab safely at the end of the night.

"Evening ladies," said a sophisticated voice behind them as they approached the entrance of the bar.

"Alan, you made it, fantastic!" smiled Tilly, wondering why Karen was blushing and seemed to have lost the power of speech. He pushed the door open for them and the party of three headed downstairs to the roped off area set aside for the mortgage company. The room was pretty full already, and they made their way to a familiar face behind the bar to order drinks.

"Better get your orders in guys, the lads down the end are doing their best to drink the budget dry!" he shouted across the music.

"What would you like ladies?" asked Alan.

"Ooh, a large glass of Rioja please," said Tilly.

"And I'll have a glass of Prosecco please Alan," smiled Karen sweetly.

Alan turned to the bar to order their drinks, but not before Tilly noticed him winking at her well-mannered colleague. Tilly turned to look at Karen, eyes wide in amusement, but Karen just as quickly looked away, suddenly distracted by some very loud laughter coming from the compliance team.

There were no tables left to sit at and after a

while the three of them split up and spent the rest of the evening mingling. There was no-one Tilly wasn't happy to talk to, as she got on with pretty much everyone in the office, and it wasn't until about three hours later that she found herself at the end of the bar again with Alan.

"So Tilly, how are you?" he asked. "We haven't had a proper catch up for ages."

"I'm OK thanks, been quite busy to be honest."

"Oh yes, I heard about your party, still having it?"

"Yes, absolutely! But no, not just that, I've actually started seeing someone."

"Ooh... anyone we know?" He looked around him. "None of these louts I hope," he laughed.

"No, my ex, Ethan, I think you met him at a few Christmas bashes?"

"Ah yes, estate agent if I remember correctly?"

"Yeah that's right, well remembered!" she patted him on the shoulder.

"So is it serious?" he asked, a genuine look of care on his face which reminded her of her father.

Tilly sighed. "Oh, I don't know Alan. Not serious yet, no, but I just don't know if I'm doing the right thing. You know, going back. He did leave me after all, who's to say he won't do it again?"

"Let me tell you something Tilly, and this is from someone who's been around the block a few times. You only live this life once, and you might as well enjoy it. So if it feels right, go for it. And if doesn't, don't. It really is as simple as that. As long as you aren't lying, or hurting anyone, then I really do believe that you should do what makes you happy."

Tilly laughed. "You make it sound so easy, Alan. If only it was."

He shook his head. "It's not always easy. Now this isn't common knowledge so keep it to yourself, but I'm sure it'll come out at some point. You met my wife, Margaret, I think?"

Tilly nodded.

"Well, we're actually in the process of getting divorced at the moment." He raised his eyebrows.

"Oh my God, Alan, I had no idea, I'm so sorry."

"No, no, please don't be. I mean, obviously, it's not ideal, but it's a mutual decision. We both realised that life is too short to be with the wrong person." He took a sip of his drink. "The hardest thing was telling the kids, but actually they've been amazing about it. You know, you've just got to do what feels right, Tilly. I did, and although I've rocked a few boats, I know that by following my heart things will be OK in the end."

Tilly was shocked, Alan had always seemed such a content man, and she'd presumed that he was happily married. She was pretty sure he was nearing 50 as well, not the typical age you imagine someone getting divorced. Or was it?

"Aren't you scared of being on your own?"

"No, you never know what's round the corner Tilly, sometimes you just have to take a chance on things!" He winked at her, a cheeky smile on his face. "Now come on, let's get another round in before I tell you too much!"

Tilly thought about what Alan had said. Yes, life was too short, and when her parents had emigrated, they'd said something similar to her and her sister. And a few years ago Jems had given her a gorgeous little ceramic heart embellished with the words "This life is not a dress rehearsal." Tilly had hung it in her kitchen and walked past it on a daily basis, but hadn't really thought about it properly for a while. Maybe it was about time she stopped treating life like a practice run. She'd grabbed the bull by the horns where the party was concerned. Maybe it was about time she applied it to her love life too.

Chapter 11
July

TILLY WAS NOT one to do things by halves, so once she'd decided that she was going to give things with Ethan a proper go, she threw herself into the relationship fully. Ethan had by now started working at Baxter and Rhinehart, and they quickly fell into a routine of spending Monday to Friday in Ethan's London flat, and the weekend at Tilly's house.

It was a warm Wednesday evening, and Tilly and Ethan were pottering around each other in the flat's small kitchen. Tilly was steadily chopping peppers and onions whilst Ethan scrolled through his online viewing diary for the following day.

"Hey Tills, check this out."

Tilly wiped her hands on a tea towel and turned to look at what he was showing her.

He clicked on the link against his 2pm viewing. A red brick townhouse filled the screen.

"What is it, a flat?"

He shook his head. "Nope. It's a house. The

whole thing," he said, raising his eyebrows. "3.2 million."

"Oh my God, I'd love to see inside. What's it like?"

"It's gorgeous, the owners have spent a fortune getting it done up."

"Why are they moving then?"

"Cos they're now spending a fortune on divorce lawyers instead," he laughed, flicking through the photos. "Look, it's stunning."

Tilly glanced at the whitewashed drawing room and enormous cream sofas.

"Bit soulless though, isn't it?"

"Yep, sadly. It'll sell no problem though. Just hope I'm the one who secures a buyer, it's a hell of a commission."

Tilly went back to chopping vegetables and tried to remember what he'd told her about his commission rates. Maybe not surprisingly for someone who worked in finance, she was generally un-phased by what people earned. It was all just numbers on a page as far as she was concerned. As long as she had money left over at the end of the month, and a good healthy amount in her savings, Tilly was content. She'd never been one for flash cars, or impressed by someone just because of their salary, but as she deseeded a red pepper she realised that Ethan was actually a pretty good catch these days for someone who *was* interested in that sort of thing. He was certainly generous, he never expected Tilly to pay for anything, but equally, he was gracious when she did.

That was one thing Ethan had in common with her brother-in-law, Andrew. The two of them had always got on well when Tilly and Ethan had been together the first time round, even if Andrew did lord it over him a little bit, for being an *estate agent*. Well, now that he worked for Baxter and Rhinehart, Ethan would be able to proudly stand his ground on that front. You couldn't do much better than them in the property field.

Her sister on the other hand… Tilly had finally plucked up the courage to tell her that she was seeing Ethan again. She'd expected her to be happy for them both, but to her surprise Mimi had been decidedly off about the whole thing. Maybe she'd caught her on a bad day, but she was so snappy that Tilly almost felt like she was having a conversation with her mother.

"Oh, I don't know Tilly, can you trust him? He walked out on you once, and he'll probably do it to you again."

Tilly had been so disappointed by Mimi's reaction. She wanted her sister to be excited for her, not negative.

"I tell you something else Tills, I really… Oscar NO, leave your sister alone… Sorry, where was I?"

Mimi's life had always been so perfect, everything had always fallen into place for her. Talking to Becky later on the phone, Tilly had asked her opinion.

"She's got the best life, why can't she just be happy for me? Maybe it's my turn to have something nice for a change. All the good stuff always happens to her, and now things are finally going well for me and she's being so damn cynical about it all."

"I'm sure she didn't mean it babe, you know what your sister is like. She's probably just having an off day. Just carry on doing what you're doing and enjoy it. If you're happy, that's all that matters."

Tilly knew she was right, it was her life after all, and apart from feeling like she was living out of a bag most of the week, she was having an absolutely fantastic time. Summer had been lovely so far this year and she was enjoying being an "us" rather than an "I". In fact she'd been so busy that between work, Ethan, and all the socialising they were doing with his colleagues, she'd barely even given her party a second thought. There was plenty of time for all that.

She went to the fridge to get the salmon and noticed a bar of her favourite chocolate on the top shelf, which she definitely hadn't put there herself. Tilly smiled. Bless him, he could be so sweet sometimes, and it was nice to have someone thinking about *her* for a change.

Ethan walked back into the kitchen, leant over her shoulder and reached around her for a bottle of white wine. "Fancy a glass? It'll go nicely with the salmon."

"Ooh, on a school night? You're such a rebel," she laughed. "Go on then, why not."

"Oh by the way, I forgot to say, the boss has decided to up the ante on Friday night and take us to Ten Degrees for cocktails. Partners too. Fancy it?"

"Is that the hotel on Park Lane, up the top?"

"Yep, that's the one."

"Oh my God I'd love to, yes please!" She wrapped the salmon in foil and popped it into the oven. "Bugger, I'm not going home between now and Friday though, and I haven't got anything here to wear." Tilly sighed, it was such a pain living out of a bag.

"Go shopping tomorrow?" he suggested. "Could you? In your lunch break?"

"Ha, I don't usually get long enough to go shopping at lunchtime. Mind you, it's Thursday tomorrow, the shops are open late so I could go after work if you don't mind?"

"Course I don't mind babe." He pulled his wallet out of his back pocket. "In fact here, take this, buy something nice." He thumbed a wodge of twenty pound notes out. "My treat. And I'll do dinner, have it ready for when you get back."

Tilly stood on her tip toes and kissed him on the lips.

"You – are absolutely the best boyfriend in the whole wide world," she smiled. "Thank you."

Maybe it wasn't so bad living out of a bag after all.

THURSDAY'S VIEWING WAS as good as Ethan had hoped, and the following day an offer had been made on the red brick property overlooking the common. Ethan was in high spirits as the two of them got ready to go out on Friday evening.

"And that, sweetheart, is very nice indeed," he complimented, as Tilly slipped on the gorgeous cap sleeved fitted dress that she'd found in Karen Millen. It was sexy but elegant, exactly the look she'd been aiming for.

Her choice of outfit had gone down well with some of Ethan's colleagues too, if the compliments she received later that night were anything to go by. It was the first time she'd been somewhere really glamorous with the Baxter and Rhinehart lot, and when she saw what the other girls were wearing she was glad she'd made the effort. They clearly knew how to shop, and Tilly felt appropriately dressed in her new purchase.

The venue itself was stunning, making Tilly feel

like she'd walked into a James Bond movie. Despite the early evening sun, the dark ceilings and mirrored bar area made it feel intimate and exclusive, with plush velvet furnishings and gorgeous chandeliers embellishing the room. Ethan led Tilly through the throng of beautiful people, his confidence helping to ease her nerves. From somewhere across the crowd came the sound of a sultry saxophone, its notes smoothing the effervescence of Friday night joy.

"Ethan! Over here mate!"

Ethan clocked the voice of one of his colleagues, and Tilly's hand slipped from his as he veered towards the group of men standing at the bar. She followed, keeping up with him as best she could in her heels, then hanging back as the boys greeted each other. Tilly kept a smile on her face as they hugged, patting backs and congratulating him on his brilliant sale.

"We're getting cocktails, what are you having mate?"

"Whiskey Sour for me," he turned to Tilly. "What do you want, babes?"

Tilly wasn't sure what she wanted to drink without looking at a cocktail list, but didn't want to delay them ordering by asking to have a look.

"Ummm, what was that drink I used to like, when we went on holiday?"

Ethan looked at her exasperatedly, shaking his

head. "I don't know, just pick something."

She ground her back teeth together, annoyed with herself for not being more prepared for the question. She could hear two girls behind her discussing what they were going to order, and picked up on a name she recognised as something she'd had before.

"Oooh I'll have a caipirinha please."

Ethan nodded and turned back towards his colleagues, adding her drinks order to theirs, and Tilly leant down to pull the strap of her very high sandal away from her ankle. It was hurting already, much to her annoyance.

She watched as the bar tender perfected the creation he was currently working on, peeling a tiny slither of orange rind and somehow making it curl exquisitely before dropping it into a very potent looking drink in a martini glass. He slid it carefully across the bar to its recipient and looked up, catching Tilly's eye and winking at her as she blushed and hurriedly looked away.

Ethan turned towards her. "You OK babe?"

She nodded, keen to get a drink inside her for a bit of Dutch courage, and wondered when some girls might turn up too.

"Caipirinha?" called a very tall blond man from the midst of the group of estate agents.

"Over here, mate," said Ethan, taking the drink and passing it to Tilly. "There we go, that'll liven you up," he laughed.

Tilly forced herself to drink slowly. She had to pace herself – the last thing she wanted to do was get drunk and let Ethan down. She sipped her drink through the short cocktail straw as he loudly discussed the intricacies of the property market with his sales manager, and Tilly hoped that her face looked more interested than it felt.

"Tilly! You came, I'm so pleased!" said a voice behind her.

She looked around and was relieved to see the partner of one of Ethan's colleagues.

"Oh hi!" she said, desperately racking her brains to remember the girl's name. She'd met so many people recently that she couldn't keep up.

"Come over here with us, we've got a spot by the window. You don't mind us stealing your wife do you, Ethan?"

The blood rose in Tilly's cheeks as she glanced at him, mortified at the presumption and hoping he wouldn't say anything that made the situation even more toe curlingly embarrassing than it already was.

"No of course not, you go ahead," he replied, winking at Tilly as she shimmied off through the smartly dressed bodies.

As the two girls walked across the room Tilly wondered if she should correct Gabi, whose name she had just remembered, on the matrimonial presumption. It seemed a bit churlish, but if she didn't say anything now then it could well manifest itself into something that was even more embarrassing when found out at a later date. She decided to be brave, despite the fact that deep down, she was quite chuffed to have been elevated to "wife" status.

"Err, Ethan and I aren't actually married."

Gabi turned around, a look of horror on her face.

"Oh my God, I'm so sorry, how awful of me!"

Seeing Tilly's smiling face she relaxed, and guffawed slightly at her faux pas.

"That is so me, I am forever doing things like that. I just presumed... You seem so natural together."

"Don't worry, it's fine, we go back a long way." Tilly rolled her eyes.

"Oh yeah? Sounds like there's a story there!"

Tilly reminded herself that she was with Ethan's colleagues, not a bunch of old school friends, and took the diplomatic approach.

"Oh no, nothing exciting, we've just known each other for a very long time, that's all." She took a larger mouthful of her caipirinha and changed the subject. "So, remind me who you are married to, engaged to, with?" she gestured.

"Oh, that one over there, the tall one with the loud laugh."

Tilly turned to look, spotted who Gabi was referring to, and caught sight of Ethan at the same time. He did look very handsome in his dark suit and open necked white shirt, and for a brief moment she imagined him as a groom, laughing and joking with their guests as she worked her way around the room in her wedding dress, before instantly admonishing herself for getting so carried away.

But her heart still swelled with pride, just knowing that she was with him, that he had brought her here tonight, and watching him with his colleagues, Tilly was suddenly so very proud of him. The thought sprung back in to her mind. *Married. Whoa...* She hadn't thought about things like that for such a long time. It was crazy to even contemplate. They'd only been back together for five minutes. But then again, they had years behind them. What if...

"Tilly, come and sit down here darling. And what are you drinking? Saffy is going to the bar."

Tilly turned her attention back to the girls.

"Sorry, I was miles away, I'll have another one of these please, a caipirinha."

"Oooh good choice, nice drink. Back in a min."

THE DRINKS HAD flowed all evening, and Tilly barely saw Ethan until it was time to go. They said their farewells and Ethan flagged down a black cab.

"Come on, Mrs Roberts, let's get you home," he teased, cheekily patting her backside as she climbed into the taxi.

"Hey you," she laughed, secretly loving the implication, and wondering if men ever thought the same way about things that women did.

The taxi wove its way through the streets back to Ethan's flat; the warm air and late night chatter on the radio threatening to send Tilly into an alcoholically charged slumber. She slipped her shoes off her tired feet, and leant in against Ethan, as he lifted his arm and put it protectively around her. She loved this so much, just being held, and feeling wanted, after such a long time on her own. By the time they pulled up outside the flat, Tilly's rather inebriated mind had decided that she really did love Ethan a lot, and that she actually did want to marry him and live happily ever after with him after all.

And when they stood next to each other, brushing their teeth in the bathroom, she edged closer to him until her thigh was brushing his, and they looked at each other's eyes in the reflection in the mirror and she decided that she should probably tell him *exactly* how she felt when they got into bed. Even though she was definitely a little bit more tipsy than she'd planned to be…

The sun shone through the curtains as Tilly slowly came to, her brain subconsciously working out where she was before her body caught up. Her tongue was dry and as she sat up to reach for the glass of water on the bedside table a nagging pain announced itself in her temples.

"Urgh….."

She lay back into the pillow and turned her head slowly to look at the other side of the bed. Ethan was already up, of course he was. He was an early riser come what may, and as her ears concentrated on the noises coming from outside the bedroom door, she recognised the familiar sounds of tea and toast being made in the kitchen along the hallway.

Tilly tried to remember how much she'd had to drink, counting the cocktails in her mind before remembering Champagne being ordered too. She'd had such a fun time, and the drinks had flowed all night thanks to the boss's credit card and a few hefty bonuses having recently been paid. Flashes of the evening came back to her as she lay very still on Ethan's white sheets. She remembered leaving, that was a good sign at least, but then… She stared into nowhere and tried to remember.

Her eyes suddenly jerked wide open.

Oh No. Please don't have said what you were going to last night Tilly Jenkins, she thought.

"Morning sleepyhead!"

Ethan appeared through the doorway with a

wooden tray in both hands.

"Thought you might be in need of resuscitation," he said, placing the tray on the end of the bed as she carefully shimmied into an upright position. Picking up two mugs and putting one on each bedside table, he went back for the large plate of buttered marmalade toast and placed it on the middle of the duvet before sliding into the other side of the bed.

"How's the head?"

"Not too bad," she lied, hating to admit the truth.

"You were so funny last night," he said, picking up a slice of white toast and taking a huge bite.

Chew faster, she thought, as he nodded to himself whilst he ate.

"Why, what did I do?"

"Oh nothing really, you were just trying to say something when we got into bed but you were so drunk that you couldn't get the words out right, and before you managed it you'd fallen asleep and were snoring your head off!" he laughed.

She jokingly slapped his leg.

"I was not snoring, I don't snore!" she protested.

"Ha! You did last night! I'd forgotten that about you, Miss Jenkins."

Tilly picked up her mug of tea and took a sip.

"Do we have to do anything today?" she asked,

her brain devoid of any weekend arrangements.

"Nope. I've got to pop into the office for a couple of hours this morning, so you can take it easy and have a bath or whatever you want, and I'll be back in time to take you out for lunch, if you fancy?"

"Ah… you really are the perfect boyfriend," she said, relieved that she hadn't let herself down too badly, and thankful that she hadn't voiced her drunken devotion.

"I know," he smiled. "Think about where you want to go for lunch and book us table if you want. One o'clock, Mr and Mrs Roberts," he winked, before disappearing through the bedroom door and down the corridor to the bathroom.

Chapter 12

August

AUGUST BROUGHT WITH it two major milestones. Four clear months until the party, and Tilly's birthday. Both of which were causing her varying amounts of stress, and one of which depended heavily on Ethan upping his game.

The Jenkins family had always gone seriously over the top when it came to birthdays. No one was supposed to go to work, and everyone was expected to participate in making the birthday girl or boy's special day as extravagant as was humanly possible. No-one outside of Tilly's family really understood the unwritten set of rules where the Jenkins' birthdays were concerned, but Ethan had been witness to a few of them, so he should at least have known how things worked.

But two weeks before The Big Day, Ethan still hadn't mentioned anything, and Tilly felt obliged to raise the subject herself.

"So... I just wondered, it's my birthday in a couple of weeks, have you had any thoughts?" she asked over supper one evening.

Ethan stopped chewing and stared at her.

"Yes yes, of course, I… um…"

"Oh my God, had you forgotten?"

Ethan took a sip of water and smiled his best estate agent smile.

"No of course I hadn't, my darling. I was going to ask you actually, if there was anything particular you fancied doing."

Tilly knew he was bluffing, but it wasn't worth an argument, so she went along with the charade.

"Well, I'm not going to have a party, cos two in a year would be slight overkill, and I haven't really thought about it that much…" she lied, "but I was thinking maybe you and I could do something together? Maybe a night away somewhere?"

Ethan nodded, ignoring the reference to what he thought of as her "ridiculous party" and clearly relieved that he'd apparently got away with having forgotten about her imminent birthday.

"That's a great idea, why don't we have a look at diaries and see when we're both free, and I'll book somewhere."

"Well my birthday is on a Saturday this year, handily, so maybe we could do it then?" she asked, raising her eyebrows.

"Yeah, OK, leave it with me babe, I'll do a bit of research and book a hotel. Somewhere posh. Get out of London. Yep, in fact I think I know just the place," he smiled.

TILLY WOKE ON the morning of her birthday to the sound of a thick wodge of mail being pushed through the letterbox and landing on her doormat. She smiled to herself as she flung the duvet back and went excitedly down the stairs.

"Happy birthday to me, happy birthday to me..." she sang loudly as she shuffled through the pile of cards and letters and turned the kettle on. The sun was shining in through the kitchen window, and all felt good with the world. Ethan was picking her up at 11 o'clock to drive her to the mystery hotel, and she felt a flicker of excitement in her stomach at the thought of the day ahead.

Unplugging her phone from the charger, Tilly tapped the Facebook icon for her second round of "post." Birthday messages had already started to drop into her timeline, and she read and acknowledged each one as the kettle boiled. It was funny, but ever since she'd sent her "Save The Date" message, she couldn't help but pay just a little bit more attention than normal to who had commented on, or liked, anything on her Facebook page. Were these the same people who would turn up at her party in December? Were they making more of a point to message her *because* of the party? She'd probably never know, and apart from her close friends, who she knew were genuine in their compliments, she began to feel a little more attentive towards the senders of the birthday wishes that were now filling the screen.

A tap on the front door startled her, and she put her phone down on the kitchen counter and went to open it.

"Morning Miss, delivery for you," the man smiled.

"Thank you," said Tilly, signing for the unknown item and resisting the urge to tell him that it was her birthday.

She shut the door behind her and took the heavy package into the kitchen, wondering who it was from. She laid it gently on the kitchen table and fetched the scissors in order to cut through the sturdy packing tape. As she opened the brown flaps of the box a sweet smell wafted up towards her, instantly transporting her to her mother's favourite candle store in the Florida shopping mall she regularly frequented.

"Ah, Mum, thank you," she said aloud, pulling a large jar from amongst the bubble wrap. As well as the candle there was a birthday card which had been signed by both of her parents, some gorgeous body wash and moisturiser that her mum knew she loved, and a beautiful necklace that Tilly instantly decided to wear that evening. It was too early to ring her parents, so she quickly tapped out a message on her phone so that they'd at least know their parcel had arrived safely, and went back upstairs to shower.

ETHAN PICKED HER up promptly at 11, gallantly placing her overnight bag in the boot of his car and opening the passenger door for her.

"Your carriage awaits, Madam!" he joked.

The journey was long, and Ethan kept the secret of where they were going to himself for so long that it actually began to annoy Tilly. They'd turned off the M25 and were heading south west on the M3, and the only piece of information that she had managed to glean from him was that the name of the hotel began with a C. She hated surprises, always preferring to know where she was going in advance, so that she could enjoy the anticipation of the destination before she even got there.

Tilly stared out of the window as the countryside opened up before her and wondered where Ethan could have booked.

"Have we been there before?" she asked.

"Nope."

"Have *you* been there before?"

"Nope."

"What county is it in then?" She looked at him, the smug look on his face now irritating her. "At least tell me that?" she begged.

Ethan chewed his bottom lip.

"Not telling you that, but I will give you one clue," he said, staring through the windscreen and squinting slightly. "It's near the sea."

Tilly sighed. That wasn't giving much away. She crossed her arms and leant back in the leather seat, her mind running through all the hotels she could think of that began with a C, by the sea.

"Ah ha!" She sat up as much as her seatbelt would allow. "I think I've got it!"

"Where?"

"Ha! Not telling you! Two can play at that game you know!"

"Nah, you're just bluffing," he laughed, "trying to trick me into telling you!"

Tilly grinned. This was suddenly turning into the best birthday she'd ever had. She'd always wanted to go to where she had in mind, a beautiful country house hotel that she'd only ever dreamt about going to before. Until now!

And Ethan knew how much she'd always wanted to go there – they'd once looked at the hotel's website when they were together the first time round, but when they saw how expensive it was... Well, that didn't really matter now that he was earning so much more money. And he *had* been dropping hints about how he was going to do something special with the incredible amount of commission he'd made the previous month.

Oh my God. Tilly was buzzing inside now. *Damn, I should've packed my swimming costume,* she thought, thinking about the amazing swimming pool she remembered from the hotel's website that she'd pored over.

AN HOUR LATER Ethan turned off the main road and headed through the small harbour town of Christchurch. Tilly was pretty sure that the hotel she had in mind was in a much more rural setting than they currently were in, and she wondered if he was bluffing.

"Ah here we go, I see a sign!" he said excitedly. "Welcome to your destination, madam!"

Tilly looked through the windscreen as they turned into the hotel entrance, a forced smile on her lips.

"Ahhhh… very nice…"

"So, had you guessed? Is this where you thought we were staying?"

"Not telling you, you'll never know!" she laughed, trying desperately to quell the rising disappointment in her chest.

A doorman opened Ethan's door, before coming round to her side of the car and welcoming Tilly to the hotel too.

Maybe it's not so bad after all, she thought,

looking at the vast entrance and chandelier adorned reception area beyond.

"Come on, come with me," he beckoned. "We've got a lot to do!"

To his credit, Ethan had thought of everything. After they'd been shown to their room, where a bottle of Champagne was waiting for them, Tilly had been ushered down to the hotel's spa, where he had booked her in for a massage. As she lay on her stomach and the therapist worked on her knotted shoulders, she began to feel the disappointment melting away, but also a bit guilty at having been such a spoilt brat. This was lovely, maybe she hadn't given Ethan as much credit as she should've done.

A few hours later, downstairs in the dining room, Tilly looked with amazement at the menu in front of her.

"Eight courses?" She stared wide eyed across the table at Ethan, who was swirling his wine around in the bulbous glass as if he were some sort of wine connoisseur. "How on earth are we supposed to be able to eat *eight* courses?" she asked.

"It's a tasting menu Tills, they aren't all massive plates of food," he said quietly. "You'll be fine.

Relax."

That was the thing. She wasn't relaxed. She had been earlier, when she'd gone back to the room after her massage, and she'd been even more relaxed by the time she'd finished her second glass of Champagne. But now she felt overdressed and uncomfortable, and although it had been lovely of Ethan to book a private dining room and this incredibly elaborate tasting menu for them both, she would've done anything to be on the sofa in her pyjamas with a takeaway and a box set.

"Good evening madam, sir."

They both looked at the waiter, who was standing proudly a respectable distance from their table, and Tilly hastily replaced the small embossed card on the white linen tablecloth.

"May I offer you the first course of your tasting menu this evening, an exquisite amuse-bouche for your pleasure and enjoyment."

Tilly watched as two apparently identical waiters entered through the double doors and each placed a small plate containing a miniature white soup ladle in front of them both.

Tilly smiled politely until all three men had left the room. She looked down at the single mouthful of food in front of her.

"I don't think I can eat all of this Ethan, I'll pop," she laughed, as Ethan picked up his spoon and examined it.

"It's amazing though, look at it Tills, it's like a work of art."

Tilly picked up the spoon and lifted it to eye level. He was right, it was beautiful. Wafer thin slithers of prawn were stacked up on top of each other, interspersed with something red but unidentifiable, edged with a pale green foam and studded with tiny capers.

"How do you eat it?" she asked.

"Down in one, I guess!"

They both ate at the same time, and Tilly's taste buds instantly came alive with the exquisite combination of flavours and textures. Neither of them could speak, just stared at each other as they savoured every bit of the delicious morsel that was now sadly gone.

"Wow. That was amazing," she said when she could talk again.

"Pretty good huh? I knew this place was supposed to be impressive, but if that's any indication of what's to come this evening, we're in for a real treat!"

"Madam, if I may…" The sommelier placed a fresh glass in front of her, and poured an inch of pale yellow wine into it. "May I present to you a delightful late picked Riesling, from New Zealand, to accompany your second course."

The waiters appeared again and slid two black slate plates in front of her and Ethan.

"Terrine of duck, flecked with apricot shards and studded with baby green peppercorns. Madam, sir. Bon Appetit."

Tilly smiled as she glanced at Ethan, who was nodding profusely at his food. He was really loving this whole experience, possibly more so than she was. She cut a small piece of terrine, simultaneously pushing from her mind the fact that it looked like something you'd serve your cat. She put the fork tentatively into her mouth.

No, the texture was just as she imagined cat food would be if you were so inclined to eat it. She swallowed quickly and took a large mouthful of wine. Oh God, how was she going to get through eight plates of fancy food? Especially if they were as, how could she put it, *experimental*, as this?

Being as well brought up as she had been, always taught never to leave food on your plate, Tilly reluctantly finished the terrine, and was rewarded with a bright orange soup as the next course, which looked much more palatable. Actually it looked rather like her homemade carrot and coriander soup, so she was surprised when the waiter described it proudly as "flavours of our great oceans, from home and away."

The soup was served with a delicious slightly oaked Chardonnay, which pleased Tilly no end, but at which Ethan turned his nose up as soon as the sommelier had retreated.

"Chardonnay, I mean who serves that these days?" he snorted.

"Actually, I really like Chardonnay, so if you don't like it, I'll drink it for you," she replied, back in her comfort zone now that she'd been presented with wine that she genuinely liked, and a course that didn't look like pet food.

"Yeah yeah, keep your hands off young lady, you drink yours and I'll drink mine."

Tilly laughed and turned her attention to the soup. She had never before had any issues eating in public, but for some reason she was suddenly gripped by the uttermost fear. She'd only ever eaten soup at home, from a chunky bowl, usually whilst watching TV, and positioned accordingly so that any drips fell back into the bowl and not down her front. What was the etiquette for eating soup in a posh restaurant? She picked up her spoon and sneakily looked at Ethan, who was skimming across the surface and sipping politely like he'd been doing it his whole life. Surreptitiously copying him, she ate her soup in the most ladylike manner she could muster, aware for the first time in her life just how much noise was created when you sucked soup from a spoon.

"Oh wow, this is amazing," said Ethan. "The flavours are incredible. You really can taste the ocean. In a good way, obviously."

Tilly nodded, managing another couple of

mouthfuls in the time it took him to speak. She was sucking in so much air each time that she was probably going to give herself indigestion at this rate. But he was right, it did taste incredible. Smoky sweet fish mingled with paprika, tomato, and something else she didn't recognise. Tilly longed for a hunk of bread to dunk in it, and a napkin tucked into her dress just in case.

Luckily the bowl wasn't a large one, so the torture didn't go on for too long, and then the waiter was clearing the table and re-laying cutlery, and the sommelier was placing fresh glasses in front of them.

"If I may…"

Tilly glanced at Ethan, wondering if he'd also noticed the way that the sommelier prefixed everything he said with "If I may." If he had, he didn't let on, mercifully not meeting her eyes. Which was probably a good thing, because after half a bottle of Champagne and three glasses of wine, Tilly would almost certainly have got the giggles.

Glasses filled, the twin waiters placed a large plate in front of each of them, with a tiny, perfect mound of white rice, and what could only be described as another work of art consisting of monkfish in a beautifully spiced coriander sauce. It was absolutely divine, and Tilly could have eaten it twice over.

Luckily that wasn't an option, as it was followed by a vintage coupe containing a tiny ball of sorbet, to cleanse the palate, and then what Tilly had considered from the menu to be the "main course."

"And here we have a pan seared pigeon-breast served with wild mushrooms and a balsamic glaze. Enjoy." nodded the waiter, reversing backwards but magically missing the sommelier who was approaching the table with a bottle of Rioja.

"If I may…" he began, but Tilly wasn't listening to him this time, because she was looking down at her plate and thinking that it really looked like…

"Oh my God."

Ethan glared at her across the table, shaking his head in the minutest fashion and telling her loudly with his eyes to shut up.

She looked down again. There appeared to be a *foot* on the edge of her plate. A claw. Small and neat and probably not meant for eating, but very definitely a pigeon leg. On her plate.

The sommelier disappeared once he'd poured the Rioja and Tilly glared at Ethan.

"I'm not eating that," she said.

He laughed, picking the adornment from his plate and reading the little tag that was attached to it, just like the one on Tilly's plate.

"It says eat me," he said, putting it back quickly on his plate.

Tilly grimaced, picking up her cutlery and pushing the claw to the side of the plate with her knife.

"That's disgusting, I'm not eating that. It's like animal cruelty."

"Oh, Tills, stop being silly, people eat a lot stranger things than pigeon feet. A guy in the office the other day was telling me about some of the things he ate when he was Hong Kong. Honestly, it would make your stomach turn."

"Yeah OK, keep it to yourself then!" She took a sip of the Rioja. "Mmmm, that's lovely. Right well you can have my pigeon foot then, I'm not eating it." She picked up the claw by its tag and winced as she leant across the table and dropped it onto Ethan's plate.

"Tilly, stop it, you're not 12, for goodness' sake." He glanced towards the door.

She looked down at the remaining food on her plate, bruised by his admonishment. Her dress was beginning to feel too tight around the middle, and she really needed to go to the loo, but there were still two courses left so she'd have to wait. She wished they could have their pudding in the room, which was obviously not possible, and although she was grateful for the effort Ethan had gone to in finding this hotel and booking the massage and the meal, she could quite easily curl up in bed right this minute.

When the waiter cleared their plates after the

foul fowl course, he asked Ethan if they would like a short break before the final two courses.

"Yes, thank you, that's a great idea," he said, leaning back in his chair and patting his stomach like some overfed Lord of the Manor.

"Certainly, sir. Just give me a nod when you're ready."

Alone in the dining room together, Ethan leant forward and stretched his hand across the tablecloth.

"Actually, would you mind if I just nipped out to the ladies' room? Powder my nose." Tilly slid her chair back and stood up, her legs a little wobbly in the very high heels that she was wearing. She walked as elegantly as she could across the dining room, aware that she'd had plenty to drink, and that Ethan was probably watching her from behind. She didn't want to let the side down.

"Excuse me, where is the ladies room?" she asked a passing waiter in the main part of the restaurant.

"Just down the corridor, turn right, and it's on the left-hand side under the archway."

Tilly eventually found where she was going and was grateful to find that it was a one person at a time cloakroom. She never could wee when somebody was listening. Shimmying her dress up over her legs, she sat gratefully down and leant her head on her hands. She was so full. And tired. And hot. She closed her eyes for a minute. Bliss.

"You OK?" Ethan asked when she got back to the table, "You were ages."

"Sorry, queue for the loo," she lied.

Ethan nodded at the waiter who had been lurking on the other side of the doorway.

"If I may…"

The sommelier filled a Champagne flute with bubbles and Tilly willed him silently to keep pouring until it reached the top, which she always did whenever anyone poured her Champagne, and which on this occasion, he did.

Two large plates covered with silver domes were placed in front of Tilly and Ethan simultaneously, and with perfect symmetry, were removed at exactly the same time, revealing a swirl of pale pink mist that spilled from their plates and onto the tablecloth.

"Oh!" exclaimed Tilly, leaning back and wondering if she should be wafting it back on to the plates.

Ethan laughed at her reaction, hands flapping like a drunken penguin.

"Madam, from us all, we wish you a very happy birthday," smiled the sommelier, before disappearing like a magician before the mist had settled.

Tilly looked at her plate. A perfect mound of

chocolate fondant was surrounded by tiny balls of deep pink cherry sorbet, and *"Happy Birthday Tilly"* was written in chocolate around the side of the plate.

Ethan smiled across the table at her. "Do you like it? Not too cheesy I hope?"

"Oh thank you, hun, I love it, that's really sweet. And it looks amazing... Oh damn, I wish I'd brought my phone with me, we could've taken a photo."

"Now that *would* be cheesy," said Ethan, before tucking into his desert.

BY THE TIME they'd finished the final course – an amazing cheese board and some incredibly delicious port, Tilly could barely move. Declining coffee, they made their way back to their room and flopped on to the bed, kicking their shoes off and laying, fully clothed, on top of the sheets.

"Oh my God, that was amazing," said Tilly. "I don't think I'll eat for a week after all that food."

"It was pretty good, wasn't it? Lara said it would be."

Tilly jerked her head around.

"Who's Lara?"

"One of the girls in the office, she comes here now and again, special occasions and all that. Talking of which..."

He jumped up from the bed and rummaged in his overnight bag, returning with a small gift wrapped box.

"Oooh, present, thank you," said Tilly, suddenly feeling the pressure of opening an unknown gift in front of him. She'd wondered when he was going to give her her birthday presents. Or present. It was quite small… could be jewellery… maybe earrings she thought as she slowly tore the paper off. Oh my God, what if it was…

She took the lid off the box and peered inside. A silver key on a Baxter and Rhinehart keyring sat on a velvet cushion. Pulling it out, she looked inquisitively at Ethan.

"It's a key, to my flat. I wondered if you would, well, will you… move in with me?"

Tilly stared at him, bemused by the unexpected and somewhat random gesture. Not a present at all, not a piece of jewellery, not a ring, which was probably a good thing if she was honest, just a key, which felt like a half-hearted and not very well thought through thing to do. Had he forgotten to get her a birthday present and had the brainwave of giving her the spare key or something?

"So? What do you think? It makes perfect sense. You wouldn't have to live out of a bag anymore, you could rent your house out to cover the mortgage, pay me a bit of rent instead which would be much less than what you're paying at the moment, plus you'd be closer to work, we could spend more time together…"

"Ethan, I…" Tilly didn't really know what to say. This was *not* how she'd imagined things going if this conversation had ever come up again. Where was the romance? Right at the end of his long list of things that would mainly benefit *him*.

She liked her house, her space. Yes it was a pain living out of a bag sometimes, but it wasn't the end of the world. And she didn't want to rent her house out to a complete stranger, who would never look after it the way she did.

"Oh. Well that wasn't quite the reaction I was expecting," he said. "Come on, let's clean our teeth and we can talk about it in bed."

Tilly followed him to the bathroom and watched as he brushed his teeth with military precision.

"It's not that I don't want to move in with you, of course I do, it's just, I don't want to leave my house completely," she sighed, staring at the floor. "And what about my party? I can't exactly fit 289 people into your flat, can I?"

"Oh my God, is that all you're worried about? Your stupid party? You're not *actually* still thinking about going ahead with that are you?"

Tilly smarted at his words.

"What do you mean? Of course I am. Why would I not?"

"Er, because it's a stupid idea, and you only did it cos you were on your own and bored. You've got me now, Tills, you don't need some random Facebook PR exercise to see how many friends you've got."

He strolled out of the bathroom, catching his reflection in the full length mirror as he walked past and running his hands through his hair admiringly. Tilly brushed her teeth quickly and went back through to the bedroom. Ethan was already in bed and staring at the ceiling, and she self-consciously undid her dress and hung it over the back of a chair. Fishing a silk nightdress out of her bag she slipped her bra off and quickly pulled it over her head, before sliding into bed next to Ethan.

"I'm sorry, I didn't mean to sound rude, I'd love to move in with you, I just wasn't expecting it now," she said, propping herself onto one elbow.

"It's fine, it was a silly idea, we probably should've talked about it first. I thought you would've liked it. Let's talk about it in the morning, I'm really tired." He reached up and kissed her, before turning over and pushing the pillow into his neck.

Tilly turned off the bedside lamp and lay on her back, staring into the darkness and wondering how her birthday had suddenly managed to go so disastrously wrong. Had she overreacted? Should she have been excited at his offer, and jumped at the chance to move in with her boyfriend? Maybe it was the way he'd presented it as a birthday gift. She knew that the hotel and dinner were her birthday present, but she had hoped for something little, just something thoughtful to open to show that he cared. That he knew her.

Tilly had had a lovely evening, but if she honest with herself, a couple of times she'd thought that Ethan was enjoying it a bit more than she was. In fact now she came to think about it, he had actually booked them *his* perfect evening. It was definitely more up his street than hers, and should've come as no surprise that it had been one of his colleagues who'd recommended it. They all liked a bit of bling, a bit of luxury, in that office.

But moving in? It wasn't a completely preposterous idea, and it would definitely make life a bit easier. Certainly would make Ethan's life easier. He never did like cleaning very much… whereas Tilly always left everything spic and span. And they shared the cooking, she generally did the food shopping too, she was much more organised than he was.

Tilly sighed as Ethan began to snore. Great, now she was never going to be able to get to sleep. Slipping her arm from under the duvet, she reached out and slid her mobile phone off the bedside table. Opening Facebook, she scrolled through the latest birthday messages she'd received.

Happy birthday Tilly! xx

Hey birthday girl, another year older ha ha! x

Hope you're having a fab time somewhere gorgeous, and being spoilt rotten!

Tilly rolled her eyes. Yes and no. She knew that sounded ungrateful, but the day seemed to have come shuddering to a halt in a rather disappointing way, and she couldn't shake the feeling that it had all gone a bit off track. There she was, laying in a huge bed with a snoring lump next to her, feeling guilty that she'd disappointed *him*, and unable to sleep. She clicked LIKE on each message and decided to post something in return to capture the moment.

Scrolling through her photos from the day, she contemplated which one to use. It should probably be one of her looking gorgeous, and preferably without Ethan in it – she didn't really want the whole world knowing they were together again. There was a good photo of her in her luxury towelling robe post massage, glass of Champagne in hand, but the name of the hotel was embossed in gold lettering across the front, and Tilly didn't really want to admit where she was. Another showed a view across the top of the white roll top bath in their lavish bathroom, through the sash windows and on to the green space beyond… Blue sky and sunshine… that could work. No-one would know exactly where she was, and it looked lush.

Scrolling further, she came to a similar shot but with a glass of Champagne and the bottle in it too – that would be perfect. Show everyone what a decadent birthday she was having. She edited the photo with a filter to make the sky look even bluer than it was, clicked to add it to the post and began to type.

> *Incredible birthday in a gorgeous hotel, full body massage, lots of Champagne, and an amazing EIGHT course tasting menu! Thank you so much for all your lovely birthday wishes!*

Clicking on "post" she waited for it to upload, and scrolled randomly for a few minutes until Facebook notified her that someone had liked it. In no time at all she had five likes on her post – it must be that time of night, when everyone was laying in bed scrolling through their Facebook feeds. Good. To the outside world it now looked like she'd had the most amazing birthday ever, AND added an element of mystery as to who she was with. That would get people wondering.

Pushing the power button to turn her phone off, Tilly put it back on the bedside table and puffed the feather pillow under her neck. Ethan snorted in his sleep, and she groaned as she rolled onto her side and attempted to get comfy with one finger in her ear to block out his snoring. He sounded like a pig. It was going to be a very long night indeed.

Chapter 13

"He did what?!" exclaimed Jemima, practically spitting out her drink. "A key? On a work keyring?!" She shook her head. "Oh my God, that man, honestly…"

Tilly, Becky and Jemima were sneaking in a cheeky post-work bottle of wine and a long overdue catch up. The bar was pretty quiet, although it was a Tuesday and the weather wasn't what you'd expect for August, so the desire to sit by the river and drown yourself in Pinot Grigio wasn't quite so prevalent as usual.

"And what did you say?" asked Becky.

"Well, I didn't really know what to say at first…"

"No?!"

Tilly glanced at Jemima, who was in one of her feisty moods.

"So I didn't say anything, and then somehow it turned into a bit of an argument and then he turned out the light and went to sleep."

"Ah, poor baby Ethan sulking cos he didn't get

his way on your birthday…"

Becky put her hand on Jemima's arm.

"Stop it. We know you don't like him. That's not what this is about." She turned back to her friend. "Oh Tills, what a rubbish end to your birthday, although the meal does sound A-Maze-Ing."

"It was. You and Rupert should so go there one day. I'll come and babysit for you, have a night with my god-daughter."

"Ooooh yes please, that would be fab! We haven't been away for ages. In fact I can't actually remember the last time we had a night away."

"Well, let's do diaries then, I'd love that, honestly. I can't believe she's four already. Don't know where the time goes. And when are you going to give that little girl a brother or sister then, Mrs?" she winked, nudging her friend.

"Oh, who knows, one day. Anyway, don't change the subject, what are you going to do about moving in with Ethan?" she said quickly.

"Dunno, but if I do, it won't be this side of Christmas, he is so not up for my party."

"What? For crying out loud Tills, this man puts the kibosh on everything!" said Jemima.

Tilly knew that. She'd been thinking about his reaction to her party a lot recently. Maybe he was right, maybe she should cancel it now that she was back with him. But then again…

"Hold on a minute," said Becky, always the calming voice of reason. "Why doesn't he want you to have your party?"

"He thinks it's a stupid idea, that I only did it to find a boyfriend and see how many friends I had. Maybe he's right."

"No no no no no, that's his opinion, not yours. Did you ever have doubts before he started whinging about it?"

"Well only about what would happen if everyone turned up. Or no-one."

"And did you think it was stupid, and decide to cancel it once you got a boyfriend?"

"No, actually, it was quite nice knowing that I'd have someone by my side."

"Well then, there's your answer, don't cancel it. Just cos it's not all about him Tills, doesn't mean you can't do something you want to do. For yourself. Crack on, I say. And if Ethan doesn't like it, Ethan doesn't have to come."

"Oh, I don't know," sighed Tilly. "There's so much to think about. The party, moving in, Ethan…"

"Well I know what I'd do," said Jemima, before draining her glass. "Dump Ethan, have the party, and live happily ever after."

TILLY THOUGHT ABOUT her friends' opinions on the

train journey back home. She'd been spending a bit more time in her own house again recently and was looking forward to just vegging on the sofa tonight with a bowl of pasta and some trashy TV, rather than watching one of Ethan's long and often boring documentaries. She knew Jemima didn't rate Ethan at all, and she also knew that both girls had her best intentions at heart, but she couldn't help the niggling feeling that it was OK for them, both happily married and with their lives mapped out ahead of them. It was very easy to judge from the outside.

She'd spoken to her mum the previous week, and finally told her that she was seeing Ethan again. Tilly had been somewhat apprehensive about revealing this information, but her mother had seemed completely un-phased by the return of the man who had previously broken her daughter's heart.

"Oh that's wonderful darling. Just be careful this time, huh? Maybe then you can actually get it right and have a proper grown-up relationship for once in your life. You're not getting any younger you know!"

Tilly had bitten her tongue and tried really hard not to react to her mother's incendiary comments, which she thought was pretty grown-up in itself.

"And now you can stop with all this ridiculous online dating rubbish and settle down with a good man. He's doing well for himself now then, is he?"

That was typical of her mum, zoning in on the fact that he was earning a decent salary. It was all about what he could offer her, the material stuff, but Tilly wanted more than just the security of an excellent wage. She wasn't stupid, she knew that there had to be some sort of financial compatibility, but surely it wasn't just about that anymore? Maybe in her mum's day, when women gave up work as soon as they got married and stayed at home with the children. Rightly or wrongly, it wasn't like that these days.

And the words her mum had used. Settle down. That was it, that was what Tilly felt like she'd be doing if she moved in with Ethan. Settling for second best. Where was the spark, the romance, the feeling that she had met The One? The initial excitement and lust had dropped off pretty quickly now that they'd got used to the routine in each other's lives, and Tilly felt like she'd slipped into some midlife monotony. She hadn't noticed exactly when things had changed, she was only just acknowledging it now. But maybe this was what being grown-up was all about?

Tilly had thought long and hard over the past few days about whether or not she should take Ethan up on his offer. Did she even want to move in with him? Her gut reaction, to her surprise, had been No, she was just too scared to admit it and face the possible consequences. But maybe she was also simply terrified of things going wrong again. It was an impossible situation, and Tilly wished she had a crystal ball to look into the future to see what she should do.

Her mind whirled. If she stayed with Ethan it was highly likely she'd have to cancel the party too, and yes, it was only one night, but it was her night. She'd planned it, pushed the go button, and if she cancelled it – for him – she'd look like an absolute fool. It was a really big deal to Tilly, and she often spent her entire journey to work thinking about her party. She even dreamt about it. Sometimes her house was full to the rafters, people knocking into furniture and queuing for the loo. Other times she was sitting all on her own with a towering mountain of food in front of her and no-one to tell her when it was time to go to bed.

But even if it was a massive flop, she still wanted to have done it, to have seen what the outcome of her crazy idea from all those months ago was.

Tilly looked across the carriage at the couple on the other side of the train. They were probably about her age, the girl was leaning against her partner's chest and he had his arm draped casually around her. They looked content, happy, comfortable in each other's company. She glanced down at the girl's left hand, where a sparkly diamond ring announced their status to anyone who cared to notice. The man kissed the top of the girl's head and the girl smiled to herself in the stuffy carriage.

Tilly closed her eyes. She wanted that. To be part of a content, happy couple. To be going home to the house that they both lived in, together. To love each other so much that they didn't even need to talk to know that they were OK.

Sneaking another peek at them, she wondered how long they had been together. Ethan had been back in her life for three months, and even though this was their second time around the block, she felt like they should still be rolling in romance. He should be pulling out all the stops, shouldn't he? Where *was* the romance?! If she was honest with herself, it all felt a bit too convenient for him, and that recurrent thought was beginning to make Tilly feel just a little bit used. She deserved better than that. All the books she'd read about relationships told her how much a man liked to work for the heart of the woman he loved. They wanted to impress them, to make an effort, and that didn't seem to be the case where Ethan was concerned.

The train began to slow as it pulled into a station. Tilly looked out of the window. Not hers, yet. They man across the carriage kissed his fiancé on the head and quietly murmured something into her hair, and Tilly watched as she smiled and began to stand up. The man gathered their bags and checked they'd got everything, before following her to the door and leaning around her to push the button. Oh my God he was so sweet. She wondered where they were going back to now, his house, hers? Their joint home? They looked so in love, so *together*. Could she have that with Ethan too?

She imagined going back to Ethan's flat tonight, wondered what they'd do. Dinner, TV, bed, not that different to being at home. But she'd be watching what he wanted to watch on television, eating the food that he liked to eat. There was no way he'd let her watch her trashy TV. Sometimes she loved being with him, others it felt like her time was being dictated by what he wanted to do.

She thought back to the day they'd bumped into each other in Holborn. Her stomach had flipped just being in his presence, how had she gone from that to this in so little time? All the years before they'd got back in contact – had she spent that time making him into something that wasn't real? She'd put him on a pedestal, she knew that much, but Tilly was beginning to wonder if in doing so she'd ignored the bad bits, if she'd idolised him, turning him into someone he wasn't. For years she'd pictured spending the rest of her life with him. And now he was back, and she didn't really know if she even wanted to spend the weekend with him. A jolt of reality hit her like a thunderbolt. Ethan wasn't right for her. He didn't love her enough, or rather he didn't love her like she wanted to be loved.

Compromise wasn't something Tilly wanted, not now, not ever.

In which case, there was only one thing to do, and deep down she realised that she'd probably known it all along.

Chapter 14

September

TILLY HAD ENDED things with Ethan as nicely as she possibly could. She wasn't one for confrontation or aggravation, so it wasn't something she had been looking forward to doing. But once she had made her decision to call it a day, the reasons just kept on coming, one after another. And by Friday afternoon, the thought of spending another night in his company without telling him was more than she could bear.

He had been surprised by her well-rehearsed speech, but didn't put up any resistance, which in itself spoke volumes. And as she had packed away her belongings in a large overnight bag, she had been surprised to feel a sense of closure wrapping around her that she hadn't experienced before. This was *her* leaving *him*, not the other way around. Last time it had been Tilly watching Ethan pack his things, but this time it was her decision, and it felt right.

And when she finally got back to her lovely

house, she closed the door behind her, dropped her bags to the floor, took a deep breath, and felt a weight lifting from her shoulders. She went straight upstairs, peeling her clothes off as she went, and took a long hot shower, washing the London dirt from her long brown hair and inhaling the bright citrus aroma of her favourite body wash.

Tilly felt free. Liberated. Independent but not lonely. If she could've captured the feeling of positivity that was rising from her, she would've done. Kept it for those dark February days when all you wanted to do was climb back under the duvet and go to sleep.

The sun was still not quite set when Tilly got downstairs, and she pulled a bottle of Chardonnay from the fridge door and rummaged for the corkscrew before realising belatedly that it was a screw top. Pouring herself a large glass, she took it outside and sat on the bench by the back door, enjoying the last of the day's rays. A gently warmth radiated from the brick wall behind her, and she leant back and closed her eyes. A whole weekend awaited, with no-where to go and no-one to see. Bliss. The garden could do with a bit of a tidy up, she noticed as she looked around. In fact, when was the last time she'd mowed the lawn? Too long ago.

THE FOLLOWING MORNING Tilly woke bright and

early, pulled her hair into a ponytail, and rummaged in her wardrobe for some old leggings, a T-shirt, and a baggy hoodie. She was pleased to see that the late summer sun was still shining, as she'd resolved the previous evening that this would definitely be a house and garden weekend, and she really didn't fancy gardening in the rain. It had been so long since she'd had a whole weekend at home on her own, and she needed to give her lovely house and garden the TLC it deserved. In a way it felt like a sort of cleansing, a fresh start, now that Ethan was no longer part of Tilly's life. Not that he'd made a mess or anything, it was just Tilly's way of refreshing things, of making a mark, a new beginning.

She spent the morning weeding and mowing, cutting back some angry thorns that were threatening to take over the borders, and tidying up her collection of terracotta pots. It was physical work, and the hoodie was soon discarded over the back of a chair, her forearms grateful for the vitamin D. She wasn't a brilliant gardener, but there were a few things that seemed to thrive in her garden without much input at all, and Tilly found that even just a little tinkering and pottering could make a real difference to the overall look.

She was so ensconced in the gardening that when she felt her tummy rumbling, she was astonished to find it was after two o'clock in the afternoon. Two pieces of toast at eight that morning suddenly felt like a very long time ago indeed.

Standing upright she groaned as her spine righted itself. She never seemed to notice how much she leant over when she was gardening, until it was time to stand up. Rotating her shoulders she looked around her. The garden looked so much better than it had done a few hours earlier. The green bin was full to the top with grass cuttings, weeds, leaves and brambles, and her nails were black with soil.

"Right, lunch," she said to a little robin who had been flitting around her garden all morning. "And then I'll start on the inside!"

After a thorough hand wash, a change of clothes, and a particularly tasty cheese, tomato and Salad Cream sandwich, Tilly was ready to tackle the indoor chores. By the time she'd stripped her bedding off and put a wash on, re-made the bed with a fresh set of sheets, dusted, hoovered the entire house *and* mopped the kitchen floor, she was more than ready to collapse on the sofa. She showered the day from her weary body and made herself a cup of tea, which she took outside to appreciate the results of her day's grafting. Sitting on the back step she surveyed her garden. The robin was back, sitting on the fence and singing its little heart out, and Tilly wondered if it was true that robins really were the souls of departed loved ones. She remembered reading about it once in a magazine, but had been told otherwise by Ethan, who had stated quite bluntly that everyone had lost someone, and that there were robins everywhere. In her mind that didn't mean anything either way, but Ethan had been one of those people who you didn't bother arguing a point with, he would always have the last word.

She briefly wondered what he was doing at that very moment, before realising that it wasn't worth her time even thinking about it, because she didn't actually care, and she smiled to herself as she picked up her mug and went into the kitchen for a rummage in the fridge to see what she could find for dinner. Closing the door to the garden behind her, Tilly shivered briefly at the evening chill that seemed to have been present the last few nights. The sun was still shining during the daytime, but there was a definite whiff of autumn in the air, which filled Tilly with joy. It was her favourite season, apart from the spiders of course, and the bite of the cooler evenings seemed to bring an anticipation with it of all the good that was to come with the change of seasons.

LATER, AS SHE chopped tomatoes and olives for her dinner, it dawned on her that she was actually having a really nice weekend, not a miserable "moping around just broken up with my boyfriend" weekend. She had had a super productive day, doing things which some may consider dull, but to her were a fabulous way to spend her Saturday. Tilly wondered if she'd enjoyed herself even more so because she was on her own – maybe the boyfriend thing wasn't the be all and end all that she'd always presumed. Maybe she didn't need a man in her life. Her venture into the world of internet dating had been a disaster, and her rekindling of the greatest relationship of her life had ended up fizzling out too. It felt like she'd tested both ends of the scale, old and new, and neither had worked for her.

She weighed out precisely 80 grams of orecchiette and tipped the little ears into a pan of boiling water as she pondered. What did that mean for her future? Was she destined to be on her own forever? And if so, did it even matter?

The only thing she really needed a man for was if she wanted children, but even that wasn't a guarantee to not be on your own. She could get married, have a couple of kids, and then the marriage might fail. How would that work out? Although she adored her niece and nephew, she wasn't sure she'd fancy raising two children on her own. She could see from watching her sister that it was hard enough even when there were two of you. Nothing was guaranteed in life if you relied on other people. It was simply too unpredictable.

She stared at the water as it bubbled steadily in the pan, her eyes un-focussing until the pasta seemed to merge into itself. But what did that mean for her now, she thought. Was it good? Bad? Indifferent?

Tilly looked around the kitchen for her phone. Eventually locating it on the hall table, she scrolled back through her call log until she found her sister's name. Mimi was always honest with her. The phone rang once the other end, before being diverted to answerphone. Tilly stared at her phone and pulled a face. Since when did her sister start cutting her off? Deciding against leaving a message, she hung up and went back to the stove and stirred the orecchiette, dislodging a few pieces that had stuck to the bottom of the pan.

Her phone pinged and she picked it up.

Sorry Tills, can't talk at the mo, call you tomorrow. Everything ok? xxx

Yes fine, just fancied a catch up. You free next weekend? x

Yes! Come and stay! Love to see you xxx

OK. Talk tomorrow x

As she dished up her bowl of pasta, Tilly wondered what Mimi was doing. Probably putting the kids to bed, she thought, as she glanced at her watch. Stupid time to have phoned. She could talk to her sister about Ethan tomorrow, and then have a proper catch up about everything else the following weekend. It felt like ages since she'd seen Mimi, Andrew, and the kids.

As it turned out, she didn't see Andrew at all anyway. He was away on a team building weekend with a few of his colleagues apparently, although as his colleagues were pretty much his only friends, she suspected it was more like a boy's golfing weekend and piss-up. And when he phoned on Saturday evening to say goodnight to the children, Tilly could hear his voice from the other side of the sofa. Definitely a few drinks down already, she thought, as he told the kids how much he missed them and couldn't wait to see them when he got back.

Once Oscar and Rosie were asleep, Mimi opened a bottle of wine and poured two large glasses. They plonked themselves on the large squishy sofa with a bowl of crisps on the cushion between them, and a huge bar of Dairy Milk within reaching distance.

"So, my lovely sister, what's happening with you?" Mimi asked.

"I've dumped Ethan," she replied, getting straight to the point.

"Gosh, that was quick! What happened?"

Tilly sighed. "Oh, I don't know, I just feel like… I wasn't getting it, you know, that all-encompassing happy ever after feeling that you're supposed to get. Like you and Andrew."

Mimi guffawed into her glass of wine.

"Yeah right. Flowers and chocolates all the way. Tilly, trust me, once you've been married for a few years and have thrown two kids into the mix I can guarantee that there's absolutely no room left for romance whatsoever."

"But you two always look so happy. That post you put on Facebook the other week, all dressed up for some romantic night out, you look like such a lovely couple."

"That, oh my God no, it was some boring work dinner with Andrew's boss, nothing exciting I can assure you."

"OK then, what about this?" She picked up her phone and scrolled through her list of friends until she found her sister's name. "There's one of the four of you, I think you were in the woods, you just look like the perfect family. Argh, here it is." She turned the phone around to face her sister.

"Ha ha, yes. No. If you'd seen the melt down about five minutes later when Rosie decided she didn't want to walk any more, and then Oscar said he needed a poo, well, let's just say that we won't be posting *that* on Facebook."

"Oh, OK."

"Anyway, we digress. So, you and Ethan, I thought you were good?"

This is what Tilly loved so much about having a sister. The way they could be completely honest with each other, and the fact that she knew she'd always get a truthful reply to a question. She filled her in on the events of the past few weeks, leaving nothing out and telling her exactly how it had been. By the time she'd finished, Mimi was nodding.

"Well, it sounds as if you're definitely done this time, my lovely. But I'm glad you're not sad about it, no point crying into your wine now is there? Talking of which, we need a top up. Back in a sec."

Mimi picked up her phone and disappeared into the kitchen, and Tilly broke off a strip of chocolate and snapped it into squares before popping one into her mouth. Tonight was definitely a night of free calories, especially as she had the joy of having her sister all to herself. Although she liked Andrew, the two girls never spoke as freely when he was around. Tilly often felt that her brother-in-law looked down on her a little, as if the fact that she wasn't married made her some lower echelon of society.

Realising that she needed the loo, Tilly hauled herself up from the squashy sofa. As she walked past the kitchen door she noticed her sister standing by the fridge, a bottle of wine in one hand and her phone in the other, texting with her thumb and smiling.

Ah, how sweet, thought Tilly. Probably a drunken message from her husband saying how much he misses her.

"Say hi from me!" she called, as she disappeared into the downstairs cloakroom.

When she got back home on Sunday afternoon, Tilly found a "Sorry we missed you" card sticking out of her letterbox. It was so annoying the way they did that, it might as well have been a sign saying "no-one home, come burgle me."

As she shut the door behind her with her foot she racked her brain as to what it was she had ordered. Nothing immediately sprung to mind, so she was going to have to go to – Tilly read the back of the card to find out where they'd left her parcel – number 22 to find out what it was.

Grabbing her keys and going back out through the front door, Tilly squinted across the street to see where 22 was. She lived on the odd numbered side of the road, so it would be on the other side. 18 was opposite… her eyes continued along the row of houses. Oh God, it was Tariq's. She ran a hand through her hair and adjusted her posture. Knocking on the door of the pristine house, she stood as straight as a soldier as she heard a rustling sound from inside the house. The door opened to reveal a pair of Sunday lounge-pant clad legs and a rather large bunch of flowers.

Tilly blushed. "Oh wow. Hi. Thanks," she mumbled, her cheeks giving away her embarrassment.

"I think these are for you," said Tariq, from behind the cellophane, as he passed the flowers to her. "They came yesterday. I was outside cleaning my car and I think the man delivering them was desperate to find someone to take them in rather than just leave them out front. I had noticed you were away last night so offered to take them in, I hope that's OK."

"Er, yeah, cool, thanks," said Tilly, wondering who the man had been and why he was bringing her flowers. It just got more cringeworthy by the minute. She stood on the doorstep for a moment, before she realised that that was the end of any required conversation and nodded at Tariq. "OK, thank you, see you soon then, have a nice day!"

"Yes, you too," smiled Tariq, not completely oblivious to the awkwardness of the situation and her toe-curling embarrassment.

Tilly walked briskly back across the street and in through her front door as quickly as she possibly could. Oh my God. That was mortifying. She pulled the card from the wrapper and tore open the little envelope.

Tilly – Thinking about you, hope you're ok

after the Ethan stuff. Lots of Love, Bex xx

Breathing a sigh of relief, she smiled at the kindness of her dear friend. To be honest she was just relieved that the flowers weren't from Ethan, or some weird stalker that she didn't yet know about. Trust Becky to be so thoughtful. She was always thinking about other people. Whenever they met or spoke it was always Becky asking about Tilly, not the other way around, and even though they never stopped talking when they were together, Tilly often left an evening with her friend not knowing anything more about her than she had done the day before. Making a mental note to call her the next day to say thank you properly for the flowers, and to ask how *she* was, Tilly tapped out a quick text just so that Becky knew she'd received her lovely gesture. Sunday afternoons were family times, and she didn't want to phone and interrupt whatever they were doing.

LATER THAT EVENING, after her dinner stuff had been washed, dried, and put away, Tilly channel-hopped through the usual Sunday night garbage until her mind wandered to party prep. A part of her wished she could fast-forward through time, to be at the end of November or something, so that everything was organised and ready to go. It was only September, and Christmas felt like ages away. She picked up her phone and searched for a calendar to count the weeks. One, two, three… Tilly scrolled through the months. 12 weeks, just under. In fact, 12 weeks from now it would all be over. Suddenly it seemed not far away at all.

Turning off the television, she jumped up from the sofa and took the stairs two at a time. Pulling her pink folder out of the chest of drawers in her bedroom, she flicked through the plastic pages that were stuffed with bits torn out from magazines. Decorations, food, lists of names; everything to do with the party was in her trusty folder. She felt like a bride with her wedding planner, it was probably just as stressful, but a whole lot cheaper, and just as much fun even if she didn't get to go home with a husband at the end of the night. Oh well.

She looked at a few pages that she'd doodled on. Despite her keenness to crack on, there wasn't much she could do right now. But next week it would be October, and as soon as Halloween was out of the way, people's minds automatically went to Christmas. That was what she'd do. Spend October thinking about food, drink and decorations, then on the 1st of November she'd send the proper invite out again on Facebook, and get a definite number of attendees so she could order what she needed. And book a marquee in a field if everyone said yes, they were coming.

Tilly felt a bit sick at the thought of that, and she shut the folder quickly in an attempt to block the image from her mind. Slipping it back into the drawer, she pulled out clean underwear for the following day, and turned to the wardrobe to find a suitable outfit for the morning. You could never be too prepared, and Tilly was not one who liked to leave anything until the last minute.

As she slipped under the duvet that night, grateful to be back in her own bed despite the lovely night away at Mimi's, Tilly felt a deep sense of contentment within. She counted out five blessings on her fingers, as she often did before she went to sleep. There was the beautiful bunch of flowers from Becky; she'd had a lovely time with her sister and the children; the sun had shone all weekend; there was a plan for her party organisation; and … she couldn't think of a fifth… Maybe everything was just good in her life. That would do, she thought as she closed her eyes and drifted off to sleep, that was all you could ever really ask for.

But on Monday morning, Tilly came crashing back down to earth with a bump and any sense of contentment went flying out of the window. As she walked through the rows of desks in the office, she could tell immediately that something was going on. Gone were the usual motivated Monday morning faces, in fact some of her colleagues looked more like it was Friday morning after too much to drink on Thursday night. There was a definite whiff of glum about the place, and as she reached her desk and shrugged off her jacket Tilly looked across the office to see Karen, who was wide eyed and slowly shaking her head in her direction.

Read your emails, she mouthed silently.

Tilly slid into her chair, pushed the power button on her computer and waited impatiently. Why did computers take so flipping long to turn on? She looked around in the hope that something or someone might give her a clue as to what was happening, but nothing was forthcoming. Most people had their heads down and seemed intent on concentrating on whatever they were doing, and even the usually chatty ones were strangely devoid of tales from their weekends.

Eventually, painfully slowly, her desktop screen appeared and Tilly clicked on the letterbox logo. The usual start of the week deluge of emails dropped into her inbox, and she scanned the rows of subject titles looking for something that might obviously be important.

IMPORTANT – Company Reorganisation.

Tilly gulped. That would be it. There had been

rumours swirling around for a while about changes heading their way, although she had tried to ignore the gossip as much as possible. As a team leader she was usually kept in the loop as to anything major, and as far as she was aware, there wasn't anything in the pipeline. Mind you, her head had been so full of party stuff recently that she could well have missed something. She clicked on the header and read as quickly as possible through the lengthy text.

Re-structuring… New faces… Streamlining… One-on-ones… Redundancies.

Tilly picked up her takeaway cup of coffee and took a gulp, the hot liquid burning her tongue. Shit. No wonder everyone looked so miserable. How did she not know about this? To be fair, she'd been enjoying the summer so much with Ethan and her friends, that she'd done very little socialising with anyone at work and may well have missed any alcoholically charged spilling of secrets.

Sighing, she wondered why it was that just when you thought things were going well in your life, a great big fat curve ball would come flying around the corner, throwing everything up into the air again.

24 hours earlier Tilly had been in a really good place; home, friends, job, happily single, healthy, and having a lovely weekend with her sister and the kids. And now suddenly she was contemplating the

possibility of losing her job, and all that that would entail. She scrolled through the email again and wondered how on earth she'd pay her mortgage without her not-to-be-grumbled-at salary dropping into her bank account every month. A lot of her colleagues were married, at least they had someone to fall back on to help pay the bills. And the younger ones these days didn't seem to worry so much about losing their job, they either lived with their parents or secretly quite liked the idea of doing something way more exciting than mortgage admin.

Maybe she should've stayed with Ethan and moved in with him after all. At least that way she'd have a roof over her head that she wasn't responsible for. At least the pressure would have been off. No, that was a silly idea, and Tilly knew it the instant the thought crossed her mind. Moving on from Ethan had been a good thing, and she wondered if she should try to convince herself that the company reorganisation was actually a good thing too. Maybe.

She glanced over towards Karen's desk. Alan was perched on the edge, precariously close to a pile of manila folders. They were talking very quietly about something or other, probably discussing whether or not their jobs were on the line too. Something tugged at Tilly's heartstrings. Although she wasn't big on the social scene at work, she would miss the office banter that flowed so easily around the office if she didn't work there anymore. It was unimaginable, the thought of not seeing her colleagues on a daily basis, not knowing anything at all about what was going on in their lives. Which reminded her, she really should organise a drink with Karen one evening after work, see what was going on with her these days.

Tilly took another sip of her latte. That would have to change too. No more wasting money on posh coffees, it would be a jar of instant for her from now on.

And what about the party? On her way to work that morning she'd been drafting the official invite in her mind and wondering if October was too early to send it. Thank God she hadn't, no-one would want to come to a party if there was just lemonade and a bowl of peanuts on offer. Tilly scratched her head and sighed. This was a textbook reaction for her, to immediately jump to the worst case scenario. The good thing about that though was that she usually then worked her way to finding a satisfactory resolution.

She sat back in her chair and cast her eye around the office, wondering who would go and who would stay. Maybe a couple of the new girls in the corner, last in first out? Or would they scale down the number of consultants? She knew the ones who didn't make their commission targets regularly, surely they'd be up there on the firing line? Tilly caught the eye of one of the compliance team, and quickly looked away. Was he thinking the same? Oh God, was everyone looking around the office and wondering whose days were numbered? Hideous.

"Tilly, can I have a word please?"

Her boss's voice cut through her thoughts and brought her back into the moment. She stood up quickly, as if she'd been caught doing something she shouldn't have been.

"Yes of course."

Tilly followed Duncan along the walkway, a dozen pairs of eyes burning into her back as she made her way to his office.

"Close the door please."

Tilly felt an uncomfortable prickle in her armpits as she shut the glass door and sat down in the empty chair.

"Right. So, I presume you've seen the email that's been sent out this morning?" he asked.

Tilly nodded, fearful of saying anything other than "Yes" that might steer her fate in an unpalatable direction.

"OK well first of all, don't panic, I'm not about to give you your marching orders," he laughed.

Easy for him to say, she thought, a tight smile on her lips.

"I just wanted to give you a heads-up. I was

hoping to have had a chat with the department leads before the email went out, but unfortunately that didn't happen." He took a deep breath before continuing, adding to the tension. "Yes, there are going to be some changes, but no, they won't be major. The first step will be to review our current staffing levels, look at if and where we can shift people around, but I don't want people thinking they're going to be out of a job next week. OK?"

Tilly nodded, the worry she'd felt earlier slowly receding.

"What I'd like you to do at this stage is to have a chat with each of your team members, reassure them of the situation, and see if anyone has any interest in working in any of our other offices. Please do make it clear that we are not suggesting that anyone will be moved against their will, it's just a stock take of the company as it were, seeing how the land lies. Is that OK?"

"Yes, absolutely," said Tilly, her management skills mindset replacing the self-indulgent fear she'd felt before. "Although like you said, a heads-up on this would have been good, no one likes surprises."

Duncan nodded.

"Oh and Tilly, I'm hoping that *you* aren't going to suggest going anywhere else, you do a great job here and I wouldn't want to lose you, OK?"

Tilly smiled. "Thank you, I appreciate that."

Striding back to her desk, she felt a glow of

satisfaction. Praise always made her feel good, and it had been a while since anyone had said something so positive about her. As she flicked open her screen all thoughts of redundancy, losing her house, and cancelling the party fell to one side, and she got to work straight away on a plan of action for her team.

Chapter 15
October

THE FIRST HALF of October flew by for Tilly, her head full of work and her body feeling the stress that she automatically seemed to absorb from her worried team. If she hadn't been so busy with everything that was now going on, she would have been completely preoccupied with party stuff, and in the semi lucid moments before she fell asleep each night her mind spun with all the things that she had hoped to be doing in October.

But thankfully the initial shock of the potential changes at work eventually diminished, and luckily no-one was required to make any moves that they hadn't suggested themselves. A couple of Tilly's team had been happy to move sideways to other departments in the company, and three of the consultants had taken up offers of relocation to offices outside of London, so everything had worked out fine in the end. If only she'd known it would've gone so smoothly, Tilly might actually have been a little bit less stressed.

By the time she stopped to breathe, it was mid-October, and Tilly was now chomping at the bit to get the official party invite sent out. She hadn't even had a chance to catch up properly with Jemima or Becky, relying instead on the joy of social media to keep her up to date (or not) with what was going on in her friend's lives. Jems had been posting before and after photographs from her most recent projects, which made Tilly instantly want to redecorate her entire house. And Becky was curiously absent, probably up to her ears in family life and all that it entailed.

Tilly did NOT want to be absent from social media, she needed to be out there and visible, so on Friday night she made herself a big mug of tea and sat down at the kitchen table with her laptop ready to get designing. Luckily for Tilly, who wasn't completely au fait with the workings of Facebook, there was a handy "Create Event" tab that guided you through the process. Easy, she thought.

The first few details required were simple enough, starting with the event name. Tilly pondered briefly on whether to call it something memorable, but decided simply on "Christmas Party." No point trying to dress it up as something that it wasn't. Like the most terrifying yet momentous thing she'd ever done in her whole life or anything.

The date had already been decided, but specifying the start and end time had her pondering for quite a while. Too early and the evening could end up either very messy or very short, but too late and she'd spend half the evening in fear of no-one turning up. Deciding on 7.30pm as a happy medium, she entered the time and put midnight to end. She didn't want to annoy her neighbours (which reminded her, she needed to let them know about her party so they didn't complain about any unexpected noise), but then she couldn't imagine many people stayed at parties past midnight anyway. Did they?

"Event Privacy" was where everything began to feel very real indeed. Private, public, or friends only. Basically zero, two billion, or 289. The latter it was then. Tempting as the first option was.

Sliding the tab very firmly to OFF on the "Guests Can Invite Friends" option, Tilly clicked through to the next tab, "Location." Oh God. Even more real. She typed in her home address and hit enter, a slight feeling of nausea as her personal details moved one step closer to being shared with the world. Well, to 289 people in the world anyway.

The final box to complete was "Description." After staring at the empty space for a not inconsiderable amount of time, Tilly got up and poured herself a glass of wine. What do you write when it's going out to not only your nearest and dearest, but also several random strangers who you haven't seen for years, and a high percentage of people who probably think you're absolutely nuts?

After several attempts and an equal number of deletions, Tilly settled on a simple description which she hoped didn't sound too desperate, or too sad.

> *I would like to invite you all for Christmas drinks, nibbles, and merriment. I am inviting every single one of my Facebook friends so no offence will be taken if you can't make it! My house is only so big after all… Strictly invitation only, please do not share! I very much look forward to seeing you. Kindly RSVP by 5th November. Thank you! Tilly x*

Hoping that "merriment" wasn't too strange a word, Tilly clicked to submit the event, and there it was. Her invite, winging its way through the atmosphere to 289 people. Just like that, with not a single stamp in sight.

Knowing that she'd drive herself mad if she sat and watched her Facebook page until someone replied, Tilly closed the laptop, switched her phone to silent, and decided to direct her attention to cooking dinner. Tomorrow she could check for RSVPs, and update her already prepared spreadsheet with yes, no, or maybes. Tonight she needed food, TV, and a chance to unwind after a very busy few weeks.

Chapter 16
November

By November Tilly had almost 80 confirmed guests. She was happy with that, if a little overwhelmed. It was certainly a decent amount of people, and as she walked around the downstairs rooms of her home she tried to imagine how they would fill the space. Actually, if people spread themselves equally between the sitting room, dining room and kitchen, plus a few outside smoking, the house might even feel quite roomy. But knowing that all good parties ended up in the kitchen… well, that would be one hell of a squeeze. Panic began to rise and not for the first time she felt like pulling the plug, until a little voice inside her head reminded her why she was doing this. She *wanted* a house full of people. A party that people talked about for years. The potential for new openings, real friendships, maybe more… Calm down, she told herself. It was more than likely that a few would drop out nearer the time, just hopefully not so many that she'd look like Billy-no-mates.

She'd also had over 100 messages thanking her for the invite, but declining due to prior engagements, family commitments, or simply the fact that they lived in another country. Tilly found it fascinating how many of her Facebook friends lived abroad, she hadn't ever really acknowledged that before. Some had emigrated since she'd met them, others had always lived abroad, and one of her old school friends was moving to New Zealand the week before the party.

Bad timing, or what?! she'd typed.

That left about 100 people who hadn't said yes or no to coming, and Tilly wondered how late to leave it before she chased up RSVPs. In all likelihood a non-reply probably meant a no show, but she was not one for presuming or speculating, so decided she'd send a follow up at the end of November. Just to be on the safe side.

Her parents hadn't officially declined the invite, but Tilly had spoken to her Mum earlier in the month, so she knew that they weren't planning on coming back to England any time soon. In fact, her mother had had the audacity to suggest that Tilly should "Ditch the stupid party idea and hop on a plane for some sunshine instead darling."

The idea actually sounded amazing, and it made Tilly think about how long it had been since she'd been on holiday. A beach and some relaxation would've suited her down to the ground any other time, especially now that November was closing in around her and bringing with it the mist and damp that often arrived at this time of year.

But no, Tilly had plans, and she needed to crack on with them.

In her opinion the most important things that she just had to get right were the drink, food, and atmosphere. So, confirming her online food order and the wine delivery from Majestic were top of her To Do list.

THE NICE LADY at the wine warehouse was incredibly enthusiastic once Tilly had explained how many people she was catering for and why, and had been positively gushing with suggestions and the offering of free samples for Tilly to taste. They had discussed the downfalls of offering too much of a choice, and come to the conclusion that if you offered red wine, white wine, prosecco and beer, then everyone would find something that they liked. There was really no need for spirits and mixers, and just the thought of all the extra glasses and paraphernalia that went with cocktails was enough to convince Tilly that she was right.

Penelope (a very surprising name for someone under 30) entered all of Tilly's party details into her magic ordering system, and came up with the apparently perfect number of bottles that she would need to cater for everyone. It sounded like an awful lot of wine, and an even larger amount of money, but Penelope explained that anything that wasn't opened could be returned for a full refund. Tilly had actually had nightmares in which she ran out of drink at the party. Imagine the embarrassment, the mass exodus… So she certainly didn't want to under order. But knowing that most people would probably bring a bottle anyway meant that in all likelihood there would be wine left over, which was a positive thought.

After choosing a "smooth and light" Pinot Grigio, an "easy drinking" Portuguese red, and a "great for parties" Prosecco, Tilly gratefully accepted Penelope's suggestion of beer choice. She didn't really know much about beer, so was happy to relinquish that responsibility to the very friendly and helpful expert sitting across the table from her. In fact by the time Tilly had finished tasting all the samples she'd been offered, she was on the verge of inviting Penelope to her party anyway, such was the joviality of the occasion.

Before the serious and down to earth with a bump part of the day arrived (paying), Tilly arranged glass hire and chiller bin hire, which to her joy were both free. The wine and everything else would be delivered the day before the party, which was perfect. She'd stared into the fridge that morning and wondered how on earth she was going to fit all the food and wine in there, so that was one less thing to worry about. And the glassware would be collected two days after the party, much to Tilly's relief. She didn't fancy having to get up at the crack of dawn the following morning to wash and dry two hundred glasses.

Once the wine order was sorted, Tilly turned her mind to food. She had already concluded that the food needed to be as low maintenance as possible, but at the same time had to be filling enough to line people's stomachs so that they didn't get completely wasted and puke on the carpet.

So after much deliberation, pleasant as it was, she had decided on large platters of "picky" food. Hot honey mustard sausages, which could be prepared the day before and put in the fridge ready to pop into the oven to heat up. Mini chicken goujons with a garlicky mayonnaise dip. Huge bowls of crisps and olives, which would be easy to top up. And a vast cheeseboard with crackers, chunks of bread, and chutney, which if she did properly would be a gorgeous centrepiece on the dining room table. She wanted nibbly food, things that could be eaten with fingers, napkins, and small plates.

And then pudding. Her brilliant brainwave. She was going to make several batches of mini chocolate and cranberry brownie bites – sweet, sticky and Christmassy, piled high and dusted with icing sugar. With a little reindeer perched on the top, like she'd seen Nigella do once. A snowy winter's mouth-watering mountainous scene.

She had – of course – already made a list of the ingredients she'd need in order to make all of this, and she had even bought the long-life items like flour and dried cranberries in advance. Everything was now safely stored in her kitchen cupboards, on a special "party" shelf. Tilly had considered prebooking an online food order for all the other ingredients, but she'd heard so many horror stories about the wrong item being delivered, or some crucial ingredient being forgotten, that she had decided to do a big shop in person the weekend before the party instead. That way she would have plenty of time to pick up any odd bits during the week if she needed too. It would be ridiculous to rely on a supermarket employee to know exactly what she needed and not let her down on a single item. That just wasn't Tilly's style.

Once the food and drink were sorted, for the time being at least, Tilly breathed a sigh of relief and took some time to think about some of the other elements of the party. The Christmas tree would have to wait until December, and decorations had to be sparkly and elegant, not glitzy and naff. Her outfit – oh God, what on earth was she going to wear – was definitely next week's Very Important Thing To Do. She needed more plates, napkins, cocktail sticks and big bowls. Tablecloths, candles, loo rolls, Christmassy hand towels…. The more she thought about it the bigger it seemed to get.

Tilly put her head in her hands, wishing there was someone to share the burden with. She wondered if Ethan would've helped if they were still together, before she remembered how negative he'd been about the party. What about her sister? Maybe not, she had been so snappy recently. Tilly wondered what was going on in Mimi's life that was making her so weird at the moment. There was definitely something odd going on; they weren't chatting as much, and Mimi never seemed to be able to talk when Andrew was in the house. She thought back to the random text at Christmas and for a brief moment wondered if there was trouble in paradise, before swiftly admonishing herself and putting such a silly thought to the back of her mind. She was beginning to sound like Mrs Mangel.

Nope, there were two other people in her life who she knew would come up trumps. Time to call in the girls.

"OH MY GOD I LOVE a party," squealed Jemima, when Tilly rang to ask for her help. "What can I do? Decorate? DJ? Make cocktails?"

Tilly rolled her eyes, wondering if the party was

about to be taken over by her excitable best friend.

"No! No cocktails! I've sorted the drinks, it's fine. But I would appreciate your help with some of the millions of other things I have on my To Do list, please...."

"What? You've got to have cocktails! Leave it to me, I am SO good at making cocktails – as you well know my love. We could do Bellinis, Mojitos, oh my God I'm going to get my thinking cap on and get plotting for you. How EXCITING!"

Luckily Becky was the calm voice of reason when Tilly phoned her next.

"Don't worry about Jems, you know what she's like. Let's get together and make a plan, you can tell us what you need doing, and I'll rein Jemima in. What are you up to this weekend?"

SO ON FRIDAY night Tilly had a girl's night in at her house. A proper food, wine, chat and sleepover, long overdue, and very welcome. She left work at half five on the dot, walked to the train station as quickly as she could, made the early train, practically jogged home, and shed her work clothes as she climbed the stairs. Quick shower, jeans and her favourite sparkly star jumper, and she was ready to go. A night in at home with her best friends was a rare treat, and she'd stashed several bottles of bubbly in the fridge in anticipation. With impeccable timing, the doorbell rang as she came down the stairs, and Tilly opened the door to see Becky's smiling, but somewhat weary face.

"Bex! Come in!" She gave her friend a big hug and ushered her in to the warmth.

"Oh my God, it is so nice to be here, it feels like ages since we had a proper girls night in."

"I know, waaaaay too long." She took Becky's coat and hung it on a hanger. "How's Delilah? Gorgeous as ever?"

"No, not this morning she wasn't, she was not impressed that I was going out straight from work, and even less impressed when she found out that I was seeing you! Honestly, you should've heard her. *I want to come, me me me!*"

Tilly laughed. "Oh bless her, my little angel, you should've brought her."

"No chance," smiled Becky, "we wouldn't have got a word in edgeways. She is four going on 14 at the moment; if you ignore her for a minute she gets a right strop on. A madam in the making I think. Poor Rupes, he's got his work cut out for himself tonight!"

In the kitchen Tilly took a bottle of Champagne out of the fridge and slid three of her good Champagne flutes from the top shelf of the cupboard.

"Oooh nice, just what I need after the week I've had."

Tilly glanced at her friend. "Oh? What's happened?"

"Oh nothing, you know, the usual, work, family, never enough sleep, anyway stop asking questions and get on with opening that bottle please. Oh, and I've bought a bottle of red and some chocs too, they're in my bag."

Tilly popped the cork and filled up two of the three flutes. As they chinked glasses the doorbell went again, and Tilly took a quick sip before going to open the door.

"That'll be Jems then, you know what she's like, she can smell an open bottle of Champagne from 100 yards!"

"Hellooooo!" Jemima whirled into the hallway, dumping her bags haphazardly on the floor and flinging her arms around her friends. "Oh my girls, my darlings, this is so lovely! Here, these are for you." She thrust a thick paper grocery bag towards Tilly, which chinked loudly as she took it. "One red, one white. Thought we could pretend to choose but actually just drink both," she laughed.

"Oh darling, you didn't have to bring anything, either of you, but thank you. Dinner's on me, obviously, now come inside and have some Champagne."

At the point at which the second bottle was being opened, Tilly realised that she'd better be a little bit organised, or else they'd just end up legless, eating crisps.

"Right, come on girls, let's get the curry ordered

and then we can do a bit of party planning before the food gets here, is that OK?"

"Argh, you're so SENSIBLE!" squawked Jemima. "But yes, you're right, although you're going to need your glass topped up in order that I can convince you to let me make cocktails!"

Becky met Tilly's eyes across the table.

"No, Jems, I've been thinking about this too, and it's just so much faff. I agree, you do make the best cocktails, but not for that many people. They'd be waiting all night! I hate to say it, but I think Tills is right."

Jemima rolled her eyes. "OK… It is your party… But please can I do something exciting? Maybe I can dress up as a … Hold on, what's the theme?"

"Er, there isn't a theme," replied Tilly. "It's a Christmas party," she shrugged.

"What? Oh my God, no cocktails, no theme, not even a flipping birthday. Remind me why you're having this party again?"

"Alright," interjected Becky, who hadn't missed the speed at which Jemima's glass was being emptied. "Go easy on her!"

Tilly took a deep breath, trying to remember why she wanted this party in the first place.

"Because I never have a party. I never do anything exciting anymore. It's alright for you two, you've got your glamourous jobs, a gorgeous little girl, fab husbands, I never have anything fun going on in my life anymore and I want that. I want people to be excited about coming here, to look forward to something. For so long now I've just been going through the motions, and I want this house to feel alive again. Does that make sense?"

Becky reached across to take Tilly's hand in hers.

"Of course it does darling, and we're here to help with whatever you need. Right. Knowing you, you've probably got a list somewhere with our names on it, haven't you?"

Tilly smiled, surprised at the level of emotion that had been stirred up inside her.

"Yes I have, and there's a shit load of stuff on there so you'd better be ready!" she joked. "Right, let's get our food order in and we can plot."

THREE CURRIES, THREE rice, two naan breads and a saag aloo later, they had constructed a master plan for Tilly's party. Which, considering the number of empty wine bottles there were in the kitchen, would be a miracle if they remembered.

Obviously, Tilly had made notes along the edge of her list, so evidence remained, and all would not be lost. She scraped remnants of curry into the bin as Becky carried some more plates over to the sink.

"I am soooo stuffed," she said. "Why do we always order so much food?!"

Tilly laughed. "It's not bad that we order so much, it's that we eat it all!" She took the plates from her friend and slotted them into the dishwasher. "What's Jems doing? She's very quiet all of a sudden."

They went into the sitting room to find Jemima sprawled on the sofa, fast asleep and still managing to look gorgeous, in the way that only she could.

"Oh bless, she's shattered," said Tilly.

Becky smiled. "You're too soft on her sometimes Tills. She's not tired, she's drunk. Again. Did you not notice the speed at which she was putting it away?"

"I did, yes, but she's always like that. Come on, let's go and sit in the kitchen. You and I can have a natter, feels like ages since we had a proper chat. What do you fancy, wine or tea?"

"Oooh, a cup of tea, that would be lovely, thanks Tills."

Tilly put the kettle on to boil and Becky lurked next to her. They had known each other almost their whole lives, and Tilly instantly knew something was coming. She looked at her sideways.

"What?"

Becky sighed and wrapped her long hair in a twirl around her hand.

"Actually, there was something I wanted to tell you." She screwed her face up.

Tilly raised her eyebrows in anticipation, immediately thinking that she was going to tell her she was pregnant, before remembering that they'd all been drinking. A lot.

Becky's nose wrinkled.

"Oh, it's a bit shit, but I wanted to tell you. I thought I was pregnant last month, that's why I've been a bit quiet, but it turns out it's not meant to be. I got my period, or miscarried, or something, I don't really know."

"Oh Bex, my love, I'm so sorry." She took her into her arms. Tilly hadn't even been aware that they were actually trying for another baby, although she had wondered for a while if they'd ever add to their little family of three. She felt a sob on her shoulder. "Oh God, I'm sorry, I didn't mean to make you sad!"

Becky half smiled, half cried.

"No, I'm sorry, I didn't mean to cry! Must be the wine." She wiped her eyes. "Actually it feels good to let it out, I can't really talk about it with Rupee, he doesn't understand what it's like for us girls."

Tilly didn't fully understand either to be fair, having never been in Becky's situation, but she hated seeing her friend upset. She was also rubbish at knowing what the right thing to say was, but she'd read enough magazine articles to know that sometimes listening was more important than talking, so she took the mugs of tea over to the kitchen table and listened as her friend filled her in on the last few weeks, secretly grateful that Jems had passed out on the sofa so that the two of them could have this time together to talk.

TILLY FINALLY FELL into bed the wrong side of one o'clock, a bit drunker than she'd planned on being, but happy to have spent so much quality time with her two best friends. She was glad that Becky had confided in her about her situation, even though she felt dreadful for her. But Bex was strong, she would get through this, and maybe even, hopefully, try again with a better ending next time. She hated seeing her friend upset yet be powerless to help. Maybe getting involved with the party planning would be a welcome distraction – Tilly knew it wouldn't lessen Becky's sadness but hoped it might at least occupy her mind enough to stop her from dwelling too much on the things she couldn't change.

Also, after sharing the load with the girls, Tilly felt much more in control of the party situation. There was still a lot to do, but she was as excited as she was nervous, maybe even a little bit more excited now that she had Becky and Jemima on board too. Tilly may be single in the conventional sense, but she didn't feel alone anymore. There was no boyfriend to talk to or to sound things off on, but she was OK with that. She still had her job, her lovely house, and although she might not have got around to joining a gym that year she felt good about herself. And the next few weeks were going to be super busy!

AT THE END of November Tilly posted once again on her Facebook page, sending a final reply request. The original RSVP date had been the start of November, but she needed to make an absolute final plan, and get definite numbers, so she knew exactly how many people she was expecting. Fear and anticipation ran through her mind, the uncertainty going against everything she stood for, and the need to know what she was dealing with greater than ever. This was it. It was finally about to happen. Three weeks left and absolutely no turning back now. Her crazy, hair-brained idea from almost a year ago was about to come to fruition. Everything she wanted was literally about to present itself at her front door. And it was terrifying!

Chapter 17
December

As it turned out, the first two weeks of December did not go as Tilly had planned or expected. The month had started simply enough, with a busy week at work and the usual lunch time buying of Christmas cards and presents slotted in amongst meetings, deadlines and festive joviality. But as she stared out of the train window into the dark evening on Friday night, trying to remember how many sets of twinkly lights she had in the loft, the weekend's plans were suddenly, and unexpectedly, thrown into disarray.

Tilly's mobile phone rang loudly in the quiet carriage, and she flipped open the cover to see her sister's name on the screen.

"Hey Mims, how you doing?" she asked.

There was a brief pause in which Tilly heard a car whooshing past, followed by a honk of a horn before her sister's frantic voice came through the phone.

"Tills, I need your help." Tilly's heart raced,

instantly wondering if something had happened to one of the children.

"Oh my God, what's happened?" she asked, causing the man opposite her to stop reading and look up from his newspaper.

"It's too complicated to explain, but I really need a favour. Is there any chance you can please come and look after the children for me this weekend? I need… I just need to sort something out, I'm sorry I know I'm not making sense but I just need someone to look after the kids for me. Can you? Would you mind? Please?"

Tilly thought quickly. A tiny flutter of annoyance ran through her, which was instantly quashed by her kind-natured, better self. She would absolutely help her sister out. Whatever the reason.

"Of course I will Mims, are you OK? What's happened?"

Her sister exhaled loudly down the phone line.

"It's Andrew, we've had a massive argument, I can't go into it now I'm sorry my love, I just need to sort some stuff out and I can't do it with the kids in tow. Can you come tomorrow morning? Please?"

BY THE TIME Tilly got home she'd also had a text from Mimi telling her to bring an overnight bag "just in case" which basically ruled out the whole weekend and meant that the massive party To Do list was not going to get a look in. Although Tilly loved her sister (of course she did), without knowing the full facts a touch of resentment crept into her mind. Tilly may not have a husband and kids, but she did have a load of stuff to do this weekend. Although... scrolling through the list she wondered if it might be possible to kill two birds with one stone.

THE FOLLOWING MORNING Tilly showered, dressed, packed a few things into a holdall, and jumped into her car. She thought the roads were surprisingly busy for a Saturday, until she realised that there were only a couple of shopping weekends left before Christmas, so of course the whole world was out there doing their present buying or heading to friends and family for pre-Christmas shenanigans.

When she finally arrived at Mimi's house, hoping for a cup of tea and some enlightenment, Tilly found her sister ready to go; bag packed and coat on.

"Thank you so much Tills, I owe you one. I promise I'll explain everything, I just can't at the moment. I've told the kids that I've got to go on a work thing with Daddy, so they don't worry, and..."

Tilly's niece barrelled into her legs from the sitting room.

289 FRIENDS

"Auntie Tilly! You're here!"

Tilly leant down to hug Rosie, kissing the top of her head. "Yes I am my darling, and when I've had a chat with Mummy we are going to have SO much fun!"

"Yaaaaayyyyy" smiled her niece, before running back into the sitting room to find her big brother.

"Right. The fridge is full of food, I've left some cash in the fruit bowl for whatever you need, and I'll text you later, thanks again for this, you really are a life saver."

Tilly looked around.

"Is Andrew here?"

"What? Oh, no, he left ages ago. He won't be back til late tomorrow night."

"So, I don't understand, I thought you had to sort something out with him?"

Mimi opened the front door. "Yes. No. Oh God it's so complicated. I promise you I'll tell you everything once this is all over. KIDS! Mummy's going now!"

Two blonde bombshells careered through the hallway, clearly unperturbed by the fact that both of their parents were deserting them for the weekend.

"Right, you be good for Auntie Tilly, I want to hear good reports when I get back please!"

"When are you coming home, Mummy?" asked Rosie.

"Tomorrow darling, but Auntie Tilly is staying here tonight and you are going to have such fun together!"

Tilly took a deep breath and tried not to be too annoyed that her sister hadn't actually told her she was definitely away overnight.

And then Mimi was gone, and Tilly was distracted from her thoughts by her two absolutely favourite small people in the world.

SEVERAL HOURS LATER, when lunch had been eaten and Tilly finally had a cup of tea in her hands, she decided on a plan of action. There was a huge IKEA in Reading, which wasn't a million miles away, plus she knew they had great clothes shops in the town, so bribing the kids with a suggestion of meatballs for dinner if they helped her choose a dress first, they piled into her car and headed into town.

Luckily the clothing section of John Lewis wasn't very busy, so the three of them wandered around the endless racks of dresses picking up anything in a size 12 that Tilly liked, and Rosie and Oscar approved of.

"Oh no Auntie Tilly, you must not wear that," piped up Oscar as she contemplated a rather over-the-top shimmery silver number.

"Why not, Oscar?"

"Because Mummy did one time and Daddy said

she looked like a flaming Christmas tree," he replied seriously.

Rosie giggled into the palm of her hand and Tilly quickly returned the dress to the rail. "OK come on then, I think I've got enough here to try on anyway. Let's go."

Oscar and Rosie squished into the chair in the changing room, and Tilly tried on each dress, before parading up and down in the ones she liked, for a critique by her niece and nephew. Some of the comments they came out with were hilarious, and when Rosie told her that she looked "Very fat indeed in that dress," Tilly swore she heard the lady in the adjacent cubicle snigger.

Eventually Tilly found the perfect party outfit. It was a dark blue sequinned mini dress, twinkly under the lights but not in a Christmas tree way. Elbow length sleeves, the length short but not in a tarty way, finishing just above her knees. Something about the way the beautifully lined fabric fell over her body made Tilly feel like a million dollars, and when the helpful sales assistant brought her some strappy silver heels to try on with it, she was absolutely sold. So much so that she purchased the shoes too, for once in her life sensibly realising that she probably wasn't going to have time to go shoe shopping between now and the party.

Then it was back into the car for the short journey to IKEA, which Tilly knew the kids would love, and was probably going to cost her a fortune even though she only needed candles.

She was right, the three of them had more fun than she knew was possible in a shop, with two small children in tow. They followed the arrows through the maze of rooms, like a giant amusement park that cost her nothing, except for the 100 plus pounds that you always seemed to spend as a minimum in IKEA. It really was impossible to go into that shop and come out with only the item you'd gone in for.

Later, as they sat in the café, bags by their feet bursting at the seams with all manner of random things that Tilly hadn't known she'd ever needed, filling their hungry tummies with meatballs and mash, she felt a great sense of satisfaction. She had managed to tick two items off her party To Do list, *and* keep her niece and nephew occupied and content all day long. They were such lovely little things, and she hated the thought that their parents were in the midst of some huge argument, which could very well derail their happy little lives if not handled properly.

Tilly pulled her phone out of her pocket. Nothing from Mimi.

"Right, let's take a picture for Mummy and Daddy, show them how much fun we're having!"

Two cherubic faces grinned at her, Rosie's fork in the air and Oscar beaming proudly with his newly acquired green rubber dinosaur pride of place on the Formica table. Hopefully a picture of the kids might spur Mimi into actually communicating with her sister. It would be nice to at least know that they were OK. Or even just where they were.

"Come on then, eat up, and we'll pick up a bag of those mini chocolate bars on the way out for the journey home," she said. "IF you both eat up all your peas."

BY THE TIME they'd left the store it was dark, and once the heating had warmed the car and they'd left the harsh lights of the industrial park, it was only a matter of minutes before both Oscar and Rosie were fast asleep in the back seat. Tilly drove carefully back to her sister's house, her precious cargo cosy and warm in their booster seats.

She was annoyed with Mimi, because she still didn't know what the issue was, and for the first time that day Tilly let herself wonder what was really going on. What had caused the argument that was so bad that Andrew had left the house? Was he having an affair? That would make sense of things at least. Her mind went back to last Christmas, that weird text on the phone. She racked her brains to try and remember what the initial was on the message, but with no joy. She was cross with her sister for not even telling her what was going on, surely she must know that she would be on her side whatever it was?

As she drove into the driveway, Tilly wondered if either of them would be back. But there were no cars in front of the house, so it looked like she was going to be none the wiser for another night. Maybe tomorrow would shed some light on the situation. Hopefully it would turn out to be just some big misunderstanding, and everything would blow over. Tensions often ran high around Christmas, maybe Andrew had been working too hard and leaving Mimi to sort everything out at home on her own. Her sister could be a bit of a drama queen considering the pampered life she led, although Tilly would never say that to her face. Yep, that's probably exactly what it was, she thought, as she turned off the engine and wondered how on earth she was going to get the two little angels in the back seat upstairs and into bed on her own.

TILLY WOKE UP on Sunday morning to find her niece asleep in bed next to her and a text message from Mimi on her phone. Rosie had obviously crept in at some point during the night, although Tilly must have been dead to the world because she had absolutely no recollection of that happening whatsoever.

She opened the message apprehensively, wondering how the day was going to play out.

Morning! Hope you had a quiet night with the kids. Just to let you know I'll be back by midday. Thanks babe xx

Tilly exhaled gratefully. At least she'd be back in Kent by mid-afternoon, get some time at home before it was back to the grindstone for five days in the office. The last time-consuming task she still had to do was compile a huge music playlist for the party, so at least if she started it that afternoon she could add to it during the week, if not get it done and ticked off the list completely. And then next weekend she could blitz the house to within an inch of its life. Sorted.

Tilly busied herself with getting the three of them dressed, breakfasted, and ready for the day, and by the time they'd played two games of hide and seek, and more games of snap than she cared to remember, it was nearly lunchtime.

Mimi arrived back at midday on the dot, looking surprisingly calm and rested. Not what Tilly had expected for someone who's marriage had appeared to be in crisis 24 hours before.

"Kids!" she called from the hallway, "Mummy's home!"

Rosie and Oscar abandoned their game and ran into the hallway, cards scattering as they did. Auntie Tilly was fab, but no-one could replace Mummy.

Tilly felt a pang of envy as she watched the mutual love fest in the hallway, wondering when, or if, she would ever experience the same. She wasn't stupid, she was well aware of the ticking clock, of her dwindling fertility, despite all the middle aged celebrity mums who filled the glossies. But without a man in her life, it was never going to happen.

"Penny for them," laughed Mimi. "What are you thinking about?"

"Sorry, I was miles away. How was your night? All OK?"

"Yeah, great, thanks, right, I need a cup of tea, and then I thought I could take my three favourite people out for lunch! How does that sound?"

"Yay!" cried the kids, jumping up and down at the prospect of going out.

Tilly contemplated the offer, whizzed the hours forward in her mind. "Tea yes, but then I'll have to shoot, I've got so much to do at home, sorry."

Mimi nodded. "OK, no worries, just us then kiddos!"

"What about Daddy?" asked Oscar.

"Oh Daddy's not going to be back until later my darling, he's got more work to do today but he will DEFINITELY be back before bedtime, so he can give you both a bath and read you a story before you go to sleep. OK?"

Seemingly pacified by this response, the kids traipsed into the kitchen, happy to just be in

Mummy's presence and watch her make cups of tea for her and Auntie Tilly. Which meant there was no chance yet again for any information about where Mimi had been, what she'd been doing, and where Andrew really was. Something did not sit right with Tilly.

After tea and cookies with her sister and the kids, Tilly packed her overnight bag and said her goodbyes.

"So next time I see you it will be CHRISTMAS!" she said excitedly, as she hugged her niece and nephew. "And next time I see YOU..." she hugged her sister, "will be at my party!" Tilly grimaced, the proximity to the big day now really ringing true.

"Oh my God, how exciting! I'd better get my outfit sorted! And book a babysitter!" she laughed, finding it clearly more amusing than Tilly did.

How had she not booked a babysitter like, ages ago?! It was the weekend before Christmas for goodness sake!

Shaking her head with only half a smile on her face, Tilly climbed into the car and waved as she reversed out of the drive. Honestly, her sister drove her mad sometimes. She'd better get things sorted and be at the party. She would never forgive her if she failed to show up at something that was so important to her.

Discarding her fears, Tilly cranked the radio up

as she hit the motorway, trying desperately to remember the names of each song she liked so that she could add them to her party compilation later on. The DJ was playing a fair few Christmas songs, and although December had been pretty mild so far, the music was definitely beginning to make Tilly feel a little bit festive.

She sang along to the old classics as she made her way back home, swept along in the musical goodwill filling the car. As she sang, she changed some of the lyrics to wish for a bit of Christmas magic, a big dollop of positivity thrown out to the universe. Well, you never know, they did say that if you wanted something badly enough, just ask. There were only thirteen days left until her party, so maybe it was time to start doing exactly that. She'd worked so hard to get where she had, everything bar the final preparation (and the music playlist, she reminded herself) was organised. From here on in everything just had to slot into place and happen. It was exciting and terrifying at the same time, but she was doing it, and nothing was going to get in her way.

Chapter 18

Wednesday - Three days before the party

THERE WAS A stillness in the early morning air as Tilly walked to the train station, that she couldn't quite put her finger on. It was usually pretty quiet at that time of day in her street, but something felt different that morning. Maybe people had packed up work already; the schools had probably finished for the term so she guessed more people than usual were still tucked up safely in their warm beds.

Lucky things, she thought, before reminding herself that she only had three days of work left before she finished for Christmas too.

As she arrived at the train station Tilly grabbed one of the free newspapers from the dispenser at the entrance and tucked it under her arm, glancing at the billboard as she did.

"Cold snap coming!" warned the sign. *You're not kidding*, she thought, it was flipping freezing.

It was only when Tilly sat down in the carriage and unfolded her newspaper that she got the full story. Weather warnings in place... Cold front heading our way... Snow forecast... Be prepared... *No, there's no need to get caught up in the panic*, she told herself. This was typical of the press. Desperate for a white Christmas and nothing else exciting to talk about. It would come to nothing, as usual. She couldn't remember the last time they'd had snow, much to her disappointment.

Tilly loved snow. She loved the way that time seemed to slow down when the world was covered in a blanket of white. There would probably be a few flakes but nothing to write home about, as usual.

WHEN SHE ARRIVED at the office though, snow was all everyone was talking about. One of her colleagues, Bill, was a secret weather geek, and was proudly holding court talking about cold fronts from the north meeting warm fronts from the Atlantic, or something like that. Tilly caught Karen's eye as she hung her coat up on the hat stand, furtively glancing towards the kitchen and making a T sign with her hands. Karen nodded and stood up from her chair.

"Oh my God, he is in his element," she said once they were in the safety of the kitchen. "He's been going on non-stop for about twenty minutes!"

"Really?"

"Yep! Apparently we're in for a shocker, on the news this morning they said eight inches of snow by the weekend."

Tilly stopped stirring the tea and looked at her friend, suddenly taking it seriously for the first time that morning.

"Oh God. That's not good. I thought it was just a fuss about nothing. I've got loads of stuff being delivered over the next two days for the party. You're still coming, aren't you?"

"Too right, try and stop me. It's the highlight of my Christmas diary! Hey, maybe we'll get snowed in and have to keep partying until Christmas!"

They laughed as they walked back to their desks, mugs of tea in hand. There was a huge pile of folders on Tilly's desk waiting to distract her from any more weather discussions, and the morning passed by quickly thanks to the sheer quantity of work she had to do. And when she popped out to grab a sandwich at lunch the sky was a perfect blue, the weak winter sunshine shattering any thoughts of the alleged blizzard apparently heading their way.

Thursday - Two days before the party

THE FOLLOWING DAY however, the weather warnings were still coming through thick and fast. Rumours were beginning to circulate about trains being cancelled, gritting lorries out en masse, and advice to only travel "when absolutely necessary." Tilly thought through the list of people coming to her party. Of the 80 confirmed attendees there were about 25 people from work and 30 from school (including partners). Then there was Becky, Jems and her sister plus their respective other halves, and about 10 random couples, if it was OK to call neighbours and local acquaintances random.

Many of her school friends were coming from quite a long way away and most of her work colleagues were heading down from London, and the niggly feeling that Tilly had fearing cancellations began to come true when the first few messages started to drop into her inbox.

Sorry Tilly, think we're going to have to bow out of Saturday night... trains looking dodgy and can't risk getting stuck...

So sorry darling, the grandparents are no longer able to babysit now due to the snow, we're going to have to bail...

And when the boss sent an email on Thursday afternoon announcing that Friday would be a half day in the office "to enable people to get home safely" before the snow hit on Friday evening, Tilly began to panic, big time. She pulled her phone out of her bag and checked Facebook. A couple more cancellations were waiting for her, and she opened up the party invite to send an update message to the people who were still on the RSVP yes list.

> *2 days to go! I'm sure you've all seen the weather forecast, but just to let you know that I'm obviously still going ahead with my party! I have food, drink, and a warm cosy house ready and waiting, and I am really looking forward to seeing you all! Get your party frocks and your scarves on and I'll see you Saturday!*

Tilly prayed silently as she shuffled down the station steps on the way home. It had been almost a year in planning, and if it didn't happen… No, she couldn't think about that. Positive thoughts only.

Dismissing the billboards outside the train station warning of heavy snowfall, Tilly ignored the pings on her phone and prayed that things were going to be OK, only checking her messages when she got home. Totting up the number of cancellations she reckoned she was down to about 50 guests. That was OK, still good! She texted Jemima and Becky with threats of defriending them if they even contemplated not coming. She needed them there more than ever, and was reassured by their positive responses.

> *It's only a bit of snow! Chill babe! x*
> *Try and stop me! I so need a good night out xxx*

Relieved, Tilly took a deep breath and exhaled.

It would be OK. Most of the time these weather predictions turned out to be way less intense than expected, and if the worst came to the worst and it ended up being just her two best friends and half of Majestic's stock in the kitchen, well, so be it!

Not that it would come to that, obviously.

Friday - The day before the party

As it turned out, the crisp and cold, blue sky weather continued all the way through Friday, and her boss's half day seemed a complete over reaction to the weather man's predictions, just as Tilly had suspected. Making a mental note to ignore the newsreaders next time they told her to stay home, Tilly packed up her desk for the Christmas break, and made her way out of town before the rest of London did too. She could use the extra time to add a few more decorations to the house and enjoy a quiet evening at home before a lot of people descended on her doorstep the following day.

Panic over.

Party ON!

Chapter 19

Saturday 22nd December

On the day of the party Tilly woke early, a nagging feeling disturbing her sleep, urging her to get up. She rolled over and snuggled back into the pillow, before the momentary comfort was rudely displaced by the sudden realisation of what day it was.

Oh my God, it's today!

Her eyes jolted open, her brain instantly wide awake. She swung her legs out of bed and sat upright, took a sip of water from the glass on her bedside table. There was so much to do. All be it for the possibly not too many people coming to her potentially not so massive party.

She walked towards the window, a little apprehensive as to what she might find beyond the glass. Opening one curtain an inch, she peered through the gap into the gradually lightening morning.

"Oh thank you, world," she said aloud, as she registered the light dusting of snowfall across the lawn and on the shed roof. Pulling open the curtains fully, she inspected the scene. Yes, there was some white stuff, but not anywhere near what had been predicted, just as she had suspected would be the case all along. It was certainly nothing to get excited about.

Checking her phone whilst the kettle boiled, Tilly noticed that there had been three more cancellations during the night, which she suspected were more likely to be down to "can't be bothered" excuses, rather than the possible inclement weather. Which was just a bit rude, and very annoying. She checked her updated party spreadsheet, that made 44 people left.

Cranking the thermostat up a notch, Tilly swapped her pyjamas for jogging bottoms and a baggy sweatshirt, perfect for house blitzing. There was no point showering now, she'd only get sweaty and have to wash again before the party. So pulling her hair up into a messy top knot, she pulled out her notebook and wrote a quick list of all the things she needed to do. The plan was to be completely ready by mid-afternoon, in order to give herself a good couple of hours to shower, wash her hair, and deal with any last-minute issues.

Her Christmas tree was obviously already decorated, and Tilly switched on the twinkly lights to set the mood for the day, a shiver of excitement reminding her of the festive joy she always felt at this time of year. Arming herself with a duster and spray, she went around each room in the house giving every surface, mirror and handle a final once over. Then she hoovered every inch of carpet, emptied the bins, and plumped the cushions on the sofa.

Covering the dining room table with a festive red and white tablecloth she'd bought especially for the occasion, Tilly laid the huge empty platters out, ready to be filled with food later on. She placed a tall pile of side plates at each end of the table, along with pots of cutlery and a couple of napkin holders that she'd found in a gift shop, with cute little Christmas trees to hold the napkins in place. She had turned the ice machine on the night before, and lifted the lid to find the cavity full of cubes ready for the beer baths, then arranged neat lines of wine and Champagne glasses on one side of the kitchen counter.

Most of the food would have to be left until later to be put out (no-one likes a stale crisp), but Tilly filled bowls with garlic mayo and cling-filmed them in the fridge, before mixing up her special honey and mustard glaze for the cocktail sausages and coating what seemed like hundreds of them in the sticky sauce, ready to be popped into the oven later. The goujons simply had to be tipped onto trays and cooked for twenty minutes, and the cheese (which she reminded herself should be taken out of the fridge by 6pm at the absolute latest) just had to be unwrapped and placed on large wooden boards, and adorned with fat red grapes, jars of chutney, hunks of bread and baskets of crackers. Easy.

She placed large bowls on the side tables ready for crisps to be poured into, and smaller ones for nuts and olives. Ever organised, Tilly had put the large white boxes of handmade chocolate brownies in her study, along with a square silver cake board and icing sugar shaker on her desk, and turned the radiator off to keep them cool. All she had to do mid-evening was pile the squishy pre-cut brownies into a mountain like arrangement, sprinkle with sugar, and perch her cute little reindeer on the top. Simple.

TILLY MARKED THE last item on the list as done, and cast her eyes over the whole page just to reassure herself that everything was in order. She glanced at her phone. To her surprise it was nearly three o'clock, four hours to go. Time to think about herself. She glanced through the window. It was almost dark outside, just a few little snowflakes were falling, making her feel even more festive and excited than she had been before. She pressed play on her completed music playlist to keep her in the mood, before closing the curtains on the snow dusted garden. Filling a bucket with hot water and floor cleaner, she quickly swished the squeezed out mop over the kitchen floor, and left it to dry whilst she went upstairs to attend to her now somewhat unkempt appearance.

AN HOUR LATER, showered and in her dressing gown with her wrapped hair in a towel, Tilly felt her stomach growl. She had been so busy prepping that she'd completely forgotten to eat anything, which was most unlike her. So as soon as she had blow dried her hair and done her make up, Tilly pulled on jeans and a jumper and went downstairs to the kitchen to quickly make herself a cheese sandwich and a cup of tea. It was still too early to put her party dress on, but now that everything else was done, it would take 10 minutes to transform herself from boring Tilly to party Tilly.

Sandwich made, she flicked on the TV in the sitting room and appeased her stomach as she scrolled through the channels. Stopping on the news, Tilly took a sip of her tea as she observed the scene in front of her.

A female newsreader, barely visible through the blowing snow and a very large hood, was earning every penny of her salary broadcasting live from – Tilly looked at the bottom of the screen – Surrey? Blinking rapidly, Tilly swallowed quicker than she'd intended. Hot tea burnt her throat and she leant forward to check she'd read it correctly. Yep, definitely Surrey. With horror, Tilly's brain finally realised that this wasn't very far from Kent at all. Images sent by viewers flashed up onto the screen, showing complete carnage across the country. Heavy snow was, and still was, falling across southern England.

"And as you can see from our live weather radar, this very large bank of weather is not showing any sign of letting up at all," said the newsreader desperately, probably wondering when she could go back inside and warm up, "bringing what we expect to be a night of very extreme weather indeed."

Tilly put her mug down on the coffee table as they cut back to the TV studio.

"Thank you, Angela," said the newsreader, smug in the nice warm studio. "So the advice tonight is to stay in, wrap up warm, and do not travel unless it is absolutely necessary to do so."

Cursing under her breath, Tilly reached for her mobile phone. It was 5pm. Two hours until people started arriving. She stood up and opened the curtains that she'd closed only a couple of hours earlier. To her dismay she discovered that a thick blanket of pure white snow had covered the bushes in the front garden, her car, and even the road, and the heavy snow that was still falling was indeed not showing any sign of stopping at all. It must have started the minute she'd gone upstairs, and not stopped since.

Her heart began to race and a panic descended upon her. Groaning audibly, fear settled as heavily as the snow had, and Tilly ran to the back of the house, yanking the curtains open to see if this nightmare really was happening.

Oh no… she thought, as her eyes filled with tears.

Flicking open her phone, she discovered another round of "I'm so sorry, the roads are impassable," or "oh no, our babysitter has just cancelled…." Tilly shoved it into her pocket, unable to face the unwelcome facts. She couldn't bear to check the spreadsheet again but knew without looking that she'd be down to about 35 people now.

"Oh my God, no. This is a disaster," she said out loud, staring at the ceiling and gritting her teeth. Grimacing as she gave into the powers of technology, she pulled her phone back out of her pocket and scrolled through the news feed in an attempt to look for an answer to her crisis, or at the very least distract herself from the reality of what she was facing.

Pictures of snowmen filled the screen, most of which had clearly been built by the adults and not the cute toddlers standing next to them. Sledging videos. Mittened hands holding steaming hot chocolate, a mini mountain of cream and marshmallows on top. And all of these pictures were being posted by people that Tilly had invited to her party. Who weren't coming. Who were living their best lives elsewhere, and not even making the effort to come to Tilly's party.

Buggers, she thought, as she put her phone face down on the counter harder than was necessary.

Although… As much as she hated Facebook right now, it was still her most reliable connection to the outside world, so she tapped out one last message on the party group thread, pressed send, and crossed her fingers.

Chapter 20

TO HER UTTER dismay, and absolute horror, only eight people turned up to Tilly's massive Christmas party.

Jemima, Hugo, Becky and Rupert had arrived shortly after 7pm for a pre-party bottle of Champagne. Jemima had clearly had a couple of drinks already, so was in high spirits. Becky was just lovely as always, as was Rupert, who Tilly hadn't seen for ages. Delilah was at home with her favourite grandma, having a very exciting snowy sleepover, and both couples had overnight bags with them in anticipation of definitely NOT going home that night.

"Oh Tills, your house, it looks amazing!" said Becky, hugging her friend close.

"Yeah yeah," chipped in Jemima. "Enough of the pleasantries please, I need Champagne, chop chop, get your coat off and shimmy along into the kitchen please Mrs!"

Tilly laughed. "Oh my God, I'm so glad you're all here. I am SO stressed."

"Why are you stressed? You've done everything, right? Now all you have to do is top up glasses and enjoy yourself!"

"No but this weather, people keep cancelling…"

"It'll be fine. Stop worrying. It's only a bit of snow, all those hard-core party goers won't let that stop them!"

Hugo and Rupert exchanged glances.

"I dunno Jems, it's pretty bad out there. A lot of people will be battening down the hatches tonight… sorry Tilly."

"That's alright Hugo, you guys are here though, and that's all that really matters. I'm sure some will come."

The five of them stood in the kitchen as they chatted, Jemima bopping in time to the music, Tilly's party playlist sending feel good vibes from the speaker in the corner of the room. *The calm before the storm,* thought Tilly. She looked at the clock.

"Why is no-one here yet though? It's half past seven!"

"Babe. Chill. No-one arrives at a party on time these days. And the snow probably means that the trains are up the spout, so I'd give it at least half an hour before you start worrying."

"Yeah I know but…"

"Stop fretting and have another glass of Champagne," said Jemima, popping a second cork. "It'll make you feel much better."

Tilly's doorbell rang, barely audible over the music.

"See, there's someone already!"

Tilly ran to the front door, relieved and excited all at once, and opened the door with a flourish.

"Mimi!"

"Hello my lovely sister, I made it! Flipping heck it's cold out there, let me in, I need to warm up!"

Tilly ushered her sister into the kitchen and took her coat upstairs to throw it on the bed, before scuttling back precariously down the stairs. All her favourite people were in the kitchen, which made her feel very happy indeed, and she filled another glass with bubbles and passed it to Mimi.

"So, where's your lovely husband tonight then?" asked Jemima, casting a quick sideways glance in Tilly's direction. The girls knew Mimi well after many years of friendship with her sister, and Tilly had mentioned the recent marital disharmony to them. Which she now realised could come back to bite her if Jemima wasn't subtle about where she was going with her line of questioning.

"Babysitting I'm afraid, we couldn't get a sitter so it was either me on my own or neither of us, and that was an easy decision to make!" she laughed.

Tilly passed a bowl of crisps around and wondered if she should try to move people into the sitting room. She had lit a fire in the hearth, and it looked so cosy and Christmassy in there, although they already seemed pretty settled in the kitchen and she wasn't exactly sure how she could herd them through.

Her phone pinged from the top of the microwave, and she picked it up and swiped it open, preparing herself for another cancellation.

Hey Tilly, it's Karen, nearly there, running a bit late due weather! See you shortly! x

"I love your dress Tills, you look gorgeous," said Becky. "A very glamourous host!"

Tilly smiled, ignoring the Facebook messages she could see were waiting for her and putting the phone back down. She was really pleased with her outfit, she just wished people would hurry up and get here so she could actually have a party *to* host.

The doorbell rang again and Tilly went to answer it. A tall man in a smart overcoat stood on the doorstep holding a bottle of red wine.

"Hi. Tariq. From over the road."

Tilly stared at him, temporarily speechless. "Oh yes, sorry, come in come in, how lovely to see you!"

Tariq noticed the very small gathering of people over her shoulder as he entered the hallway. "Oh gosh sorry, am I too early?"

"No, no, not at all, it's just that not many people are here yet because of the, you know, the snow. Please, let me take your coat and introduce you to everyone."

They jostled awkwardly around each other whilst Tariq took his coat off with the bottle of wine still in his hand, Tilly then attempting to take both from him at the same time therefore having no hands to shut the front door behind him.

"Here, let me," said Tariq, closing the door against the cold.

Tilly led him through to the kitchen and blushed as everyone stopped talking to turn and stare at the handsome man who had suddenly appeared in Tilly's house.

She gestured to each person in the group, one by one. "This is my sister, Mimi, my friend Jemima and her husband Hugo, this is Becky and her husband Rupert, and everybody – this is Tariq, my neighbour."

Tariq shook everyone's hand in turn and Tilly stood like a lemon before remembering that she still had his coat in her hand.

"I'll just run this upstairs, Mims can you get Tariq a drink please?"

She ran up the stairs as quickly as she could in high heels, lay his coat carefully on her bed and went back downstairs before Jemima said anything embarrassing about her.

As she walked back into the kitchen Becky glanced at her, raised her eyebrows and smiled.

"What?" mouthed Tilly.

Becky ignored her and took another sip of her drink, before joining Jemima in the inquisition of the new man in their midst.

"Is your wife coming too?" she asked, a classic line that always provided the information that she *really* wanted to know.

"No, no, I'm not married."

"Girlfriend?"

"Er, no, I don't have a girlfriend."

"Boyfriend?" chipped in Jemima.

"Jems!" Tilly interrupted the interrogation, "I'm so sorry, you'll have to excuse my friends, they are so nosy."

Tilly glared at Jemima, mortified at the barrage of questions that Tariq had been subjected to. She wasn't going to be able to leave her alone for a second at this rate.

"Becky, why don't you show everyone through to the lounge, and Jems, you can stay here and help me with the oven," she instructed, in a tone of voice that left Jemima in no doubt at all as to what she really meant.

Becky smoothly moved everyone into the sitting room, and Tilly could hear murmurs of appreciation as they caught sight of the Christmas tree and sparkly lights.

"Right. Stop being annoying and help me get this food cooked," whispered Tilly, peeling cling film from trays of sausages, and passing them to

Jemima to put in the preheated oven.

"I'm not being annoying. I'm checking him out for you! He is seriously hot, Miss Jenkins!"

"Shush, stop it, he'll hear you. Anyway, it's not like that, he's my neighbour for God's sake!"

"And that is exactly your problem, Tills. You can't see a good thing when it's right in front of you! What does he do for a living?"

"I think he's a lawyer, I don't know, ask him if you're so interested!"

"Oh I will," she said cheekily, sliding a second tray of chicken goujons into the oven before stomping through to the sitting room to interrogate further.

Tilly set the oven timer for 20 minutes and opened the fridge door to see if there was anything else that needed to come out. Satisfied that everything that could be on the table already was, she shut the door and picked up a bottle of wine to take through to the sitting room.

The doorbell rang and Tilly's heart skipped a beat with excitement. Who was next? She put down the bottle and went to the front door to find not one but two friendly faces from work.

"Karen! Alan! You made it!"

Faces flushed red from the cold, they bundled into the hallway and ruffled the snow from their hair.

"It's really coming down out there now," said

Alan, "I hope you've got a shovel to get us out!"

Tilly laughed, thinking how funny it was that they'd arrived at exactly the same time.

"Here, let me take your coats. I think I might put them in the utility room to dry off, you're nearly soaked through! Come with me to the kitchen and I'll get you both a drink."

Drinks poured, Tilly took Karen and Alan through to the sitting room and introduced them to her sister, who was steadily working her way through a bowl of cashew nuts, and her friends. The fire was crackling warmly, and Christmas songs were filling the room with festive love. Happy faces encircled her, and Tilly smiled to herself with a little glow of satisfaction. All she needed was for another 30-odd people to come through the door and tonight would be the night she'd always hoped for.

But no-one else knocked on Tilly's front door that night. The 289 people she had invited to her "party to end all parties" had resulted in eight people in her sitting room. Nine including herself. By half past eight she started to feel slightly sick with the realisation that this might be it. That no-one else might turn up. She went to the kitchen and picked up her phone. More messages apologising for not being able to get there. Texts from people she knew,

Facebook messages from those she knew less well.

Another song about snow replaced the last jolly seasonal tune. *Flipping snow*, thought Tilly, it had a lot to answer for this year. It was so embarrassing. Not in front of her close friends, but Tariq, Karen, Alan, they didn't really know her as a person, and this was now how they'd always remember her. As the girl who had no friends at her party.

"Penny for them." Becky put her hand on Tilly's arm. "You OK?"

"Oh Bex, this is hideous. Why did I ever think this was a good idea?" She shook her head.

"Babes, it's not your fault, you didn't make it snow. No-one else is bothered that not everyone has made it. And anyway, they're all having a ball in there, they're getting on like a house on fire."

"Really?"

"Yes. Now fill up your glass and come in, it's not a party if you're not there. Oh and by the way, your neighbour, he smells delicious. Come and stand near him, that'll cheer you up!"

Tilly rolled her eyes and followed Becky back into the sitting room, picking up a bottle of red and a bottle of white on the way to replenish everyone's glasses. But just as she put the half empty bottles back on the sideboard there was a slight flickering of lights, a faint crackling noise from somewhere in the kitchen, and then suddenly the whole house was completely and utterly plunged into darkness.

Chapter 21

"Shit."

"Oh my God oh my God oh my God!"

"Whoa…"

For a brief moment Tilly thought she'd gone blind, before she realised that no-one else could see anything either. Within seconds her eyes adjusted to the dark, the fire in the hearth the primary source of light. A few candles dotted around the room created little puddles of light on the sideboard and bookshelf. The music had been silenced so abruptly, that the quiet filled her ears, permeated only with the whispers and murmurings from her nearest and dearest.

"What the fuck?" piped up Jemima, breaking the stillness in the room and spurring the men into action.

"There must have been a power cut…" Hugo, stating the obvious but with no idea what to do.

"Let's check if the streetlights have gone out, see if it's the whole road…" Rupert, always the logical one.

"Don't worry, it'll probably come back on in a minute…" Alan, calm and unphased.

Tariq put his hand on Tilly's elbow. "Do you want me to check the fuse box? I imagine it's in the same place as mine?"

"Thanks," said Tilly, "I know where it is but I'm not the greatest when it comes to DIY. Let's go."

Tariq pulled his phone out from his pocket and switched on the torch, shining it in front of Tilly as they made their way to the utility room. Tilly opened the cover of the fuse box and Tariq shone the phone light on the row of switches. Becky was right, he DID smell gorgeous. Tilly blushed in the darkness, embarrassed to be thinking such thoughts about the semi stranger who was standing so close to her.

"Yes, the main switch has tripped, lets re-set it and see if that works."

He clicked the red switch to ON as Tilly held her breath with anticipation.

Nothing.

"Looks like the whole street is down," called Rupert from the hallway, shutting the front door quickly behind him in an attempt to keep the cold dark night out.

The group reconvened in the sitting room, the fire now their central port. Tilly couldn't actually believe that her diabolical evening had managed to get even worse than it already was.

"Oh guys, I'm so sorry, I've dragged you from all over town for my stupid party, to which no-one has come," she glanced at Tariq, Karen and Alan, "and now the power has gone off and I can't do anything about it." She stifled a sob. "It's a flipping disaster!"

"Don't be silly," said Becky. "Actually I think it's quite exciting. Come on, let's get some more candles, bring the wine in here, and we'll be fine in one room! To be fair, it's probably a good thing that there aren't that many of us, can you imagine trying to herd 200 people around your house in the pitch black?!"

"I agree, and we'll always remember your party Tilly. Just think, years from now we'll look back on tonight and reminisce about it," said Karen. Tilly smiled back, noticing for the first time the lack of any gap between Karen and Alan on the sofa opposite.

"I suppose so, and I guess it's not like I'm having a four-course dinner party or something," she laughed. "Oh bugger, I forgot about the oven!"

Leaping up, Tilly disappeared towards the kitchen before remembering there was no light in there. She picked up a tealight in a small china holder and realised that she was going to have to get something sorted if they were going to be able to move around the house without crashing into things. The oven was off, nothing was going to burn, so she went back and summoned her sister.

"Mimi, can you give me a hand please? I need to get some more candles lit so we can see properly."

Mimi stood up and followed her sister into the kitchen.

"Right. We need a plan of action. We've got no idea how long this is going to go on for but we might as well get set up in case it's for a while." She put her face in her hands. "OK, let me think. Fridge and freezer need to stay shut to keep the cold in. Heating is now off so the house could get cold pretty rapidly. I suggest we stay in the sitting room and if it gets really dire I've got some throws and blankets upstairs."

She opened a cupboard door and started pulling candles out. "Mims, take these and put some in the loo, the hallway, and the sitting room please."

Jemima slunk in though the double doors. "I don't suppose I could trouble you for another bottle could I please my darling? Red if you've got it?"

"Jems, I'm a bit busy at the moment my lovely, I tell you what, why don't you take a few bottles of red through and leave them on the coffee table. That way they'll pick up the warmth from the fire and not get chilly."

Karen appeared behind her. "Can I help Tilly?"

"Oh, thank you Karen, I don't want you to work though, you're my guest!"

"Don't be silly, let me help, that's what friends are for," she replied.

Tilly looked around her. "OK, thank you. If you can grab one of the big plates from the table in the dining room I can get this food out of the oven, it was about done when the power went off anyway so we might as well take it out and eat it before it either dries out, burns, or goes stone cold!"

Karen nodded and got to work on the hot food. The white wine and fizz was keeping itself chilled in the beer buckets but Tilly grabbed another couple of bottles to take though to the sitting room. Her phone pinged from where she'd left it on the kitchen counter and she picked it up to see who was texting her. She could see from the home screen that it was a text from the power company, so she flicked open the message to see what it said.

> *Dear Customer, we are sorry to inform you that due to a mains failure some homes in your area may have lost electricity. Please be assured that we are working as quickly as we can to restore power. We estimate that this will be in approximately 2-4 hours.*

Tilly rolled her eyes. Useless. Oh well, they'd just have to get on with it, no point crying over spilt milk. Or failed mains, in her case.

When they were all back around the fire, perched on sofas, chairs and the floor, Tilly took charge.

"Right guys. Here's the plan. I've had a message from the power company and it's gonna be a few hours before they fix it, so... The food and drink needs eating and drinking just like before. As the power's off for a while it'll get cold, so let's stay in here with the connecting doors shut and keep the party around the fire! I've got plenty of logs, there are candles in the kitchen and downstairs loo, the only thing I can't sort is music, but I have enough wine to sink a ship so I'm sure it won't matter!" She raised a glass. "So cheers everyone, thank you for coming to my teeny weeny massive party!"

"Yay, let's get pissed!" chimed Jemima.

Glasses chinked and the conversation quickly resumed amongst them, the boys discussing the benefits of winter tyres, the girls chatting about Christmas plans. Eager hands slowly demolished the hot food, and Tilly realised how hungry she was. She looked around at the group of people who were with her on this crazy night. Reaching for her phone to take a photo, she realised that the intrusion of technology would completely destroy the happy moment, so left it where it was. She had everything she needed right here. This could stay a happy memory in her brain, not in her phone.

BECKY CAME BACK from the loo and plonked herself on the sofa next to Karen and Alan.

"So, how long have you two been together then?" she asked.

"No, no, they aren't together, they just work together," interjected Tilly.

Karen and Alan glanced at each other, a hint of a smile passing across her lips as he nodded his head at her.

"Well actually…"

Tilly put her glass down as her mouth fell open.

"Nooooo!"

Alan reached across to take Karen's small hand in his, a smile as big as a Cheshire cat's now lighting his eyes up.

"Oh my God!" squealed Tilly, completely blown away by the revelation. "I can't believe it! How? When? Why didn't you tell me?!" she laughed.

"It's been nearly a year!"

"Wow! How did I not notice that?!" She thought back to their Solstice drinks in June, the body language between them both, Alan's comments about life being too short to not follow your heart, all of it now making perfect sense. And Karen's blushes in the office. How had she not seen it? It was right there in front of her and she hadn't had a clue.

"Well, I did not see that coming!" she laughed, raising her glass in the air by way of a toast. "Cheers, congratulations!" She stood up and gestured to Alan to get up from the sofa. "Come on Mr, swap places with me, I need to quiz your GIRLFRIEND about this, and find out all the gory details."

Alan, good natured as always, duly swapped places with Tilly and left the girls to discuss the things that only women did. He was old enough to know how things worked, and he secretly quite enjoyed watching the lady he loved happy in her skin and enjoying the attention that she deserved.

As soon as Tilly sat down in the warm space that Alan had left, she angled herself towards her colleague – and now friend – and started to quiz her.

"So… how did you both end up together? Oh my gosh it's so romantic, I just love it!"

Karen filled the girls in on how they met; it wasn't the most exciting story in her opinion, but the smile on Tilly's face in response was making her feel like it was maybe a big deal after all.

"So, have you ever kissed in the office when everyone's gone home?" she teased.

Karen tapped Tilly on the leg good naturedly. "No silly, of course not, we're not like that. Although he does sometimes leave cryptic Post-it notes on my desk," she smiled.

"Oh my God, I love it, I am not going to be able to look at you two in the same way again! Does anyone else know?"

"Nope, you're the first person from the office to find out!" she blushed. "We didn't want to make a big deal of it in case people started treating us differently, plus although this obviously didn't happen whilst Alan was still married, we didn't want anyone gossiping about us in case, well, you know how people can be."

Tilly nodded. "Don't worry, your secret is safe with me. And I certainly won't be posting any photos of tonight online, so no-one will see you both here."

9.30pm

BECKY WAS FLICKING through her Facebook pictures, showing the girls photos of Delilah.

"Oh my gosh, she is so cute," said Karen. "I'd love to have a little girl one day." She glanced coyly at Alan, who knew she wanted to have a baby and wasn't totally averse to the idea himself, even at his slightly more advanced years. "Do you think you might have any more children?"

Becky smiled at her phone, admiring a particularly angelic photo of her daughter she'd recently posted online, and which had received 98 likes.

"What? Oh, er, well, I don't know, it's complicated," she said, before promptly bursting into tears and rushing from the room.

Tilly glanced at Rupert and they simultaneously

stood and followed her quickly through the candlelit kitchen to the downstairs cloakroom.

"Bex, sweetheart, what's wrong?" Tilly put her arms around her friend as she sobbed into her shoulder.

Rupert lurked in the doorway, the small room not built for three adult bodies at the same time.

"It's the, it's the baby thing," she sniffed, "I just don't know how long I can keep going."

Tilly thought back to the conversation they'd had the night of the takeaway curry.

"Oh darling, I know you're having a rubbish time, and I'm sorry I don't talk about it much, but I never really know what to say, and I…"

"No Tills, it's not that, it's something else," Rupert interjected quietly. He glanced at Becky, a knowing look passing between them. Tilly swallowed, scared of what he was about to say.

Becky sat down heavily on the closed toilet seat, pulling a wodge of tissue from the loo roll to blow her nose loudly. She looked up at her friend, and across to her husband again. Rupert nodded imperceptibly.

"We're trying to adopt a baby, well maybe a young child, but hopefully a baby," she explained.

Tilly nodded, relieved that it wasn't anything more serious, as she'd briefly feared, and crouched down next to the loo to listen to her friend talk.

"Go on."

Becky took a deep breath, exhaling slowly and steadily before she started to talk.

"We started looking into it a few months ago. Just in case I couldn't get pregnant again. It takes ages. We've registered with an agency, and have been to a meeting with some other couples going through the same thing. It's horrible, it feels like a competition." Her eyes welled up again and she swallowed, composing herself. "But it's OK, we passed the first test, they liked us."

"Of course they would, you're an amazing mum." Tilly patted Becky's leg affectionately.

"So now we're in the next bit, lots of forms. SO many forms. We're going to a class after Christmas, to talk about the effect adoption has on you and your family. As if I don't already know." She looked at Tilly. "It's exhausting Tills. The fear, the pressure, the constant worry that you're not good enough. Or the thought that somewhere a baby is being born right this minute, and we aren't far enough down the line, and that maybe right now it doesn't have a home, and I could do that, I could be its mummy…" she collapsed into tears again, at which point Rupert managed to squeeze into the cloakroom as well and hold his wife as she sobbed her heart out.

BACK IN THE sitting room, Hugo was drunkenly probing Tariq about his love life.

"Seriously mate, you seriously telling me you're single? I know we've only just met but I'd have guessed you were shacked up with some hot babe!" He counted out Tariq's attributes on his fingers. "You're a lawyer, you've got a nice house if you live down this road, gonna guess a nice car, and I can tell even with your clothes on you work out, so what's the deal?"

Tariq laughed politely. He did indeed work out, and saw guys just like Hugo flexing their muscles in the gym all the time.

"Yes, you're right, and yes, to my mother's great annoyance I am still very much a single man. Not that that would be the case if she had anything to do with it though!"

"Argh…. Does she wanna find you a wife?" his words slurred a little. "Arranged marriage eh? God I couldn't put up with that!"

Alan caught Tariq's eye and raised his eyebrows, a slight shake of his head at Hugo's potentially provocative line of questioning. He hadn't met Hugo before, but he had sussed him out pretty quickly. A bit brash, loud and over confident, not the sort of person Alan would normally socialise with. But he was Tilly's friend, and he certainly wasn't about to disagree with something Hugo had said for fear of causing an argument. So in typical Alan form, he lightened the conversation as he always did in situations like this.

"So Tariq, what would your ideal partner be like?"

Tariq sighed.

"Well to be honest I'm a little bit of a romantic at heart," he laughed, surprised how comfortable he felt talking so openly to people that he'd never met before. "It's not so much about what someone looks like, it's more about personality, how you click with someone. You know?"

Alan nodded.

"I just don't really get to meet many ladies to be honest. I work long hours, I'm not a big drinker, I do go to the gym but apparently you're not supposed to look at people these days when they're working out. It's crazy, when did smiling at someone become offensive?"

"Oh mate, tell me about it, the world's gone mad. What about on-line dating? It's quick and easy! Just stick your photo on, add a few likes, and off you go!"

Alan glanced at Hugo, wondering how on earth he knew so much about dating apps when he was apparently a happily married man.

"No, no, not for me, I'm old fashioned I'm afraid," offered Tariq. "I just want to meet someone normally. I have faith that one day I'll bump into my perfect woman, it will be as it's supposed to be."

Alan liked Tariq. He didn't know anything

about him other than what he had learnt tonight, but they seemed to have similar outlooks on life. He thought about how he'd got together with Karen, how their friendship had blossomed so naturally into more than that, after he and his wife had separated. It had been so straight forward, so easy. Maybe Tariq was right. He was obviously a man of faith and morals, hopefully that would stand him in good stead.

"YOU LOOK FINE darling, no-one will know you've been crying." A little white lie was definitely required here. "Anyway, it's so flipping dark in there and everyone's been drinking so stop worrying about it. Come on."

Tilly took her friend by the hand and led her through to the kitchen.

"Where's your drink? Here, let me get you a fresh glass and some nibbles and – oh I know, hold on!"

Tilly went through to her study, which was very slightly illuminated by the light coming through the venetian blind from the snow outside. It was funny how that happened, the night seemed less dark, the world a touch more silent, when the ground was covered in a carpet of white.

Deciding against attempting to construct the planned cake mountain during a power cut, Tilly picked up the whole box of chocolate brownies and carried it through to the kitchen.

"Here we go, double chocolate brownies, handmade by yours truly, two types of chocolate AND cherries, just what we need. Bex, you get the biggest one in the box."

"Oooooh thank you my lovely. And… I wanted to ask you actually, now that we've broached the subject, would you be one of my referees on the adoption form? Please?"

"Of course I will, anything for you. And I promise I won't tell them about the time we hitched a lift across Waterloo Bridge in the back of that police van!"

10.30pm

IT WASN'T HER imagination; it was definitely getting darker in the sitting room. Tilly's supply of candles was rapidly diminishing, and as she was rummaging blindly in the back of the dresser she heard Tariq's voice behind her.

"Are you OK Tilly, can I help you with something?"

AND SO IT was that five minutes later the two of them were trudging across the silent snow covered street, wrapped up in coats and scarves for the short journey to Tariq's house. All the streetlamps were off, the only light was from their torches, and as they stepped out onto the front doorstep the scene in front of them brought them up short. They stood for a moment, in awe of the silence around them, so quiet that Tilly could actually hear the very faint sound of snow falling through the air.

"It feels like we are standing in a picture postcard," whispered Tariq.

"I know, but why are we whispering?" giggled Tilly.

They set off diagonally across the street, no need to look for cars. Tilly had swapped her heels for wellies, and she crunched through the snow satisfyingly. Tariq was still wearing his leather shoes, and she found herself worrying about tide marks on the pristine leather.

Candles flickered in several windows along the street, and a little girl in pink pyjamas stared from her bedroom window at the two of them as they made their way past her house. Otherwise, there was no-one to be seen. Everyone else was wisely tucked up at home, probably in bed thanks to the absence of television or light.

Tariq pulled a small bunch of keys from his coat pocket and slid one into the lock on the front door. Tilly looked around the porch as he pushed the door open. It was very neat, even the door knob was shiny.

Stomping her feet to shake off the snow, she slipped her wellies off and followed him into his house. Instinctively he reached up to turn the hall light on, before remembering that it wouldn't be working, and he pulled his phone back out to use the torch on that instead.

It was a bit strange being in someone else's house in the pitch black, and Tilly was relieved when Tariq pulled a small camping style lamp from the understairs cupboard and handed it to her.

"Here, turn this on and wait for me, I'll fetch the candles and be back in just one minute," he said. "Are you OK?"

She nodded. He disappeared up the stairs and Tilly stood stock still against the wall. She felt a little bit out of her comfort zone standing in a house she hadn't been in before, in the dark, and her ears worked overtime listening to the sounds of an unfamiliar house as he moved through the rooms above her.

After what felt like an eternity, Tariq came back down the stairs and handed her a canvas shopper half full of church candles.

"Can you hold this please Tilly? Just a second, I have a big box of matches somewhere, in case we need them too," he said, disappearing into the sitting room. Tilly watched him move through the dark, the light from his mobile showing glimpses of his life. The house was certainly very neat. Tilly could see a leather sofa, with a book laying on one armrest, and she wondered briefly what he was reading.

"Here, got them. OK let's go. Ready?"

They headed back down the hallway and Tariq took the bag from Tilly so that she could put her wellies on, then they made their way back through their own snowy tracks to Tilly's house.

11.30pm

JEMIMA WAS DRUNK. To be fair, most of them were pretty tipsy, although Jemima was definitely the loudest of the group. She was standing in front of the fire, holding court with her stories about some of her most high profile clients.

"And then this one woman, I mean, honestly, more money than sense. You should've seen what she wanted in her bedroom. Gaudy is not the word. Picture this..."

Tilly had heard this story before, and she needed a wee, so she slipped away through the kitchen to the downstairs cloakroom. It was really quite chilly in the rest of the house now, and she shivered as she sat down on the cold toilet seat. It had turned out to be such a random evening, but despite the lack of guests, the weather, and the power cut, Tilly was surprised to acknowledge that she was actually having a really good time. She was surrounded by people who she genuinely liked, with no chance of being stuck talking to someone she barely knew, other than a once brief contact that had turned into a social media connection.

And it was amazing what came out when you actually spent time talking to someone. She thought she knew everything about Becky – she was one of her best friends, but the adoption revelation had blown her away. Who would've thought that she'd been carrying around such a huge secret these last few months.

And Tariq – he was fitting in so well with her friends, it was brilliant to finally have made a real life connection with her near neighbour.

As she walked back through the kitchen she found Jemima rummaging in her cupboards.

"Tills, there you are babe. We need shot glasses. We're gonna play a game!"

Oh God, thought Tilly, *here we go*.

"I haven't got any darling, I'm not a shot sort of girl, you know that!"

"Oh God, you're so straight!" she laughed.

Tilly brushed the comments away, Jemima could be pretty cutting when she got drunk, but Tilly knew that she didn't mean it cruelly.

"Oh, I know what I've got. Here, pass me that candle, I need to see down here."

Tilly rummaged in the back of a cupboard that was stuffed full of random items. Somewhere, she was sure, there was a packet of paper cups left over from a picnic she'd had with her sister's kids last summer.

"Yep, here they are." Tilly pulled a stack of brightly coloured children's cups out. "What do you want to put in them?"

"Oh, I dunno, what have you got?"

"Rum? I've got a bottle in the dresser that I haven't even opened."

"Yes!" squealed Jemima, before she shimmied back into the sitting room to announce the game to her new found audience. "Perfect!"

"OK. I'LL START. Never have I ever… snogged someone famous!" Jemima announced gleefully as she kicked off the game five minutes later. She then promptly downed her drink with a flourish and slammed her paper cup down onto the coffee table.

Tilly looked around the group, who were all holding their paper cups in anticipation and staring at Jemima.

"Sorry," said Mimi, "What do we do? Drink if we have, or drink if we haven't?"

"Oh you lot, haven't you ever played this before?" Jemima shook her head and refilled her cup. "Drink if you've done it. Don't if you haven't. That's it! God – only me, wow, you're all so boring!" She looked to her left. "Rupert. Your turn! Think of a question!"

"Hold on, who did you snog?" asked Karen, who was slightly inebriated and getting more confident as the evening progressed.

"Oooh I know this!" interrupted Tilly, "that bloke off the telly, you know, the sexy Scottish one who does the Amazing Spaces thingy!"

"He's not Scottish, he's from Sunderland you wally!" laughed Jemima. "And yes, it was George Clarke. A long time ago! But he was a great snog," she laughed. "Right, next!"

Rupert raised his cup. "Never have I ever… stolen from a shop!" he downed his rum as Tariq and several others looked on in horror.

"Hold on, hold on, you'll have to explain that one," laughed Becky. "I know the truth, but no-one else does, and now they're all gonna think you're a thief!"

"I stole a penny sweet from the newsagents at the end of the road when I was five years old. I've felt guilty about it for the whole of my life," he said, reaching for the rum bottle.

"Oh…"

Hugo and Alan downed their drinks too, laughing conspiratorially and leaning across to high five each other.

"Mimi, your turn."

"Hmmmm… OK. Never have I ever… pretended to go to the gym but read a book in the café instead!" she gabbled, picking up her drink and downing it quickly, before pulling a face and wiping her mouth with the back of her hand.

"Mimi, you are so bad!" teased Tilly, wondering if that was really the worst thing her sister had ever done. "Bex, you're up."

Becky pondered. She was so kind, no-one who knew her would ever think she was capable of anything worthy of winning a drinking game.

"OK. Never have I ever… kissed a married man!" she said, winking at her husband.

Becky, Jemima and Mimi all picked up their cups and downed them, as Karen leant forwards, hesitated, frowned at Alan and sat back again. "Nope, you were definitely divorced!"

"Oh, fuck it," said Hugo, knocking his rum back and winking at Tariq. "Might as well play the game properly!"

Midnight

RUPERT BROKE THE silence. "Whoa there! Mate! What?" He was aghast at what Hugo had just announced. Silence descended upon the group like tumbleweed, the crackling of the fire suddenly the only sound in the room. All eyes turned to Jemima, who had slunk back against the sofa, and shut her eyes in horror.

"Why, oh why, would you say that?!" she

slurred. "You bloody idiot." She pushed herself up from the seat, her height in heels making her look statuesque in the candlelight against the other eight seated bodies, and wobbled out of the room.

"Sorry, sorry!" he shouted after her.

Becky and Tilly followed their friend into the kitchen, shutting the door firmly behind them.

"What the actual fuck?" she was saying, not very quietly at all. "Why would he say that?"

The girls were speechless, not sure if it was true or a wind up, the implications of it being true bouncing around in their heads.

"What's he talking about, Jems?"

Jemima picked up an empty glass and topped it up generously from the nearest open bottle of wine. Taking a large swig in an attempt to calm her nerves and compose herself, she turned to her best friends in the world.

"Do you know what? Fuck it. I'm fed up of these lies. It was going to come out one day anyway. Hugo, my husband, the supposed love of my life, is gay." She took another mouthful of wine. "There we go, I've said it." She stood up straight, took a deep breath, and was surprised to find herself feeling relieved, not sad or shocked as she would have expected.

"What?" said Tilly.

"I knew there was something going on," said Becky, shaking her head. "Oh Jems. I'm so sorry darling."

Tilly was astounded. She had not spotted that coming in a hundred years, and was struggling to deal with the reality of the huge bombshell that had just been dropped so casually in her kitchen.

"I don't understand. How can he be gay? He's married to you."

Jemima sunk down to the floor, the girls following suit to sit on the cold tiles.

"In name only babe. To be honest I've known for ages. Our marriage is a sham, I knew that within a few months of being married to him. Why do you think we've never had children?"

"Oh Jems, I can't bear it!"

"It's fine, I accepted it a while ago. I'd be a shit mum anyway," she laughed, a little hysterically. "I just didn't think it would come out like this."

"But hold on, what about when he had that fling? When you almost left him?"

"With a man," Jemima nodded, reaching up for the rest of the bottle. "Why do you think I drink so much?!"

BACK IN THE sitting room Karen, Alan, Tariq and Mimi were feeling decidedly uncomfortable with the awkward position they'd found themselves in. Rupert was berating Hugo for having upset Jemima in front of everyone, whilst simultaneously apologising profusely on his friend's behalf for having ruined their evening too.

Hugo at least had the decency to act vaguely contrite, and when pushed he put his hands up and nodded his head slowly.

"Ok, OK, I'm sorry everyone. Especially you guys…" he glanced over to Karen, Alan and Tariq. "You've just come for a nice drink, never met me before, and here I go, ruining everyone's night."

A chorus of No's washed back to him.

"Maybe you should go and see if your wife is OK," suggested Tariq.

If it had been anyone else Hugo probably would've punched them, but something about the way Tariq spoke to him hit exactly the right chord.

"Yeah, you're right mate, good call," he slurred, before pushing himself up from the sofa and wandering slowly to the kitchen.

Rupert looked at his watch and was relieved to see that it was well after midnight.

"Gosh, is that the time?" he announced, breaking the awkward silence that Hugo had left behind. He wasn't a night owl and had actually been ready for bed at the point that Jemima had suggested they play a game. He knew that he'd have to be on good form the next day; a hangover with two small kids *and* the grandparents staying for lunch was not a good combination. He stood up.

"Guys, I'm really sorry, but I'm going to call it a night. Early start tomorrow. It was great to meet you all, we should do it again sometime." He reached forward to shake Tariq and Alan's hands, and to kiss Mimi and a yawning Karen on the cheek. "Maybe with the power on next time!"

They all said their farewells and Tariq moved over to the hearth to add another couple of logs. The warmth had dropped noticeably as the fire had died down, and as there were only four of them left in the sitting room it didn't feel quite as cosy with the extra space between them all. He had also discovered over the course of the evening that Tilly was really rather lovely indeed, and he didn't want her thinking he was useless. He wondered why he had never talked to her properly before. All this time living over the road and their paths had barely crossed. He sat down on the vacant sofa next to Mimi just as Tilly walked back into the room, a bottle of wine and another plate of cheese in her hands to add to their supplies.

He stood up again immediately.

"Tilly, would you like to sit here?" he asked politely.

"Oooh yes please, shove up Mims, there's room for the three of us."

Mimi did as she was told.

"Are they OK?" she asked her sister, referring to Jemima and Hugo.

"Yes, although they've decided to call it a night and head to bed. I think Jems is a bit traumatised about the way it all came out in front of everyone, and Bex and Rupes are knackered so they've gone to bed as well."

"Maybe we should make a move too," said Alan, looking at Karen, who was beginning to fall asleep on his shoulder.

"No, don't be silly guys," said Tilly. "I've no more spare rooms but you are welcome to crash on the sofa. It's still snowing out there and the trains probably aren't even running anymore. Honestly, I've got loads of blankets, you're welcome to stay."

Alan glanced at Karen, who nodded briefly before closing her eyes again. "I think that's a yes," he laughed. "OK thank you Tilly. Thats very kind of you."

"Where am I sleeping then?" asked Mimi.

"In with me, silly," laughed Tilly. "You don't get your own bedroom, this isn't The Ritz!" She looked over at Tariq. "You're also very welcome to stay if you don't mind a sofa, your house is probably freezing by now."

"No no, it's fine, I don't mind a bit of cold. My mother sent me some brushed cotton pyjamas only last week, they will come into their own tonight!" he laughed.

Tilly blushed slightly at the thought of Tariq in his pyjamas, thinking it rather sweet and at the same time wondering why she was imagining him brushing his teeth in her bathroom.

"So this is it then," announced Mimi. "The last ones standing! I think we need bubbles."

Making her way to the drinks area, she rummaged in the beer bath until she found an unopened bottle of fizz. Using her fingers to deftly pick up four fresh Champagne glasses she took them back to the sofa and popped the cork. She filled the glasses and handed one each to her sister, Tariq and Alan, bypassing Karen who was by now snoring gently beside him.

"I would like to make a toast." She announced. "To my lovely sister, for having us tonight, come what may. To Tilly!" They all chinked glasses and drank the icy cold bubbles, which was decidedly refreshing after possibly too much red wine and certainly rather a lot of cheese.

"And to friendships," added Tilly. "To you lot, who have made this the perfect evening. Cheers!" They chinked again. "I thought when I organised tonight I was going to have a hundred people here, a house full of friends, but tonight has made me realise that you don't need hundreds of people to be happy. You only need the people that matter. And you guys matter to me, I'm so grateful to have you here. Thank you all for coming."

"Thank you for having us," said Alan, "it's been a delightful evening. And you've been a wonderful host," he smiled. "So what are you doing us for breakfast then?"

Iam

"OK, TIME FOR me to head home," said Tariq, as he set his empty glass down on the coffee table. He stood up and turned to Tilly. "May I trouble you for my coat please?"

"Ooooh yes, it's on my bed, in my bedroom, I'll just go upstairs and get it for you." She blushed, wondering why she'd mentioned her bed to Tariq. Although maybe that was only awkward in her head, and maybe she shouldn't really have had that last glass of Prosecco.

Tilly tiptoed upstairs to retrieve his coat without disturbing the others. Turning on the bedside lamp, she wondered briefly why it wasn't working, before giggling quietly to herself at her stupidity. She felt through the items on her bed and picked up a long wool coat from the top of the pile, breathing deeply as she smelt his wonderful fragrance. "Stop it," she said, before tiptoeing back down the stairs to hand it to him.

"Well, thank you so much for having me Tilly, it has been a really rather wonderful evening."

"You're very welcome," she replied. "Come anytime. I mean, not too early, but, yes, anytime," she said, smiling broadly at him and telling herself silently to shut up.

He leant forward to kiss her on the cheek. "I'll see you soon," he smiled. "But not too early. Thank you again."

Tilly opened the front door and let Tariq out into the snowy night, watching the little glow of light from his phone torch as he crossed the street towards his empty house. The cold swirled around her feet and she shut the door quietly, before pushing the draught excluder against it in an attempt to retain any warmth that was left in the house. They were going to need all the help they could get tonight.

When she walked back into the lounge Mimi was picking up glasses, and Karen was completely horizontal on the sofa, fast asleep and snoring softly.

"Tilly, would it be OK to borrow a couple of blankets please?" Alan asked. "Or a throw or something?"

"Yes yes, of course, I'll just go and get some, hold on a minute."

She disappeared up the stairs again, taking a little tealight candle in a jar with her to put in her bedroom. She pulled two woollen blankets from the bottom of the chest of drawers and took them back downstairs.

"Ok, so you know where the bathroom is, help yourself to water and whatever you need, I'm afraid I don't have any spare pillows but you can always use the scatter cushions," she offered.

"You're so kind Tilly, that's great, thank you so

much," said Alan, tired himself and looking forward to going to sleep. "I'll blow out all the candles too, don't worry," he smiled.

"Oh yes, the candles, thank you Alan."

Mimi appeared in the doorway holding two large glasses of water. "Come on Tills, stop waffling, it's cold and I think Alan wants to go to sleep. Let's go!" she whispered.

"Night Alan, sleep well."

"Good night Tilly, thank you for a lovely evening."

Tilly climbed the stairs wearily. It was over. The evening that had started as a complete disaster had ended up going not only surprisingly fast, but (shocking revelations aside), very well. She yawned deeply. Her pyjamas were going to be so very welcome after hours in a party dress.

TEN MINUTES LATER Mimi and Tilly were snuggled in her bed, pyjamas on and teeth brushed. The bathroom had been as cold as ice but there was no way either of them would've gone to bed without cleaning their teeth. Make up still on yes, but clean teeth were non-negotiable.

"It's flipping freezing in here Tills!"

"I know, stop whinging. Do what Mum taught us. Run in the bed."

They both rolled onto their sides and wiggled

like hamsters running on a wheel, before Mimi burst into laughter at the preposterous sight they must look.

"It works though, doesn't it!"

Tilly slid her legs down the bed, grateful for her fluffy bed socks.

"Oh my God, what a night. I'm so glad you came. Even though I haven't really had a chance to chat to you properly all night."

"I know, I was thinking the same," she sighed.

"Are you alright, Mims?"

There was a silence in the darkness, and Tilly let it pass, gave her sister room to think.

"Not really, no."

Another silence. Tilly bit her lip, letting the gap do what it had to do. She knew something was going on after the previous weekend's events, but had no idea what it was.

"Do you know what, I've had such a great time tonight. Laughing, chatting, just normal stuff, you know? Meeting new people, getting out of the house, being me. It felt so… liberating."

Tilly nodded, kept listening.

"And I actually think I enjoyed it even more cos I was here on my own. It's the first time in ages that I've had a proper laugh. You know, I didn't miss Andrew being here at all."

Tilly listened to her gut and took a chance. "Are you guys OK?"

Another pause.

"I dunno. Actually yes I do. No, we're not." Mimi took a sharp intake of breath. "We don't do anything together anymore. Family stuff, yeah, of course, but during the week I feel like a single parent most of the time. And we never, you know. If I'm brutally honest I think we're only staying together for the sake of the kids."

Tilly's eyes widened in the darkness, her forehead creasing as she raised her eyebrows. She'd known something was a bit off, but no-where near as bad as what she was hearing.

"I actually think he might have had an affair."

"What?"

"I found a message on his phone a few months ago. I didn't recognise the name and it was pretty flirty. Do you know what though, I didn't even care. It was almost like someone had waved a magic wand for me and I could switch off my marriage, just get rid of it all and live a nice easy life with the kids."

"Oh hun, that's awful, my gosh I didn't realise you felt like this."

"That's what our argument was about the other week. I'd been too scared to confront him about the message, but it kept creeping up on me so I did. I knew he'd deny it and of course he just turned it around on me and had a go at me for looking at his phone. So I decided to see what I could find out on my own. That's where I went that night."

"And what did you find?"

"Nothing. Complete waste of time. And now he's acting like nothing's happened, that we're all fine and it's Christmas as normal, and I'm dreading it Tills, I'm just getting so fed up of playing happy families, I feel like I'm living someone else's life and nothing is real."

Tilly couldn't help but notice the irony of someone who appeared to have it all actually feeling the complete opposite.

"I just feel as if I'm stuck at home like the trophy wife. I used to have a career, be my own person. Sometimes I look at you and wish we could swap places, you're so independent, you've got your job, your house, a great social life…"

Tilly snorted.

"And now I'm… what? The cook, the cleaner, the nanny, the dutiful wife who makes the house look nice. Is that it? I feel as if he's lost all respect for me since I've been a stay at home mum. Like that's all I'm good for."

"Babe, you're not just those things. You're an amazing mother, a lovely sister, and you deserve to be happy. Don't ever say anything but. You're worth so much more than that."

"But am I? If I applied for a job I probably wouldn't even get an interview. I've been out of the game for so long now."

"Is that what you want? To go back to work?"

"No. Yes. Maybe. Oh, I don't know."

"Well why don't you have a look at what's out there? Maybe that's what you need, a few days at work, it might give you a bit of self-worth, if you know what I mean. A bit of time for you to be you again."

Mimi sighed. "I don't even know if I fancy him anymore. Is that bad?"

"Er, well yes I suppose that is a bit of an issue," she laughed, "but it's probably just cos of how you feel right now. Maybe you need a bit of counselling. There's no shame in it these days. Maybe you should give it a go for the sake of your sanity. And for your family. Oh Mims, I wish you'd talked to me about this before, I had no idea it had got so bad. I thought you were happy. You're like the perfect family on Facebook."

Mimi guffawed.

"Yeah, the camera never lies huh?"

When her sister was finally asleep, Tilly lay in the darkness, happy in the knowledge that her nearest and dearest were all under her roof, problems and all. The night had brought so many revelations, in all manner of shapes and sizes, and at that exact moment in time Tilly couldn't have guessed the outcome of any of them if she'd tried.

Becky and Rupert adopting – wow – that wasn't something she'd seen coming. Tilly wondered if they'd get a baby, and how that must feel to become parents literally overnight to another child. She wasn't sure if she could do it.

And Hugo. Oh my God. That had come completely out of the blue! Poor Jems, she must have been struggling keeping things to herself for so long. No wonder she drank the way she did. Although a part of Tilly did admire Hugo for finally coming clean about things – there was no point living a lie forever, you only got one shot at this life. In this case, it was probably better for everyone long term that things were out in the open.

As she went through her friends and the revelations that had just kept on coming, she smiled at the newfound knowledge about Karen and Alan. They were both such lovely people, and it made complete sense that they were together, but how funny that it had taken her party to uncover their secret.

And Tariq – no revelations here other than the fact that he was single, gorgeous, and smelt divine. Walking to work past his house would never be the same again.

Mimi snorted in her sleep, before rolling over and resuming her dreams. Poor Mims. Tilly hadn't realised how unhappy her sister was. Despite her initial scepticism she did feel sorry for her. It must be miserable chugging along with no goal; throw in a bit of doubt about your marriage and you've got a recipe for disaster. She didn't know how that was going to work out, but at the heart of it were two little children who needed their Mum and Dad, and who Tilly adored to the ends of the earth. *Please God don't let their lives be ripped apart*, she said silently into the dark room.

All these revelations, the grievances that had been aired tonight. She didn't know what was going to happen. But what she did know was that together, as friends and family, they would all get through them.

Tilly was so grateful for her lovely friends, tonight had brought that into sharp focus. She wasn't alone in this world, and she had a small group of people around her who meant the world to her. Some with new beginnings, others with a lot of work ahead of them. Family, old friends, and maybe some new ones too.

One of whom was just over the road in his brushed cotton pyjamas, brushing his teeth and thinking about the girl across the street.

Chapter 22

The day after the party

TILLY WASN'T SURE what woke her first. Her bladder, her headache, or the strange noise that was coming from downstairs. She could hear a man's voice, and a low buzzing sound in the distance, which gradually increased in volume as she stirred from her hungover slumber. There was a ticking noise too, which as she surfaced, Tilly recognised as the sound of the heating coming on, as the hot water made its way through the creaking pipes to the radiators.

"Uuuurgh, what's that noise?" murmured her sister from the other side of the bed.

"I think the electricity has come back on," replied Tilly, sitting up slowly to see how bad her hangover was. "Oh, I don't think we should've had that last bottle…"

As she tiptoed down the stairs Tilly realised that the man's voice was in fact Shane MacGowan singing "Fairytale of New York," which was apt seeing as the Christmas tree lights had all sprung back into action again and were flashing away over a bundle of blanketed bodies on the sitting room sofa. There didn't seem to be much movement from underneath them though, so Tilly left Karen and Alan sleeping in peace and crept into the kitchen instead.

The fridge hummed contentedly as Tilly rummaged behind the bottles of wine for a carton of milk. Tea was required quickly, and in large quantities. She filled the kettle and took great satisfaction in flicking the switch on for the water to boil. It was funny how you took such simple actions for granted until they were taken away from you.

Pulling eight mugs from the cupboard, Tilly popped a teabag into each one.

"Morning Tills. Thought I heard someone up and about. Oh, the powers back on!" Becky hugged her friend close. "How's the head?"

Rupert appeared in the doorway behind her.

"Oh good, tea, just what I need," he smiled. "Morning Tilly, how's the head?"

"Oh God, was I that drunk last night?" she laughed, desperately racking her brain to search for anything embarrassing she might have said or done.

"No, you're fine, I'm only teasing. Two sugars for me please."

By the time the tea had brewed Mimi had appeared in the kitchen too, looking as bleary eyed as

Tilly felt. Placing the mugs on the kitchen table she busied herself toasting thickly sliced bread, and placed a large plate of buttered toast on the tablecloth. Hungry hands demolished it in a matter of minutes, and Tilly started on a second batch just as Karen and Alan entered the kitchen, sleepy and slightly dishevelled after their night on the sofa. It was the most relaxed Tilly had ever seen her colleagues, and it had to be said that it rather suited them.

"Morning guys, help yourself to tea, I'm just making some more toast."

"Thank you Tilly, much appreciated. And if I may, could I possibly trouble you for a couple of paracetamol? I seem to have woken up with a little bit of a headache. I don't know why," smiled Alan.

ONCE THEY WERE replenished by the tea and toast, Becky and Rupert politely made their excuses and packed their overnight bags ready for the journey home.

"Thank you so much for having us Tills, it was such a great night. Sorry I cried on you."

"Don't be silly, it's fine, I'm just so glad you told us what's going on. I'm so excited for you both!" Tilly hugged her friend and opened the front door. "Safe journey home, go easy on those roads, they'll be treacherous. And give Delilah a big kiss from me when you get back, tell her I'll see her soon."

"Will do, and say bye to Jems for me, I think it'll be a while before she surfaces."

Tilly breathed in the crisp morning air as she waved her friends off, watching them fondly as they crunched their way to the car. The snow had stopped falling and the air felt fresh. A new day. She glanced the other way along the street towards Tariq's house before closing the door and heading back inside.

"Right. I'm just going to pull some clothes on and I'll be back in a minute," she announced. "Help yourself to more tea, toast, whatever you want, I won't be long."

She was desperate for a shower but felt guilty leaving her guests for too long, so she pulled on jeans and a baggy sweatshirt, splashed her face with cold water, and almost as an afterthought, put some mascara on. Just in case.

By the time she got back downstairs somebody had folded all the blankets neatly in the sitting room and placed the scatter cushions back in their original positions. Karen had donned marigolds and was making a start on the dirty glasses, whilst Alan was filling the kettle in anticipation of another round of tea.

"Oh Karen, you don't have to do that!" exclaimed Tilly.

"It's fine, actually I quite like washing up," she smiled. "Who do you think washes all the mugs at work?"

It's funny, Tilly thought to herself, if she'd ever even considered having two of her work colleagues round for a sleepover, she would never in a million years have expected to find Karen and Alan folding blankets and washing up the following morning. Just 24 hours had turned them from colleagues to friends, and she really liked that, very much indeed.

A knock on the front door jolted her from her daydreams, and she went to open it with slight trepidation. She wasn't expecting anyone, and didn't usually get unannounced visitors. So she was very relieved to see Tariq's smiling face on her doorstep. And even more relieved that she'd put some mascara on earlier.

"Good morning," he said, looking unusually but comfortably casual in a deep blue sweater and jeans. He was wearing a collared shirt under the sweater and one lapel was caught just inside the neck, which gave him a slightly dishevelled look that Tilly had not seen before.

"Good morning to you," she replied, smiling at him coyly. "Come in. Oooh have you got power too?"

"I do, yes, I was rudely awakened by many lightbulbs going on this morning," he laughed. Tilly immediately imagined him in his pyjamas again and tried desperately not to blush.

"Would you like a cup of tea? We're enjoying using the kettle," she laughed, ushering him through to her kitchen.

"Well actually I thought I'd offer to help you tidy up, but if you're drinking tea I would love to join you, thank you."

As Tilly followed her neighbour into the kitchen she noticed how deliciously fresh he smelt. Clean but not over powering. How did he manage that so early in the day after such a late night? Tilly supposed it was because he hadn't drunk half as much as the rest of them had; he had been much better behaved than all of them, and she hoped, not for the first time that morning, that she hadn't made a fool of herself.

"Good morning Tariq!" Alan greeted him like an old friend, clearly happy to see him again. "You're up and about early, my friend."

"Oh yes, I may not have been, but my mother rang me at the crack of dawn as usual," he grimaced.

Over tea, Tariq explained how his lovely but opinionated mother sometimes disapproved of the way his sister was bringing up her children "in the modern way," and often called her son to have a little moan about it. He clearly loved his mum dearly, but Tariq and his sister were living a rather different life to the one she had hoped they would live, or at least so far as a strict Hindu upbringing was concerned. Tilly wasn't sure how he could do anything more to make his mother proud, he was a practising lawyer with strong family values, he was smart, presentable and polite, what wasn't there to like? In fact Tilly thought that even *her* super critical mother would approve of him.

When they'd finished their tea, Tariq helped Tilly carry the vast quantity of empty bottles out to the recycling bin, and Jemima and Hugo finally materialised just as they were coming back inside.

"Aye aye missus, where have you two been then?" croaked Jemima, clearly slightly the worse for wear.

Tilly rolled her eyes. "To the bin, Jems, tidying up whilst you slept through it all!" She hugged her friend to show that she was only teasing. It was typical of Jemima to sleep through any tidying up, they were all used to it after many years of friendship. "You OK? You look like you need coffee."

"I need more than that," she said sheepishly. "I'm really sorry about last night."

Hugo was lurking in the hallway, trying and failing to fit his washbag into their shared overnight bag. He was clearly embarrassed about the previous night's revelations and was keeping his distance from the gang in the kitchen. Tilly went to find him.

"Morning Hugo. You alright?" she asked gently.

"Oh hey Tills. Listen, I'm so sorry about last night. I didn't mean to ruin the evening."

"What? Don't be stupid. You didn't do anything of the sort. I just hope you're OK, that's all." They hugged in the hallway, and Tilly felt his pain in the silence between them.

"We're gonna head off if that's OK, I feel a bit weird mingling after last night, I'm sorry, do you mind?"

Tilly shook her head. "It's fine, do what you've got to do, we'll catch up soon."

Jemima joined them in the hallway too and slipped her arm through Tilly's. "Thank you for having us, my darling, I love you so much and will ring you very very soon, I promise. Have a lovely Christmas sweetie."

MIMI LEFT NOT long afterwards; she would have stayed with her sister all day if she could have, but she was keen to get back and see her children, plus she had a mountain of wrapping to do. Even if she wasn't exactly enthralled about going back home to her disinterested husband and boring marriage.

"So I'll see you in two sleeps my lovely sister," she said, hugging her close. "Come as early as you want, you know the kids will be chuffed to see you, and it never feels like a proper Christmas til you get there, so don't be late!"

LATER, WHEN THE washing up was done, any uneaten dried up food and remnants of candles disposed of, and the bin emptied, Tilly, Tariq, Karen and Alan sat at the kitchen table with a huge platter of leftover cheese, baguettes, chutney and grapes. Tilly had offered wine to her last remaining guests, but all had declined, opting instead for mugs of tea which surprisingly, went much better than they'd expected with cheese.

It was lovely to feel warmth in the house again after the previous night's chill, and Karen commented on how different Tilly's house looked in the daytime.

"You've got a lovely house Tilly, you've made it just perfect."

Tilly blushed. She didn't really have anyone round these days so it was nice to be complimented on her home. And even more so as it came from someone so genuine. It struck her that she didn't really know what the inside of any of her lunch companion's houses looked like (except a bit of Tariq's in the dark), but it didn't matter a jot. They could live in a bedsit or a mansion, it wouldn't make any difference to the people they were. She wondered idly if Karen and Alan would ever move in together, get married, have babies... Who knew what the following year would bring?

When they left after lunch Tilly watched the two of them trudge hand in hand down the snowy street, and it filled her heart with joy to see two such lovely people walking into their future together.

AFTER EVERYONE HAD finally gone, she sat and surveyed the scene. There was still a fair amount of tidying to do – hoovering, furniture moving and that sort of thing, but over all her house had survived the night pretty well. Her Christmas tree was still flashing away happily to itself, and she left it on to maintain the post-party / pre-Christmas festive spirit. She wondered briefly whether she should post something on Facebook about the previous night's events, but realised, to her great disappointment, that she didn't have a single photo of the evening.

But then it dawned on her that it didn't actually matter. The people who mattered were the people who were there last night. And they knew what happened because they had bothered to make the effort to get to her party. They didn't bail at the first sign of trouble. Abandon their plans and let people down because they couldn't be bothered to put on some wellies and a warm coat. It dawned on her how many people hadn't even bothered to contact her to apologise for not showing up. They were probably all too preoccupied with prepping for their own Christmases. She picked up her phone to scroll through Facebook. Bearing in mind that she had invited every single one of the people who were visible on her news feed, there were a surprising number of people who were having a perfectly lovely time – some with mutual friends too, she did notice – without a second glance at the weather! A couple of her friends had even posted pictures of nights OUT from the previous evening. Had they no shame?!

Sometimes she wished she could just remove all traces of herself from social media. It could be so toxic, so false, and she hated that so many of her thoughts involved a desire to post things online, or read about what everyone else was doing. It was often the last thing she looked at before bed, and the first thing she checked in the morning. Why? Did she ever benefit from doing so? No of course not.

She put her phone face down and exhaled. Who cared that she couldn't put her own Facebook post online? Maybe what happens during a power cut stays during a power cut. No one else needed to know. Or deserved to. It was their evening, their discussion, their party. Although she also knew that the repercussions of last night's revelations would be felt by all involved for a while to come yet.

But it was over. The party had happened, even if it was a party for nine, not 289. It was done, a year of worrying had passed. And it had been OK. In fact it had been more than OK. Her house had not been trashed. It had not been an absolute disaster. Some people had come, others hadn't.

The friendships she already had, had deepened. New relationships had formed. Incredible truths had come out. Nothing had been broken, she had survived, and for some reason Tilly felt like a slightly better person because of it.

Chapter 23
Christmas Day

"MY BOY! MY boy is here!" Tariq's mum stood up on her tip toes and planted a kiss on the side of his cheek. "Come in my baba," she glanced over his shoulder. "No young lady for me today then?" she teased, patting his waist and tutting with her tongue. "Oh, another year older, another inch wider, don't leave it too long baba!"

"Hello Maa, Happy Christmas."

Tariq leant forward and embraced his mum, her smell so familiar and her love for him so deep. It had become a standing joke by now, the lack of spouse. His sister Tanvi, on the other hand, had done everything the way his mother had approved of. Finished her A levels, gone to university, met a nice boy, and married as soon as they'd graduated. Her degree had gone to waste, in Tariq's opinion, but their mother would hear none of that, grateful only that she had met a nice Hindu boy from a well reputed family. Tanvi's husband Zahir was a good man, and was indeed the lucky one himself, Tariq thought. She was a lovely girl from a decent family, she had provided a healthy heir and a spare, and was a dutiful wife, mother and daughter. Tanvi had ticked every single one of the boxes you were supposed to, but Maa would not be happy until Tariq did the same. And everyone knew it.

"Oh, why don't you let me find you a nice wife?" his mother begged. She didn't understand her son's desire to marry for love over duty. It was his duty, surely, to follow the rules that had been passed through generation after generation, to marry appropriately and continue to provide for the family.

"Yes Maa, I will, one day," he smiled, mouthing "help me" to his sister and brother-in-law over his mother's shoulder.

"Uncle, Uncle!" two little dark-haired cherubs ran through from the back of the house and hurtled into his legs.

"Oh, hello you two," he crouched down to the same level as his smiling niece and nephew. "Happy Christmas!"

"Happy Christmas to you too Uncle," they chimed, huge grins spreading across their faces. "Did you bring us a present?"

Tariq laughed. "You'll have to wait and see!" He smiled, ushering them through to the kitchen, where a large pot of mutton curry was simmering on the stove. It smelt divine, and once again Tariq was glad that his mother had never bowed down to the traditional roast turkey. His mother's mutton curry had to be tasted to be believed, and Christmas Day in their household was a feast for the senses.

The year his beloved Papa had died, no-one had really known what to do, how to deal with that first Christmas without him, and so they'd simply gone through the motions of their traditional Hindu Christmas, laying an empty space for him at the table and remembering the good times. It had been such a shock, him dying so young. Tariq and his sister had only been in their 20s, and their mother seemed far too young to be a widow, but the whole family had pulled together and got each other through it, with love and strength and plenty of tears.

Tariq had only just finished his training contract at the family law firm he worked for when his father had been diagnosed with cancer, and he had thrown himself into work in an attempt to distract himself from the sadness. He knew his father would have wanted him to carry on as normal, and so by day he worked every hour that he could, and spent every evening and weekend with his parents. When his colleagues were heading to the pub after work he would make his excuses and go back home; he sometimes wondered if they thought he was boring, or stuck up, or didn't drink, but his family were his priority and that would never change. When the time came and his father passed away, Tariq felt a sense of relief that he hadn't missed a single minute of his dad's life that he should have been around for, and in the months afterwards, his dear Maa needed him even more than before.

And now, over 10 years on, life was continuing happily around them. His mother still lived in the family home, a handsome 1930s detached house in a small-ish village just outside Croydon, where their father had once owned a successful homewares shop. They'd bought it when Tariq and his sister were young, in the days when you could buy a nice family house for three times your salary, and Maa had no plans to move anywhere else. She had some lovely friends in the village, a peaceful life, and Croydon was only a bus ride away if she wanted something a bit more interesting.

"So, my lovely boy, what has been going on with you?"

Tariq wondered how much he should tell his mother. The truth was that there wasn't actually anything to tell yet, but Tariq hadn't stopped thinking about Tilly since Saturday night, and there wasn't really much else in his head right at that minute.

"Oh, nothing Maa.... Well... I did go to a party at the weekend."

Tanvi glanced at her brother. He wasn't normally a party goer, so the fact that he'd mentioned it piqued her interest. She knew him so well, and there had definitely been a glint of something in his eye when he'd come through the door earlier.

"Oh, what was that then, a work party?"

"No, no, it was a girl over the road."

Tanvi's mind went into overdrive.

"Oh, someone nice?" she asked provocatively.

Tariq blushed.

"Ha ha, thank you my lovely sister, don't get Maa started! Actually, it was quite eventful, the whole street had a power cut and we had to eat everything in the fridge!"

Tariq entertained them with some of the tamer stories from the evening, glancing at his sister every time he said Tilly's name. Sometimes he really hated the way she knew him inside out and back to front.

Tariq's mum listened patiently as her son regaled them with the events from Saturday night. It was good to see him so animated, and she wondered if there was more to this girl than he was letting on. *Let it be,* she thought, time would tell if this was something she needed to know about.

At one o'clock on the dot Maa gathered everyone in the kitchen to help carry the vast number of dishes to the dining room table. As well as mutton curry she had made a huge chicken biryani, and the steaming dish was placed in the centre of the table along with puri flatbreads, paneer, lentil dahl, and pakoras.

"Zahir, would you please give thanks for us?"

Her son-in-law stood and offered a prayer to thank God for the food spread before them, before raising his glass to Maa and silently towards a photograph of her late husband, before taking his seat.

"Eat! Eat!" Maa waved her arms in the air and smiled at her beautiful family, grateful for her children and grandchildren. All she needed was a lovely wife for her dear son and her life would be complete. She smiled at him across the table, and silently sent her own prayer for God to send her precious boy everything he deserved.

SOME 50 MILES west, Tilly was also thinking about Tariq. Her sister was talking non-stop about some random television programme she'd seen, and Andrew was playing with the kids in the sitting room, more so to keep his distance from his wife than to entertain his children, Tilly thought. There was definitely an atmosphere in the house, things weren't as jovial as they usually were, but Tilly topped up her glass of Champagne and carried on daydreaming whilst her sister rambled on about God knows what.

She wondered what Tariq was doing today. She couldn't remember where he said he'd be for Christmas, and picturing him at home she suddenly wished that she was going back to Tonbridge later on too. She could've accidentally bumped into him in the street. Maybe she would've invited him to hers, they could've shared a bottle of wine and a box of chocolates on the sofa. Maybe he'd put his arm around her shoulders whilst they were watching TV….

"Tills! Hello, anyone there?!" Mimi interrupted her thoughts.

Tilly put her glass down on the kitchen island, focused on her sister.

"What were you thinking about? You were miles away!"

"Oh, nothing, sorry, I'm just tired, that's all. So anyway, come on, how are things with you and…" she nodded her head towards the doorway.

Her sister shrugged. "Dunno. Nothing. It's like nothing's happened and nothing's changed. We're just going through the motions and Christmas is filling our time." She put down the canapé she was decorating and sighed. "I was thinking about what you said though. As soon as the kids are back at school I'm going to talk to him. See if we can do some counselling, sort things out. We can't keep going on like we are."

Lunch was a slightly subdued affair, albeit it delicious. Her sister did do a great roast turkey, it had to be said, and the kids were hilarious trying to work out the corny Christmas jokes in the crackers. But Tilly was glad when they had finished eating, the table was cleared, and they could collapse on the sofa to watch a Christmas movie together.

Halfway through the film, just as Tilly was nodding off, the old-fashioned phone in the hallway began to ring.

"Ooooh that'll be Grandma ringing from Florida!" said Mimi, pushing herself up from the sofa. "Come on kids!"

They all traipsed through to the hallway, except Andrew, who disappeared into his study leaving the rest of them to talk to his in-laws.

"Hellooooooo!" they chorused, hoping it was indeed Grandma, and not a neighbour calling about a lost cat or something. Even though the landline ringing on Christmas Day was only ever Grandma.

"Hello everyone," said the male voice at the other end of the line. Tilly and Mimi glanced at each other.

"Dad?" They mouthed silently.

"Grandpa!" squealed the kids excitedly. "Guess what? We got presents from Santa!"

Mimi waited whilst the kids let of steam about the gifts that had come down the chimney, and listened as best she could as her dad told them in great detail about what they would be having for breakfast, which made Oscar and Rosie laugh because it was the middle of the afternoon. When they'd finished she took the sticky handset off them and shared the earpiece with her sister.

"Hey Dad, you OK? Mum OK?"

"Er, yes we're fine, your mum's just having a bit of lie in, I was bored so I thought I'd ring my favourite daughters."

It was good to hear his voice, but it didn't escape the girls that their early riser mum was still in bed. On Christmas Day.

"Is Mum alright Dad? It's unlike her to stay in bed late."

"Oh yes, she's fine, nothing to worry about, we'll give you a ring later if you want, we're off to the clubhouse for Christmas lunch at one, but we'll ring you before we go, is that OK?"

"Of course it is Dad, ring us later, love you."

Mimi put the phone back in its cradle and looked at her sister. "It's not just me, that is weird, isn't it?"

Tilly nodded. "Yep, I thought the same. Let's see what she says when they ring back."

Good to their word, Gloria and Bob did indeed ring back before they went off to their Floridian style Christmas Day lunch. Tilly had listened carefully to her mum's every word, listening for any clues as to what was really going on. She did sound a bit tired, that was all, but maybe she was just worn out from too much golf or too many social events. She was in her seventies after all; Tilly sometimes had to remind herself of that. It had been a while since she'd seen her parents, maybe she should think about a trip to Florida in the new year. Escape the winter and check on how her parents were.

Later that night, when the kids were asleep, the washing up had been done, and Tilly finally had a minute to herself, she dug her phone out of her bag for her usual late-night addictive scroll through Facebook. There was notification of a text message, which she clicked on, expecting it to be from Becky or Jemima. But there was no name announcing the sender, just a number that she didn't recognise. She clicked on it, expecting it to be spam.

> *Hi, it's Tariq, I just wanted to say Happy Christmas, I hope you've had a lovely day. And thank you again for a great night on Saturday! T x*

Tilly's heart skipped a beat, and a smile spread

across her lips. He'd been thinking about her too! Sinking back into the pile of pillows on the bed, she realised how long it had been since she'd felt that little flutter of excitement over someone. It was a good feeling, and she liked it. A lot. He was so lovely, so normal, and from what she'd seen so far, so uncomplicated.

Should she reply? Tilly looked at her watch. It was after 11 o'clock, probably too late to be texting men she didn't know *that* well. But then again… she looked at what time the message had been sent. 10 o'clock. That was pretty late. And she didn't want to appear rude by not replying. Oh gosh, it was a minefield!

Tilly pondered the subject for a few minutes. They were grown-ups, they weren't kids in the playground. Most people who were up at 10 o'clock on Christmas Day night would be up at 11, she guessed. And she didn't want him to think she didn't care. Before she changed her mind, she opened the message again and tapped out a reply.

Hi Tariq, thanks for your message. Yes lovely Christmas at my sister's, hope you've had a good day too.

She paused, wondering how bold to be. Sod it. She continued typing.

Hopefully see you soon. Tilly x

Over in Sanderstead, in his old childhood bedroom, Tariq heard his phone buzz and picked it up expectantly.

"Yes!" he said to himself, a smile on his face. Christmas Day was turning out to be a very good day indeed this year.

Chapter 24
New Year's Eve

TILLY, ALONG WITH Jemima and Hugo, had all gathered at Becky and Rupert's house for New Year's Eve. None of them had alternative plans, or even fancied going out anyway, and trying to get a babysitter on December 31st was always a nightmare, so it was logical that they all went to Becky's for the evening. Plus she had plenty of room for them all to stay, which meant there was no worrying about trying to get home amongst a sea of drunken revellers.

Delilah had been pretending to be asleep in her bedroom when Tilly arrived, and as soon as she heard the front door open, she rushed excitedly to the top of the stairs so that she could show her favourite Godmother her new pink pyjamas. They were decorated with fairies and were *very, very comfortable*, apparently.

Becky had made one of her famous chilli con carnes, which was simmering away happily on the hob, and after a glass of Champagne to kick the evening off, Delilah was returned to her bed, and the five of them sat around the vast kitchen island helping themselves from large ceramic serving dishes in the centre of the granite slab. It was a delightfully relaxed and informal evening, and huge bowls of rice, guacamole, sour cream, chillis and grated cheese jostled for space amongst several bottles of Chilean Malbec, which Rupert had already got bored of pouring for everyone.

"Don't wait for me to top you up guys," he laughed, "I think we've known each other long enough not to be shy!"

Becky smiled at her husband. They were in a good place right now, and she was excited about what the new year might bring for them as a family.

"Come on then peeps, we need to make one wish each for the new year. What do you want 2019 to bring you?" she asked the group.

They all sat and stared at her, nervous of their answers for all sorts of different reasons. Hugo stared despondently into his wine glass.

"OK. I'll start then," said Becky, "even if it is obvious after the other week. I want us to adopt a baby!" She raised her glass into the air in a silent toast, before everyone else caught onto the gist and joined her in a *Cheers!* and a grand chinking of glasses.

"Hold on, hold on," interjected Tilly, the wine bolstering her confidence. "I think that before we start plotting for next year, we need to do a bit of a summary of this year! See what we've achieved, or what we could've done better, yeah?"

"Good point babe," said Jemima, grateful for the extra time in which to think about what she could say. "How has your year been then?"

Tilly knew the answer to this already. She had been reminiscing all day about the last 12 months. She'd even gone so far as to dig out the list she'd made at the start of the year. Last Christmas she had been lonely and miserable but had made a plan and had stuck to it. Well, most of it anyway, plus there had been a few unexpected additions. She'd joined a dating site, been to several work nights out, and had somehow managed to lose weight without even trying. She'd planned, held, and survived her "massive Christmas party." She hadn't had sailing lessons or joined the golf club but figured you can't do everything. She'd also got back with, and broken up with, her ex, and survived a company re-shuffle. Not a bad year, all in all.

"I think..." she looked around at her friends. "That it's been a pretty good year overall. Not least cos I've got you lot as my friends!"

"Yeah... and maybe a *new* friend too, eh Tills?" teased Jemima.

Tilly blushed, wondering how much to tell them.

"Hmmmm. Well actually, I might be going for

dinner with him next weekend…" She smiled, cocking her head sideways and turning even redder.

"No waaaay! Oh my God! Tell me, tell me!"

The boys looked at each other, confused. Jemima noticed their mutual glances and helped them out.

"Tariq, you wally, the bloke at the party, remember?"

Realisation dawned across both their faces.

"Oh…. Of course… Yeah he was nice, I liked him, good job, Tills."

"Thanks Rupes. Right, let's not digress, who's next?"

They worked their way around the group choosing their high points of the year, and then in turn their wishes for 2019 – the elephant in the room obviously being Hugo's recent revelation and the subsequent slow destruction of his marriage. But being the decent and supportive friends that they were, no-one pointed out the obvious and moved swiftly past any glaring omissions, until they'd all had a go and could safely move onto something slightly less contentious.

Tilly updated the girls on how things were going with Tariq, and the boys slowly drifted out of the conversation and into their own debate about rugby versus football. They weren't interested in the he-said she-said palaver of girly pre-date gossip, but Bex and Jems most definitely were. They'd both really liked Tariq; thought he was polite, funny, and handsome, and had decided that he'd be perfect for their lovely friend. It was about time she met someone nice.

"Is it silly that I wish we were a bit further down the line?" she asked.

"What do you mean?"

"Well I just wish that – don't take this the wrong way, cos I love you guys whatever, but tonight, it's just me on my own again. I'd love it if we were already a couple and he was sitting here too, chatting to the boys about football."

"Stop!" said Jemima, holding her hand up. "You absolutely cannot wish this into an established relationship already. Two reasons. One, you don't even know whether or not he's suitable long-term material yet. For all you know he might have – I dunno – really smelly feet, or an annoying habit that you just can't tolerate. You never know. And two, don't whizz past those magic bits. That first kiss. The long weekends where nothing else matters but the two of you. The getting to know each other. Discovering each other's personalities. If he's right then you've got all the time in the world to be just another couple eating chilli with their friends. And if he's not, then you need to suss that out! One step at a time my lovely."

Tilly and Becky looked at their friend.

"Whoa. That's the most sensible thing I think

I've ever heard you say. When did you become so mature?"

Jemima swirled her wine around the glass. "We've all got to grow up one day," she said nonchalantly.

AT A QUARTER to midnight they all went through to the sitting room and put Big Ben on the television to count the new year in together. Whilst they watched the build-up and waited for the dongs they each reminisced in their heads about what had changed since last New Year's Eve. They were all another year older of course, and Tilly definitely felt in a better place than she had done the year before, but for Becky and Jemima it was as if everything and nothing had changed at the same time. On the surface they were still the same people – same jobs, same house, same car, but delve deeper and they were both standing on a precipice waiting for monumental changes to their lives. A year from now Becky and Rupert could have another child in the house. Jemima and Hugo could be divorced and moving on with their lives. Both such huge changes. But as the year drew to a close they were all feeling safe amongst friends, comfortable in the knowledge that whatever the next twelve months threw at them, they would always have each other. And as Big Ben chimed the new year in, they were all silently making their own very personal wishes for the year ahead.

Becky was wishing for a baby sister for Delilah. She didn't want to sound greedy, because she knew how lucky she already was having such a lovely husband and a happy, healthy, beautiful little girl. But in her heart she yearned for two children, to even the family up and give her daughter a brother or sister. She'd grown up in a family of four, it had just felt balanced for some reason, and she longed for Delilah to grow up with the support of a sibling, learning to share, being part of that unique bond that only brothers and sisters have.

Rupert was praying that his wife would see her dreams come true and that they'd complete their family. If he was totally honest, he'd be happy having just one child, he didn't feel such a strong desire for a second one as she did. But he knew how much Becky wanted another baby, and now that the adoption thing seemed to be taking flight, she was on a mission for it to come to fruition. Each time she'd miscarried it had broken Rupert's heart, holding his beloved wife in his arms as she'd sobbed onto his T-shirt. His pain had been more for her than for their mutual loss, and he knew that women often felt that pain more deeply than men did, but either way it had hit him hard. Becky was such an amazing mum, and he just wanted to see her happy.

Jemima was making a resolution to drink less

and get her life back on track. Ever since Hugo's revelation she'd slowly been adjusting to his truth that, if she was honest, she had secretly suspected a long time ago. Jemima was a fighter. That old expression of "what doesn't kill you makes you stronger" could've been written for her, and she knew that as things unfolded in the new year she'd have to take control of her life again. She was already planning on expanding her interior design business, knowing that throwing herself into work would be exactly what she needed. And cutting back on the booze had to be part of that. She couldn't work harder if she was hungover, so she'd been drinking less and had already noticed how much better it was waking up earlier in the morning, clear headed and ready for the day.

Hugo was hoping that in being true to himself, he wouldn't hurt Jemima any more than he had already. Although he wasn't *in love* with his wife in the traditional sense of a marriage, he did love her dearly. They'd shared a good few years together, built a home together, and apart from the most recent revelation, knew everything about how each of them ticked. It was going to be a wrench working things out, living separate lives, but he didn't want to hurt Jemima financially or emotionally, he owed her that at least. He just had to find the right way forwards.

And Tilly was just thinking about her date with

Tariq. She was excited, a bit nervous, and couldn't wait for the following weekend. It was so strange to think that they'd lived so close to each other for so long, just across the street, when all this time there could've been a mutual attraction. They'd been happily passing each other's front doors, oblivious to the ins and outs of each other's daily lives, and sitting on their respective sofas in the evenings maybe even watching the same television programmes. It was so funny, yet so exasperating at the same time!

And Tilly's party had created this situation where she suddenly felt like she knew him so much better, almost as if they'd known each other their whole lives. She knew that sounded crazy, she couldn't really explain it, but finally, after a long time of being either alone or in the wrong relationship, Tilly felt like this might, just might, stand a chance.

Chapter 25
January 2019

THE NEW YEAR dawned bright and fresh. The snow had long melted and crisp January days had arrived, the best type of winter in Tilly's opinion. It also made dressing for her first proper date with Tariq much easier. Rain was never conducive to looking good – mackintoshes and umbrellas wouldn't quite cut it in the style stakes. Perusing her wardrobe, Tilly decided on a beautiful wool dress, black tights and knee-high boots, and she hung the dress on the back of her bedroom door in anticipation of her date the following day.

Tariq had booked a table at a lovely little Italian restaurant in Tonbridge, which Tilly had been to before and so knew it was a great place for a first date. The food was delicious, the ambience cosy and intimate, and best of all they could walk there and back. They'd arranged that Tariq would knock for her at 7pm, and as Tilly got ready for their date her tummy suddenly started fluttering with nerves. All week long she'd been excited yet cool, calm and collected, so she was surprised to feel anxious about his imminent arrival.

The doorbell rang a couple of minutes after seven, and Tilly slipped her coat on before she opened the front door. Tariq was standing on the doorstep looking very handsome indeed, with a smile on his face which put Tilly a little more at ease.

"Good evening," he said. "Are you ready?"

Tilly nodded, fishing her keys from her evening bag to lock the door and promptly dropping them onto the doormat. They both leant forward at the same time to retrieve them, almost but not quite bashing their heads in the process.

"Oh my gosh, sorry, I'm not normally a butterfingers," she laughed. "Actually if I'm honest I'm a bit nervous, it's ages since I've been on a date!"

Tariq smiled.

"I'm so glad you said that, I've been nervous all afternoon! I don't know what's wrong with me, it's not like we haven't met before!"

Ice broken, they walked the 10-minute journey into town chatting easily about their respective Christmas and New Years Eve's. By the time they reached the restaurant all tension had dissipated, and Tariq held the door open for Tilly as they entered. The delicious smell of garlic and pasta filled Tilly's nostrils as they entered the warm space, and they were greeted by the owner, who led them through the busy restaurant to a lovely table for two in the corner.

"I am so hungry," Tariq said as they studied the menu. "I must admit that I went online today to look at the menu, and my stomach has been anticipating it ever since!"

Tilly laughed. "I do exactly the same," she admitted. "I love pre-reading the menu."

Tariq ordered a bottle of Chianti, and over steaming plates of spaghetti vongole (Tariq) and cannelloni (Tilly) they talked non-stop all night. They had so much in common that Tilly couldn't work out how on earth their paths hadn't crossed already. They often got the same train into London, they both shopped in the same places and for the brief period that Tilly had been a gym member, it had been at the same gym that Tariq was a member of. There were none of the uncomfortable silences that you fear on a first date, and unlike previous dates Tilly could recall, Tariq asked her questions about her life and had actually listened to her replies, rather than just blabbering on about himself. He really was lovely, which made Tilly wonder why on earth he hadn't already been snapped up by someone.

Almost as if he'd read her mind, Tariq asked her the same question.

"So I don't mean this in any way rudely, but I can't believe you aren't happily married to some lucky man Tilly. You are, if I may be so bold, a lovely girl, and I feel very honoured to be your date this evening."

Tilly blushed. She didn't really want to go over the failures of her disastrous relationship with Ethan, but equally she didn't want to appear the eternal singleton.

"I guess… I don't know, I suppose I've just never met the right person," she said. "I have had relationships, obviously, but nothing that, well, you know, went all the way."

Tariq nodded. "Yes, same here, life can be unpredictable sometimes."

The waiter arrived at their table to clear away the empty plates, and Tilly wondered where the conversation would go from there, and if Tariq was thinking the same as thing as her. Luckily the manager bustled over to the table to top up their wine glasses, and to venture as to whether or not they might care for dessert. Tilly wasn't sure that she had room for anything else, but when the cheery Italian started extolling the virtues of Zabaglione, which he considered *the most superior dessert* in his humble opinion, she was sorely tempted. And when he explained that it was the perfect dessert for lovers, as it was made for two, they both got the giggles and felt that they had no option to say anything other than "Yes please."

It was absolutely delicious, a light sweet

whipped pudding that slipped down extraordinarily easily. Tilly had never had it before, but was extremely glad that they'd decided to take up the manager's recommendation. After pudding the waiter brought two tiny espresso coffees along with a complimentary small glass of amaretto for each of them, which they enjoyed with paper-wrapped amaretti biscuits. It was the perfect end to a perfect meal.

When the bill came Tilly leant down to her bag for her purse, wondering what the etiquette was these days with regards paying on a first dinner date, but happy to go halves with Tariq. It was always an awkward moment, and she didn't want to presume or offend.

"Oh no, Tilly, this is on me, please, put your card away," Tariq said firmly but kindly.

Tilly hesitated. "Are you sure?"

"Oh yes, absolutely. It has been a delight spending this evening with you, I wouldn't dream of letting you contribute. Even if you never want to see me again!"

Tilly smiled.

"Well thank you Tariq, that's really kind of you. But I can safely say I would love to see you again." She blushed, suddenly realising that he wasn't actually asking her out, and that the words had come out before she'd properly realised what she was saying. Clamping her hand over her mouth, she laughed as she looked at his smiling eyes. "Ooops! I didn't mean it to come out quite like that!"

"Oh no, please, go ahead, it saves me working out how to ask you out on another date!"

The manager brought their coats and bid them both farewell as they stepped out into the cold night air. Tariq offered his arm, which Tilly accepted, and they walked back along the high street admiring the Christmas lights that were still strung across the shop fronts and around the lamp posts. Winter definitely had a more romantic feel to it than summer did, and as Tariq smiled down at Tilly he saw the lights reflecting in her eyes, giving her an almost ethereal, sparkly appearance.

Tariq hadn't felt like this before. It was as if he was properly awake for the first time in his life, and the possibilities that lay ahead of him felt truly magical. He had enjoyed himself so much that he didn't want the evening to end. He had even thought that he couldn't wait to tell his mum about this wonderful girl who had suddenly appeared in his life, which spoke volumes. The logical, rational side of him was still there, but it was as if he was more open to certain opportunities, more aware of his feelings, than he ever had been before.

Way too soon, they were back in their road, and Tariq graciously walked Tilly all the way to her front door. As she dug her house keys out of her handbag she turned towards him.

"Thank you so much for a truly wonderful evening, I've had the best time," she smiled.

"You're very welcome, I enjoyed it very much too."

A silence hung in the air between them, neither of them sure what to do.

"Um, do you want to…" Tilly cocked her head as if to invite him in.

"No no, it's fine, I'll leave you in peace," said Tariq, which was completely the opposite of what he really wanted to do.

"OK. Well, thank you again." She fiddled with her keys awkwardly.

Tariq leant very slightly forward, hesitated, then kissed Tilly on the cheek.

"Goodnight then Tilly, see you soon."

"Goodnight."

Tilly let herself into the house, her heart racing and her mind whirring. She felt like she was 16 years old again, being kissed at a school disco. She could feel the warmth of Tariq's kiss on her cheek and she subconsciously put her fingers to her skin as if to rub it in. Closing the front door behind her she grinned like a Cheshire cat in the dark hallway, excitement and nervousness running through her body.

Meanwhile Tariq was also crossing the road with a huge smile on his face. Tilly had completely and utterly blown him away. She was absolutely gorgeous, everything he had hoped for, and although he hadn't wanted the evening to end, he didn't really know where to start. It was as if there were a million things he wanted to say to her, but was terrified of scaring her away. He knew he had to be patient, but he didn't want to waste another minute not being with her. This dating game was so confusing, and he'd been out of it for most of his adult life so a lot was unknown. But the one thing that he did know, completely and utterly, was that Tilly Jenkins was the girl for him.

Chapter 26

Across London in Jemima and Hugo's beautiful townhouse, the atmosphere couldn't have been more different. Tensions had been high for the past few weeks, and things were getting harder as each day went by. There was a reason divorce lawyers were at their busiest in January. Christmas and New Year often seemed to bring things to a head, and the start of the year had escalated emotions and were spurring Hugo on to sort his life out.

Jemima was ploughing herself into work like there was no tomorrow and had taken on a huge commission that was filling her every waking hour. Which was good, because she needed the distraction. Even sitting across the dinner table from Hugo was becoming painful. They weren't arguing, it was just the underlying knowledge that their relationship was slowly disintegrating, and all the emotions that that entailed. They both knew that divorce was the right thing to do, but it still hurt.

Jemima tutted as her mobile rudely interrupted

her thought process. If that was another request from Hugo's lawyers.... She picked it up and was pleased to see Tilly's name flashing at her.

"Hey babe, how's it going?"

"Oh my God, I cannot stop thinking about him!" squealed Tilly. "Help me!"

Jemima laughed. It was so good to hear her friend happy, finally. She'd been through some tough and often lonely times, but Tariq being in her life had illuminated her.

"Go on, tell me, I want to hear EVERYTHING."

Tilly filled her friend in on their date, their texting, the way he made her laugh. It was so sweet it almost made Jemima nauseous, but she listened regardless and hoped that things always stayed so positive. Those early days were so full of promise, the happy ever after that everybody dreamt of so within your grasp. Jemima couldn't imagine ever meeting anyone ever again though. How could she trust someone after the bombshell revelation that Hugo had dropped on her? The person she knew better than anyone? Or so she'd thought.

"Anyway, enough about me," said Tilly, aware that she'd been blabbing on for a considerable amount of time. "How are you, darling? How are things going?"

Jemima hesitated, wanting to talk about what was going on but scared of bursting Tilly's little bubble of love.

"Oh you know, working like mad as usual!"

"Jems. This is me babe. Don't give me flannel. Tell me what's going on."

"Aaaargh you're so annoying, how do you always get me to talk!" she laughed, before sighing and lowering her voice. "Yep, it's shit. Hugo's lawyers are like a dog with a bone, they seem to think that this divorce needs to be done like yesterday. I honestly think we'd be better sorting things out ourselves. Every time a question is asked it's another hundred quid for a letter asking it. Oh and to top it all off, it looks like we're definitely going to have to sell the house."

"Oh no, you love your house! It's gorgeous."

"I know, I do, but it's *our* house, not mine, and I don't think we've got any option. We need two homes now, not one, and even if I stayed here Hugo would need half the equity to put down as a deposit for somewhere else, and I can't afford to cover that."

"Oh God, that's dreadful babe, after all the work you've done."

"Yeah, but maybe it's meant to be. Maybe a fresh start is what I need. A chance to make my mark on somewhere new. It'll probably have to be smaller, maybe in a less expensive area…"

"Oooh come and live in Tonbridge. It's lovely down here and we could see each other all the time."

Jemima laughed. "Can you imagine, we'd never get anything done! No, as much as I'd love to live nearer to you, I need to be in London, that's where most of my clients are. We'll have to wait and see what happens, nothing's decided yet."

Tilly thought about what Jemima had said. She was being remarkably positive about things, considering. She had put so much love into renovating and decorating her beautiful home; it had been a wreck when they'd moved in and it had taken a long time and a lot of money to turn it into the showpiece that her house had become. Every single thing that Jems had learnt along the way as an interior designer had been applied to the makeover, and she had chosen the best bits of everything for each and every room. Being in the trade herself had meant that most items had been sourced at cost – Jemima's services weren't cheap and Tilly dreaded to think what the bill would've been if she'd been doing it for someone else. Every time she went round to Jemima and Hugo's, Tilly felt like she was walking into a life-size Susie Watson catalogue. The pastel pinks, candy stripes and bobble edged curtains all absolutely what the white walled house was crying out for.

To be honest Tilly had seen a remarkable change in her friend since the news had come out about Hugo. And weirdly, it was all for the better. Most people would have lost the plot, such a huge revelation swinging like a wrecking ball into their lives. But with Jems, it had almost been the opposite. She was drinking less, working harder, and looking into the future more than she ever had before. It was as if she'd been set free to do what she wanted, and if Tilly hadn't known better she might even have thought that Jems had known what was coming. What she was sure of thankfully, was that her friend was going to get through this and probably even end up happier because of it.

Hugo, on the other hand, was wobbling. He wouldn't admit it in a million years, but since the new year had dawned and reality had hit, he had realised just how much his life was going to change. And not necessarily for the better.

He knew he was right to finally tell the truth, however hard it was. His marriage to Jemima had been a front, a wall for him to hide behind. Whether or not he had hidden because he was scared to do what he wanted or ashamed for others to know that he was gay, he had never quite worked out, but bar a few minor indiscretions he'd managed to keep his feelings hidden and get on with life and work, and act as the good husband. But as more and more of their friends started families, the void between the truth and the lie seemed to widen, and then he began to wonder if there should be more to life than he was living.

He should've known that Jems would be the strong one in all of this. That was what had attracted him to her in the first place. Her outrageous and forthright personality. Her sheer determination to do whatever the hell she wanted. And he hated himself for what he'd done to her, set her up for a doomed marriage from day one.

But now he was paying the price. His divorce lawyer had explained to him that even though they didn't have children he should expect a 50/50 split of all their assets. To be fair they both earnt similar amounts of money, and had bought the house together, but the reality was that one pot of money, however healthy that might be, was considerably smaller when split in half. And with the London property market being as ridiculously over inflated as it was, he knew that he wasn't going to be able to afford anywhere near as nice a home as they lived in at the moment.

Luckily they'd bought a wreck and done it up, so at least they'd made money on the house. And although he enjoyed living at the level of luxury that they did, he didn't need anywhere near as large a property just for himself.

It was way too early to be looking at flats, but the seed had been sown and Hugo knew that he would be taking a step back so far as the property ladder was concerned.

On his way back from work that evening, he'd sat opposite a heavily pregnant lady on the tube. She had actually looked a bit like his wife, and tears sprung to his eyes when he imagined Jemima pregnant. Had he deprived her of that forever? He hated himself, for taking away her chances of motherhood. How was she ever going to have become a mum when their relationship was purely platonic? He wondered if she might meet someone else, start a family with someone other than him. She was still only in her 30s after all. Maybe it wasn't too late. He closed his eyes and leant against the tube window as it sped through the dark tunnels. A vision of his wife holding a baby swam through his mind, a little pink bundle in her arms. And another man standing next to them, with his arm around her shoulders.

Hugo shook himself awake as the tube jolted to a stop at the next station, glad to be rid of the image. He peered through the anonymous bodies filling the carriage to see which station they were at, before realising with a start that it was his stop. He leapt up and just about managed to get off the train before the doors closed firmly shut behind him.

Chapter 27

February

Becky was having a somewhat in-depth conversation with Delilah about why she had to wear shoes to school.

"But Mummy I don't like soooos," she said, eyes brimming with tears. "I just want my pink socks, not soooos…"

"But darling you have to wear shoes to school, they keep your feet clean, and nice and warm, and anyway these are very nice shoes…" she implored through slightly gritted teeth, wondering not for the first time that day why everything was so flipping difficult. Brush your teeth, eat your breakfast, put your shoes on…. Sometimes she felt like motherhood was just an endless string of petty battles.

Her phone rang and she abandoned the shoes to see who wanted her now.

"Hi, is that Becky?"

"Yep."

"Becky it's Sandra, from the adoption agency, is now a good time to talk?"

Becky glanced at Delilah, who had taken the phone call as an opportunity to escape her mother and was now making her way back to the lounge to find her doll, and get as far away from those shoes as she possibly could.

"Yes, yes of course, how are you?"

"Good, good, yes. Ummm, I know this is rather sooner than we'd talked about, but I think we may have found a match for you."

Becky sat down on the staircase.

"Oh my gosh, wow." She took a deep breath. "I don't know what to say!"

"Don't worry, that's normal, these phone calls are often a bit of a shock. Shall I tell you a little bit more about the situation?"

"Yes please, that would be great, sorry."

Becky listened as Sandra told her about a baby who was currently being cared for by short term foster parents, whilst a more permanent home was found for her. She swallowed as she processed the word. *Her.* A baby girl. Her mind instantly began to picture two little girls sitting at her kitchen table and she had to make a concerted effort to bring herself back to the present and pay attention to what she was being told.

"So what we'd really like to do is come and see you and Rupert, tell you both a little bit more about everything, and if you're happy, arrange a time for you to meet her, how does that sound?"

"It sounds incredible, yes, thank you so much Sandra, that's amazing!"

THREE DAYS LATER Becky and Rupert were sitting opposite Sandra and her colleague Heidi. Becky had made a pot of tea and placed a plate of very posh chocolate biscuits in the centre of the large wooden table, although Rupert had told her more than once that they weren't going to get a baby based purely on their choice of biscuit.

It suddenly all seemed to be happening very quickly indeed. They'd gone through all the relevant stages, the meetings, the training, the checks and the references over the past few months, but they'd been told all along that this last bit, the part where you literally had to sit and wait for the phone to ring, could take months. Not this time! They had only just finished the penultimate stage of the adoption process the week before, and Becky felt, for the first time, absolutely terrified.

"What if we get an awful child?" she'd sobbed to Rupert that morning. "What if she hates us? How will we deal with that?"

Rupert had done his best to calm his wife down. He was anxious too, but he knew that Becky was just panicking. He also knew that they weren't going to be thrown a random kid and left to their own devices. They could spend as much time as they wanted with a baby, or child, before committing to anything. And even then, there was a period of time before which anything was legally binding. Everyone needed to be happy. The two of them, the social worker, the adoption panel, and not least, Delilah.

"Right," said Sandra, bringing the room to attention, and cutting straight to the chase. "So the match we have for you is a six-week-old baby girl, she is looking for a permanent placement with a loving family, and is currently being cared for by a local foster family. Her birth mother has agreed to give her up for adoption due to personal circumstances, and has actually moved up north already in an attempt to move on with her life. In this particular case, she doesn't want any contact with her child or the adoptive parents, and the father is not listed on the birth certificate so there isn't any issue on that side either. In fact this is a pretty clean case, no complications. How does that sound so far?"

Becky glanced at Rupert, who was biting his lip and nodding at the information he'd just been given.

"Yep, that all makes sense."

"Ok, so the baby's mother is white Caucasian, as we believe was the father; she has thick brown hair and dark blue eyes. Well, blue at the moment – they obviously still might change colour. I must say, I did notice that she has very similar hair to your daughter!" Sandra smiled. She rooted around in a manilla folder until she found what she was looking for. "Here we are, here's a picture of baby Daisy."

Becky took a sharp intake of breath. *Daisy*. She knew that you could change a baby's name when you adopted them, but Daisy was such a sweet name. Leaning forward to take the photograph from Sandra, she leant sideways to share it with Rupert.

"Oh my gosh, she's so beautiful," she said, tears welling up in her eyes. A cute little bundle in a pink Babygro smiled up at her from the photograph. It broke her heart to think that someone could have abandoned such an adorable baby, and she wondered what sort of person her birth mother had been.

"Can I ask why her mother gave her up for adoption?"

"All I can tell you at the moment I'm afraid, is that she has had issues with drug use in the past, and that she didn't feel ready – she's quite young – to raise a child."

Becky shook her head. "Gosh, I just can't imagine what that must be like," she said, looking at Rupert for reassurance.

Heidi nodded.

"It's very hard to imagine until you're in someone else's shoes. Over 2,500 babies are given up every year for adoption, and everyone has a different story. It is very difficult, but it is what it is."

Sandra stepped in. "But luckily there are also many couples like yourselves who are desperate to give a home to an unwanted child, and all we're here to do is to facilitate the journey and match up children with parents."

"I hate to ask, but you mentioned drug use," said Rupert. "Does that mean there could be issues with Daisy, might she have any problems?"

"No, Daisy's mother abstained from any drug and alcohol use during her pregnancy, and Daisy has been tested to check for any issues that her mum's history may have caused. But I can assure you that she is a healthy, happy little girl; her foster parents have kept us up-to-date with how she's getting on, and all she needs is a permanent home with stability for her to feel secure in."

Becky looked at the photograph again.

"She's adorable, don't you think Rupes?"

Rupert nodded and squeezed his wife's hand. He had known her long enough to know that this little bundle in the photo was everything that Becky had been hoping for.

"Yes she is. And I think we should see if we can meet her in real life." He looked at Sandra and Heidi. "If that's OK of course!"

Sandra smiled. "Yes absolutely, but it doesn't happen overnight. You have to wait until the match has been approved by the panel before you can actually meet her, and you might not be surprised to hear that there are some very organised next steps to climb. While I get that ball rolling, I can send you some more details about how Daisy is getting on, and also we can show you some videos of her that have been taken by her foster parents."

Rupert held Becky's hand tightly. He knew she had probably already been imagining them going to collect Daisy the very next day.

"Once the panel reads the reports about Daisy, and about you as a family, they will decide if you're the best match for her; they obviously take into account the baby's needs, and if you are in a position to meet them."

"Oh gosh, are we in competition with another family to adopt her?" asked Becky.

"No, there's no competition, and you can go to that panel meeting too – you have the opportunity to voice your opinion as to why you'd like to adopt Daisy and why you think you'd be good parents for her. If the panel then says yes, which if I'm honest I don't see any reason they wouldn't, it comes back to us for the final approval."

"Oh my gosh there are still so many hurdles," said Rupert, running his hand through his thick hair and rubbing the back of his head.

"Don't worry, a lot of this sounds way more complicated than it is. We just have to make sure that everything is done correctly. Once that's all happened, we prepare what's called an Adoption Placement Plan. This is where we arrange a series of introductory meetings, so that you can get to know Daisy and she can get to know you. Obviously because she is such a young baby it's slightly different to if she was an older child, but we just want her to be familiar enough with you so that when the time comes for her to move in with you, she knows who you are, the sound of your voice, your smells etc. Sometimes with older children this can take time, but the first few months of a baby's life are so critical, we find that the earlier young babies can be placed in their permanent home, the better it is long term."

Becky thought back to when she'd brought Delilah home from the hospital where she'd been born. It had been such a steep learning curve for all three of them, but the one thing she had felt more than anything was the strong instinct to protect her baby girl. And even though she wasn't related to Daisy, and hadn't even met her yet, Becky just wanted to fast forward to the moment that she could gently scoop her up in her arms, hold her close, and promise her that she was going to love her and protect her, for the rest of her life.

Chapter 28

Tilly was sitting at her desk in London working her way through a cheese and tuna toastie when her mobile phone pinged. Rolling her eyes at the interruption to a long-awaited lunch, she picked it up and was surprised to see "Dad mobile" on the screen. Her dad very rarely sent text messages, and she frowned as she flipped the screen open with her thumb.

Can you ring me when you get a minute please. It's important. Love Dad x

Tilly swallowed her mouthful and wiped her hands on a paper napkin.

"I'm just popping out for a minute, got a weird text from my dad," she said to Karen as she shimmied past her desk.

"OK. Everything alright?"

"Not sure, I'll be back in a min."

Tilly made her way out towards the lifts and slipped though the emergency exit door into the stairwell. It was a good place to make personal calls from, as no-one ever used the stairs. She scrolled through her contacts to D and tapped her dad's mobile number. There was a few seconds delay before the phone line connected to America and rang only once before her dad answered.

"Hold on," he whispered, before a muffling sound filled her ear for a minute. "Sorry darling, I'm here now, are you OK?"

"Yes I'm fine Dad, I'm at work, you OK? You said it was important?"

"Yes. Well. The thing is, don't worry, everything's OK, but we're in hospital," he said, instantly causing Tilly to worry.

"Oh my God, what's happened?"

"Well, it's fine, don't worry," Tilly wished he would stop saying that and get on with saying whatever he was trying to tell her, "it's your mum, darling, she's had a bit of a funny turn, and they've brought her into hospital to check her over."

"Oh shit, is she OK? What do you mean, a funny turn?"

"She's OK, yes, the doctors here are very good and are doing lots of tests. She's had a scan, and it looks like, well, they think she might have had a mini stroke."

"Oh God, Dad..." Tilly's eyes filled up with tears, the distance between them feeling greater than ever.

"Darling it's OK, she's alright, they said she'll

be OK, they're going to keep her in overnight whilst they're working out exactly what happened."

"Is she going to be OK? I mean, she's not going to…" Tilly's words faded away, she couldn't even bring herself to say the words and voice her worst fears.

"No, no, no, darling, the doctors are really looking after her, it's not like the NHS out here, they're very good you know."

Tilly half laughed through her tears.

"Oh Daddy, I can't bear being so far away from you both. What happened? How did you know something was wrong?"

"Well you know how your mother can be a bit of an insomniac. She'd gone downstairs early this morning, I felt her get out of bed then I fell asleep again, and I don't know how long after it was when I got woken up by a loud crash."

Tilly put her hand over her mouth, the image of her mother collapsing causing her eyes to fill with tears again.

"Well, I went straight downstairs to see what had happened and found her standing in the middle of the kitchen looking very confused indeed. The coffee pot was smashed all over the floor, so I picked my way through the glass, luckily your mother was wearing her slippers, and when I realised that she couldn't speak properly I sat her down on the sofa and called 911 straight away."

"Oh Daddy, that's awful, thank God you were there."

"I know, and at least we were at home. The ambulance came very quickly, the paramedics were so wonderful, honestly, they took us both into hospital and whisked your mother off for tests while a lovely young lady sorted out my feet."

"Your feet?"

"Yes, the glass, the coffee pot shattered into a million pieces."

"Oh Dad! Are you OK?"

"Yes yes, I'm fine, I'm back with your mother in a private room and waiting for the test results to come back. In fact, I'd better go back in – listen, can you ring your sister and let her know what's happened? I texted her too, but you rang back first."

"Yep, of course, and please can you give Mummy a big kiss and tell her that I love her so so much."

"Of course I will darling."

"Text me back as soon as you hear anything, oh gosh I wish I was there, I feel so useless being so far away."

"Don't worry, everything will be fine, I promise I'll text you when I know more. Love you, darling."

"Love you too, Daddy, bye, bye…"

Tilly hung up and took a deep breath. She suddenly felt every single one of the 4,500 miles away from her parents. She was standing in a stairwell in central London and her mother was lying in a hospital bed on the other side of the Atlantic Ocean. She could've died, and Tilly would've been none the wiser. Her eyes filled up all over again and she allowed herself one big blub before wiping her tears with her sleeve and trying to compose herself enough to ring her sister.

Mimi was on her way to a Pilates class at her expensive gym when Tilly rang.

"Hey babe, how you doing?"

"Not great, did you get Dad's text?"

"Yeah, just seen it, I'll ring him after my class. Is everything OK?"

Tilly bit her tongue at the arrogance of her sister prioritising her workout regime over their father. "No, not really, Mum's in hospital."

"Oh shit." That had stopped her in her tracks. "What's happened?"

Tilly filled her in on the morning's events, just about managing to keep her emotions at bay until the part where she said how far away they were, and that she just wished they were in America with their parents. Her voice cracked and she desperately tried to suppress the sobs that were threatening to engulf her again.

Mimi clicked into big sister mode.

"OK. Right. Yes. Let me think. Now listen Tills, you know the hospitals out there are brilliant, Dad has done absolutely the right thing by getting Mum in as soon as possible, and it sounds like from what you've said that Mum's stable, yes?"

"Yes."

"OK, well I agree, we need to be there. To make sure Mum's OK, and just in case, well, you know, in case anything changes."

"Oh God, don't say that, she has to be OK, she's only in her 70s!"

"I know, and I'm sure she'll be absolutely fine, but I bet Dad would appreciate the support too. We should book a flight and go out as soon as possible. Can you go tomorrow? I'll book us flights."

"What? Hold on a minute, I have got a job you know, I can't just swan off at the drop of a hat!"

"Well, talk to your boss then! Tilly, this is important, we need to be there. And if you can't go, I'll go on my own, Andrew will have to look after the kids."

Tilly sighed. "Sorry, I didn't mean to snap."

"No it's fine, I'm sorry too, I didn't think."

"You're right though. We'd never forgive ourselves if something happened and we weren't there because of work, for flips sake. And I hate the fact that we are so far away. OK, I'm going to talk to my boss now. I'll text you as soon as I can."

TILLY WALKED BACK through the office, knocked gently on Duncan's door, and tentatively pushed it open.

"Ah Miss Jenkins, what can I do for you?"

She stood at the corner of his desk, unsure how to start the conversation, but when Duncan noticed her red eyes and asked if she was OK, it was enough to tip her over the edge and start her crying again.

He stood up and hurriedly closed the door before pulling a handful of tissues out of the faux leather covered box on his desk. He wasn't very good with crying women and didn't really know what to say, so he perched on the edge of his desk and waited until she'd calmed down enough to speak.

"So I was wondering," she said, after filling him in on her mum's situation, "If it would be possible to take some time off so that I could fly over to be with her? Please."

Duncan was very understanding, and also very relieved that that was all it was. For a moment he'd feared that one of his most loyal employees was about to hand her notice in, so a few weeks away was no problem at all.

"Absolutely, you should go Tilly. Take as much time as you need."

Tilly made her way back to her desk to text her sister.

All good, I can go whenever. Have you spoken to Andrew?

Yes, he's fine to look after the kids. I'm on my way home now to look at flights, can you go tomorrow if there are seats?

Yes. Call me when you get home, I've got to sort out a few bits in the office but it won't take long x

Twenty-four hours later Tilly and Mimi were at Heathrow Airport waiting to board a flight to Miami. Everything had happened so fast that Tilly barely had time to take it all in. They'd managed to get seats on the lunchtime flight, only "down the back" as Mimi had sniffily pointed out, but they were seats nonetheless and it meant that they were on their way to their parents.

Mimi had access to a lounge (of course she did), so rather than roughing it in Wetherspoons with the rest of the world in the terminal, they were safely cocooned in a pair of very comfortable chairs overlooking the runway, a glass of Champagne in hand.

"Does this feel a bit weird, drinking Champagne when Mum's just had a stroke?"

Mimi looked at her sister like there was something wrong with her. "No of course not, it's free, and it's there to be drunk."

"Oh OK. And are we really allowed to eat any of that food too?" asked Tilly.

"Yes of course, get whatever you want. And make sure you pick up a bottle of water and a couple of packets of crisps for the journey too. God knows when they'll feed us on the plane."

Tilly made her way over to the hot buffet. She felt like an imposter, as if she wasn't good enough to be there, and she politely spooned a small amount of rice and some interesting looking chicken dish onto a plate.

Making her way back to their seats, she balanced the plate on her knees and picked daintily at the food.

"I'm so glad we're going, Dad sounded really pleased when we phoned him, don't you think?"

Mimi drained her glass of Champagne and nodded. "Yep, he certainly did. We're doing the right thing flying over, and God knows I could do with the break."

Tilly stared at her sister. "Mims, this is not a flipping jolly, we're going to look after Mum. And Dad." She paused for a second. "Hold on a minute, I thought you were overly keen to book flights. Is that what this is really about? You just wanted a holiday?"

"No, of course not, don't be silly. I just meant

that it would be quite nice to worry about something other than the kids and Andrew and the boring day in, day out, you know what I mean."

"Hmmmm."

Tilly wasn't so sure. Her sister always seemed to have an ulterior motive when it came to things like this, and it certainly wouldn't be the first time she'd dressed something she wanted to do up as a good deed for others.

Mimi stood up and looked towards the bar area. "Do you want a top-up?"

Tilly shook her head. "No thanks, I haven't finished this one yet."

She watched as her sister sauntered over to the bar, wondering how they had ended up so different to each other. How could Mimi possibly feel justified in turning this trip into some sort of luxury break? Their lovely mum was in hospital for goodness' sake. Surely she wasn't thinking it was anything other than being a loving and supportive daughter?

Mimi sat back down on the leather seat and angled herself towards the window, Champagne glass in hand. "Here, take a picture of me on my phone please."

She handed her iPhone to Tilly and adopted her best *look at me relaxing in the club class lounge* face.

Duly snapping a photo, Tilly rolled her eyes and

handed the phone back to her sister, who promptly uploaded it to Facebook with a *"Cheeky glass of champers in the lounge – enroute to Miami"* comment for good measure.

THE FLIGHT WAS long, chilly, and a bit boring, but Tilly did manage to watch two whole films and eat rather a lot of aeroplane food, which she secretly quite liked. When they landed it was late afternoon in Miami, and by the time they'd collected their cases and found the hire car, Tilly was beginning to feel quite tired. The time difference was starting to hit her, but her sister had slept for most of the flight and only drunk water on the plane, so was happy to drive.

"Thank Mims, I'll have a nap and then I'll take over. How long is the journey?"

"Just under three hours. Don't worry, you sleep, I'll wake you up when I get tired."

Tilly gratefully accepted, and after she'd navigated them out of Miami airport and onto the main road heading west, she reclined her seat and was asleep in less than five minutes.

Two hours later she woke up to a dark America, and a remarkably empty three lane highway stretching before her.

"Oh my God, how long have I been asleep?"

"A while!" laughed Mimi. "Don't worry, it's

fine, we're nearly there and I feel OK. You can navigate the last bit and entertain me if you like, we should be there in just over half an hour."

BOB WAS STILL at the hospital when his daughters arrived. They'd arranged that he would wait for them until they got there so that they could see their mum briefly, then the three of them would go back to the villa for a shower and some sleep before they went back to hospital the following morning.

"Daddy, oh I've missed you so much, how are you?" asked Tilly, giving him a big hug and a kiss on the cheek.

"Oh, I'm OK, pootling along," he smiled, ever his cheery self. "Your mum's awake, I told her you were on your way."

"How is she, any change?"

"She's doing remarkably well actually! I will warn you though, her speech is still very slurred, but that's quite normal apparently so don't worry."

He hobbled a little as he led them through the pristine corridors to a private room, where the girls were surprised to see their mum sitting upright and looking quite normal.

"Mum!" Tilly practically ran to the bed to give her mum a hug, the relief causing her eyes to fill with tears again.

Bob pulled up a couple of chairs and he and

Mimi sat down whilst Tilly perched on the edge of the bed.

"How are you Mum, how are you feeling?"

Gloria smiled at her beautiful daughters and nodded her head.

"Myyyyy fluvely guuuurls," she said slowly, before rolling her eyes in exasperation and waving a hand at her face. "Saaaaweee."

"Oh Mummy, don't apologise, you've had an awful time, and you will get better, I know you will," said Tilly, stroking her mum's hand gently. She was shocked at how badly her speech had been affected, and she hoped she wasn't out of order thinking that, but regardless, in her view, positivity was the only way forward. Her mum was going to make a full recovery and that was that.

WHEN THEY FINALLY got back to the villa later that night, Tilly asked her dad what the doctor had said about her mum's prognosis. Apparently, the tests they'd done had confirmed that she had indeed had a small stroke, and had determined that the most likely cause was high blood pressure. As she had responded so well during the first 36 hours, the lovely young American doctor had stressed that although the first few days and weeks were the most critical, they would treat the blood pressure, and once they'd got the right level of medication, she would in all likelihood make a full recovery.

"So, did they say why she had a stroke? And could she have another one?" asked Mimi, who had been distracted by something on her phone, and had therefore not listened properly.

"Yes darling, they said it was a combination of age and high blood pressure, just one of those things that could happen to anyone at any time. It was nothing she'd done or anything like that. They gave her aspirin straight away and then some blood thinning medication so that she wouldn't have another one, which she'll keep taking to prevent any clots forming."

Mimi grimaced. "So will she have to take it forever?"

Bob nodded. "Probably yes. Most of our friends rattle as they walk these days, they take so many pills, it's just one of those things when you're as old as we are!" He laughed, patting his daughter on the arm. "Make the most of your lives whilst you're young girls, it goes by so quickly! Talking of which, how are my lovely grandchildren?"

Mimi showed him some photos on her phone that Andrew had sent. Oscar and Rosie had made some get well posters for their grandma and were proudly holding them up to the camera, big smiles all round. Mimi felt a bit sad when she looked at their little faces, so far away from her now. But they looked clean and happy and Andrew obviously had everything under control, which she was very grateful for. He had actually been amazing when she'd asked him what he thought about her flying to America and leaving the children at home. She'd expected some huffing and puffing and "My job is so important", but he hadn't hesitated in saying yes. She knew it was right to go, she wanted to, but although she'd never admit it, Tilly hadn't been that far off the mark when she'd suggested that she was keen to get away. The sisters hadn't had a chance to talk about things properly, but Mimi and Andrew had been doing a lot of talking over the past few weeks.

When the kids had gone back to school and normal post-Christmas day-to-day life had resumed, Mimi had taken the plunge and asked Andrew if they could have a chat one evening when the children were in bed. Over mugs of tea at the kitchen table they'd had a proper heart to heart, with Mimi being totally honest with him about how she was feeling. When she'd first started talking, she was wary of the can of worms she could be opening, but to her surprise Andrew had agreed with her, and admitted that he'd often felt the same, like their marriage had got lost under everything else that was going on. Tentatively Mimi had then raised the subject of her previous suspicions, and when he replied she was glad she'd been bold enough to ask.

The text she'd seen had been from one of the younger girls in the office who had – he admitted – been a bit flirty with him, but when his eyes filled up with tears as he related the story, she knew categorically that he was telling the truth.

Phoebe had joined the company a year and a half ago, as an Office Administrator. She was keen, hardworking, but fresh out of college and a little naïve. At a work night out not long after she'd joined, she'd got rather drunk, and when Andrew had found her feeling somewhat the worse for wear outside the ladies' loo, he had looked after her until one of the other girls from the office had taken her home.

The following day at work Phoebe had been profusely apologetic, although Andrew wasn't really bothered at all; he was more concerned that a young girl could end up so drunk at work drinks. He'd brushed it off, told her there was no problem at all, but from that day on Phoebe had put Andrew on a bit of a pedestal, making sure that any admin he needed doing was prioritised, ensuring he always had coffee, and smiling every time she saw him. She was so much younger than him that he had seen her as more of a daughter figure, but before he realised what was happening, she'd started occasionally messaging him, mainly on a Friday night when she had clearly had a bit too much to drink. Sometimes they were a random *Hello* but sometimes he'd just receive a notification that she'd deleted a WhatsApp she'd sent, never even knowing what had been written. He had saved her in his phone as P in case any of his colleagues had seen a message from "Phoebe" on his mobile – it was an unusual name and he didn't want to raise any unfounded suspicions, although looking back on it, this looked even more dodgy than it was. He didn't reply to any of her messages, although this never seemed to deter her, and by early summer it was happening so frequently that he'd had no choice but to talk to HR about what had been going on. He'd hated the feeling that he was "dobbing her in" but he knew what the workplace could be like these days, and had come to realise that in one fell swoop things could change very quickly indeed.

Shortly afterwards, Phoebe had quietly left the company to go and work for a luxury goods retailer, and Andrew had never heard from her again. There was no longer any issue, but the whole incident had been a little scary towards the end, and had put a considerable amount of stress on him whilst HR were investigating the situation.

Andrew had never been a good liar, so as she listened, Mimi knew he was telling the truth and that she had no reason not to take what he was saying at face value.

"Oh honey, why on earth didn't you tell me? It must've been terrifying! I do watch the news, I know what things can be like these days," she said, reaching across the table and taking his hand in hers.

"I don't know," he replied, "probably because at the beginning there was nothing to tell, and then when it got a bit more heated towards the end I didn't really know where to start."

She nodded, it wasn't really something you could drop into conversation over the kid's supper, and most evenings by the time they had any time to themselves one or other of them was nodding off on the sofa.

Continuing the conversation, which by now had turned into a full-on heart to heart, Mimi tentatively told Andrew how taken for granted she sometimes felt, and to her surprise he admitted that he'd felt exactly the same, working day in day out and feeling like all he was doing was providing for three people he barely spent any time with. It was liberating to talk so openly to each other, and rather than being the confrontational evening Mimi thought it might have been, they'd ended up in mutual appreciation of each other, talking like they had when they'd first met all those years ago. Andrew looked across at his beautiful wife, wondering why this conversation hadn't happened weeks or months before.

"Do you fancy a glass of wine?" he asked.

"What on a school night? You rebel. Go on

then, I think we deserve it after all that."

Andrew walked over to the wine rack, pulled out a nice bottle of red and collected two wine glasses.

"Come on, let's go and sit in the lounge."

They snuggled up on the sofa, flicked on the TV and watched an episode of Gogglebox with their wine, laughing and enjoying each other's company for the first time in ages.

And the following weekend, when they'd taken the kids down to the seaside for a blustery winter walk, they'd actually discussed moving down to the coast permanently, something they'd often thought about but never taken seriously. Andrew had the opportunity to work from home full time, so it was a realistic possibility. It would be a totally different lifestyle, but they'd all be together, and they'd have more time to do things as a family. Not having to commute would mean they could eat dinner together every night, and the kids would love growing up near the beach. It was a big decision, they both needed time to think about it before taking the plunge, and Mimi knew the time away from home would give her the headspace to think things through. And so, being in Florida put some distance between them at exactly the right time, giving them both some space to consider all options, and process the conversations that they'd had.

THE FOLLOWING MORNING Tilly and Mimi woke up bright and early, thanks to a combination of jet lag and the bright Florida sunshine filtering in through the bedroom shutters. Perching at the breakfast bar in their parent's vast kitchen, the two girls drank coffee whilst finally catching up on each other's lives. When their dad appeared, Mimi took charge and made them all scrambled eggs on toasted bagels, which they ate at the kitchen table with large glasses of freshly squeezed Florida orange juice.

As soon as they'd finished breakfast, they set off to the hospital, keen to spend as much time with their mum as possible. When they arrived, they were impressed to find that a speech therapist had been allocated to Gloria, and the sounds of long drawn out vowels greeted them as they entered the room.

"Good! Well done Gloria!" The therapist's beautiful America accent praised her efforts. "OK, so you know the exercises you need to do, just keep working on them and I have no doubt you will be speaking just as you were, in no time at all!" She smiled at them as she gathered her things and left the room, heels clicking on the shiny floor as she went.

"I am gooooo…. Goooing to beeee fiiiine," said Gloria, smiling at her family and patting the bed for someone to sit next to her. Tilly slipped into the spot she'd vacated the night before and gently tucked her mum's hair behind her ear.

"You look well this morning Mum, did you sleep OK?" she asked.

"Welllllllll…. It's not my own bed," she said slowly, "but it's oh kay."

The girls spent the rest of the morning chatting away, filling their mum in on events of the last few months, whilst Bob ensured they had enough coffee and snacks to keep them all happy. It was lovely having so much time to natter face to face with their parents. Often in a phone call the smaller, less important items fell to the wayside, so having the opportunity to talk about so much was an absolute treat.

"Ooooh," said Mimi. "Guess what Mum, Tilly's got a boyfriend!"

Gloria looked at Tilly, who gulped. She wouldn't ordinarily have talked about something so premature with her mum, but these were extraordinary circumstances, and plus her sister had well and truly dropped her in it now anyway, so she had no choice but to tell her mum (and dad, who was half listening, half reading a golf magazine in the corner) about Tariq.

Her mum listened with interest, and when she'd finished, Tilly waited for the usual negative comments to come. But for once, they didn't.

"He sounds niiiiice," she said, patting her

youngest daughter's hand. "I just want you to be haaaapppy," she nodded.

Tilly swallowed, feeling a little emotional about her mum's response. Something had clearly softened in her, which was a positive change so far as Tilly was concerned. Maybe the stroke had made her reassess things. She certainly appeared less snippy and judgemental than Tilly had experienced previously, which was definitely a good thing.

OVER THE NEXT few days the girls fell into a bit of a routine. They spent the morning at the hospital, then went back to the house for lunch and a swim, enjoying the time with their dad and each other. In the afternoon they'd return to the hospital for a few more hours with their mum, leaving before dinner was served. Tilly caught sight of the hospital food once, and was astonished to see that it looked absolutely delicious, nothing like the slop they served up back home. Sometimes they'd pop to the mall on the way back to do a bit of shopping for the kids, before heading back home via the Cheesecake Factory or Olive Garden for a bite to eat.

One evening, as Bob was watering his vegetable plot (a very British thing to do, Tilly thought), he asked the girls if they ever grew anything at home. Faced with shaking heads, he berated them.

"Oh you must! Look at these tomatoes. They

are so much tastier than anything you'd buy in a shop. Especially you Mimi, you should get out in the garden with the kids, give them some seeds and show them where their food comes from."

Mimi knew her dad was right, in fact she'd often thought about building some raised beds at the end of the garden for exactly that reason. It got her thinking about life at home, and that evening when she was laying in bed she contemplated the life she currently led and the discussion she'd had with Andrew before she came away. The reality was that being in America had made her able to step back and see things with a much clearer eye. She missed her house. She missed the kids – hugely – and to her surprise, she missed her husband. The distance between them had made her realise that they didn't need to move to the coast to be happy. They could stay exactly where they were. Moving would just be a sticking plaster.

If they stayed where they were, Andrew could still take the job working from home, it would mean that they'd have more time together if he didn't have hours of commuting either end of his working day. She smiled. They could even have lunch together, every day. They simply needed to get back to being the people they were before their lives got lost in a sea of parenting, school runs, work, and the relentless monotony of family life.

As she leant to turn the bedside lamp off, Mimi

knocked the novel she'd been reading onto the floor. Reaching to pick it up, she smiled at the pretty bookmark that the lady in her local bookshop had given her. She'd been so friendly, and whilst they'd chatted Mimi couldn't help but notice the "Part Time Staff Wanted" sign on the wall behind her. Thinking about it properly for the first time since, Mimi wondered if she should apply for the vacancy. Working a couple of days a week in a bookshop would be great fun. Enjoyable, sociable, probably pretty stress free, and it would certainly give a bit of structure to her day. She didn't want to go back to working full time, and she'd given up trying to climb the career ladder when she'd had her children. Mimi's main purpose in life now as a mum was to be there for Oscar and Rosie whenever they needed her. It wasn't just a need, she *wanted* to be there for them. To make their lunches, to do the school runs, to be there if they felt poorly during the day. She hadn't given birth to two children simply to give them to someone else to look after, that was for sure. But a little part time job would suit her down to the ground. It wasn't as if they needed the money, Andrew more than provided for all four of them, but a bit of pin money – her own earnings – would be very satisfying indeed.

Closing her eyes, Mimi imagined being back in her own bed. She missed her family. Missed the life she'd previously thought of as boring. It wasn't boring at all, she'd just got stuck in a rut. When she'd phoned home earlier Andrew had told her that the past few days had made him realise how much she did.

"I'm exhausted," he'd laughed. "Come home!" He was only teasing, she knew that. He'd also told her how much he was enjoying being with the kids, and she knew that they were having a great time with their daddy, but it was good that he could finally get to see first hand what her daily life consisted of.

ON THEIR FIFTH day in Florida, Gloria was discharged from hospital, to their surprise but great relief. She'd been sent home with a very comprehensive care plan and a follow up appointment with the same doctor who had looked after her. There were strict instructions to eat healthily, to have less salt in her diet, to drink less alcohol (much to her dismay), and to keep active and check her blood pressure regularly. Her doctor had said that any memory problems, confusion, or visual difficulties would gradually improve, and in fact her speech was getting better already.

It was wonderful to have their mum back at home in the villa, and Bob cooked them a special dinner that evening, whilst the girls attended to

Gloria's every need. It felt very special to be together as a foursome, just like the old days.

"You should come out to see us more," said Bob.

Gloria nodded in agreement. "Bring the chiiillldren," she smiled.

Tilly and Mimi had both been thinking exactly that. It had been so nice to see their parents, it was crazy that it had taken a dramatic event to get them over there. America wasn't *that* far away, plus the weather was so much better than at home! It had crossed both their minds that it most certainly wouldn't be so long before they were over there again. Mimi wanted her children to spend time with their grandparents too, and not just be a face on a screen. Plus, if this week had taught her anything, it was that you never knew what was around the corner. Life was there to be lived, enjoyed, not postponed for another day.

And family was so important. Your family were the people who knew you better than anyone. Who had been there through thick and thin. Tilly knew she was lucky having such a lovely mum, dad, and sister; not everyone had it as good, and she knew now that she wanted to make the most of her time by seeing them as often as she possibly could.

When Tilly went to bed that night she found a

text message on her phone from Tariq, asking how her mum was. He was so thoughtful – he'd messaged her occasionally but left her alone enough to enjoy the time with her family. It was the perfect amount of contact, and if she didn't reply straight away he left her in peace. There were certain people in her not too distant memory who actually would've got quite cross with her for not replying sooner. And although she was having a lovely time in Florida, it was nice to know that she had something – *someone* – to go home to.

All too soon it was time to pack their cases and head home, but the girls were so glad that they'd made the trip, and pleased beyond words that their mum was OK. Gloria and Bob had absolutely adored having their children to visit, and were quite sad to see them leave.

"Make sure you come baaa…. back soon," said Gloria. "Maybe you could even bring that nice boy…. boyfriend with you!" she smiled, a twinkle in her eye.

Tilly smiled. She liked this new version of her mum. It might've taken a crisis to get them together, but she felt like it had changed her mum's attitude. Gone were the comments about why she wasn't married, as if she needed a man to make her complete. She may have teased her about bringing Tariq to Florida, but Tilly knew one hundred percent that it was out of pure love for her daughter, just the way she was. No expectations, just a welcome to anyone Tilly might want to spend her time with. Her mum hadn't said a bad word to her all week, she'd just been lovely the whole time they'd been there. Which made it all the harder to leave.

When they arrived at the airport, and took their bags to the check in desk, the girls were stunned to find that Andrew had upgraded their seats on the journey home. Tilly couldn't hide her excitement when the check in lady handed them their boarding passes, although Mimi just looked relieved.

"Thank God for that," she laughed, "I don't think I could stomach a night flight in economy."

"You're such a snob," teased Tilly, thrilled at the thought of a flat bed home, and liking her brother-in-law even more than she did already.

A few glasses of Champagne (this time safe in the knowledge that their mum was OK), a four-course meal and a seat that reclined to a fully horizontal position definitely made the trip back to cold rainy England a whole lot easier. And of course, Mimi posted several photos of her return journey on her social media.

Chapter 29
March

LONDON WAS COLD. Compared to Florida it was practically Baltic. Tilly pulled her scarf more tightly around her neck and hunched her shoulders against the icy wind that was blowing down High Holborn. Shivering despite her wool coat, she wondered how her trip to America seemed like a distant memory, even though she had only been back a few weeks.

"Tilly!"

She turned, looking for where the voice was coming from, and saw Karen walking as quickly as her smart boots would let her on the frozen pavement.

"Hello my lovely, you OK?"

"No, I'm frozen! It's March for goodness' sake, it's supposed to be spring isn't it?!"

Tilly laughed, and they chatted as they made their way to Gianni's for frothy hot coffees and maybe a cheeky pastry, just because.

As they stood in the queue Tilly noticed that

Karen was smiling in a way that wasn't normal for half past eight on a weekday morning. She frowned at her friend.

"Why are you smiling like that? It's your first day back after leave, you're supposed to be grumpy."

Karen looked at her, grinning again and biting her lip.

"Alan and I are moving in together. We've found a really nice flat and we're going to take it."

Tilly's eyes opened wide. "Oh my God! That's so exciting! Where is it?"

"Not a million miles from you actually, Oxted. It's on the main trainline into London, seems like a really nice town."

"Yes, it is, oh wow. I'm so happy for you both!"

"Thank you. Anyway, enough about me, how was Florida, how's your mum?"

Tilly summarised her trip as they walked to the office. There was so much to catch up on and the five minute walk wasn't nearly enough time to fill her in on everything. It would be great if Karen moved nearer to her, they could actually socialise like normal people, without having to plan their evening around train times out of London.

"You'll have to come round when we get the keys – hey, how's it going with Tariq, is he still on the scene?"

Tilly nodded, a smile on her face.

"Well then, you'll both have to come round for dinner. Ooooh how civilised. A dinner party for four."

Tilly grinned. She liked the sound of that very much. Being a couple made her feel part of something much bigger than just her own life. It was nice. Normal. She and Tariq had seen each other a lot since she'd got back from Florida, and sort of naturally settled into a pattern of getting together once or twice a week for supper at each other's houses, and then going out properly at the weekend. Things seemed to be developing comfortably between them, no pressure, no rush, just a mutual understanding that what they had was very good, and very right. Tilly felt like she'd known him forever, but at the same time was loving hearing more about his life each time they talked. His family sounded so lovely, she just hoped they liked her as much as she liked Tariq.

And as her best friends and sister had all met him at the party, they all knew who he was, what he did, where he lived, and what he looked like, so there was no big announcement to make or public parading of the "new boyfriend." He just seamlessly fitted into their conversations and invites as if he had been in Tilly's life forever.

TARIQ WAS EQUALLY smitten with Tilly. He had missed her so much whilst she was in America, but had refrained from messaging her too often in case he looked like some sort of lovesick schoolboy. He'd surprised himself how easily they had slotted into each other's lives, how well they got on, and how natural it was being intertwined with someone else's daily life after having been single for so long. It had felt surreally familiar just popping round to Tilly's house, which should've felt strange after having spent years walking past her front door. But the weirdest thing was that it just felt so *normal* being with Tilly. He couldn't explain it, but when he tried to tell his mother how he felt, she just smiled, nodded, and patted her beloved son on the arm.

"You'll see *beta*. All is good, do not worry."

And that was, for now at least, all she had to say on the subject. Tariq was a little flummoxed. He was thinking crazy thoughts about a girl he'd only known for a few months, and the one time he would've actually welcomed his mother's advice she was barely saying a word.

His sister, however, was more forthcoming on the matter. He had met up with Tanvi the previous weekend, keen to share his innermost feelings with the person who knew him better than anyone, but to his surprise she had been quite stern with him.

"Right, listen bro. You absolutely must not say

any of what you've just said to me, to Tilly. She'll run a mile. I agree with you though, she does sound really lovely, but if you come over all lovey dovey too early on in the day you'll ruin everything."

"Ah but she's perfect Tan, she's the kindest, sweetest, prettiest girl I've ever met, and I can't believe she's been over the road from me the whole time. You wouldn't believe the crazy things I've thought, it's madness!"

Tanvi smiled at her brother. He had it bad, she could see that, but he was a little bit naive where romantic relationships were concerned, and she didn't want him going in all guns blazing and scaring away the person who'd made him shine in a way that she hadn't seen before.

Tariq knew that Tanvi was right – to be fair his sister was always right when it came to matters of the heart. How did girls do that? It was mind boggling to him. What she'd said was so frustrating, but the truth was that he really didn't want to mess this up. For the first time in his life, he understood what people said when they talked about "The One." Tariq wanted things with Tilly to go all the way. As preposterous as it sounded to a man who did everything by the book, followed the letter of the law and dealt with black and white facts and guarantees, he already knew without a shadow of a doubt that he wanted to spend the rest of his life with Tilly Jenkins.

Chapter 30
April

THE FIRST FRIDAY of every month was earmarked in Tilly, Jemima and Becky's diaries for drinks and a catch up whenever possible, although Becky had blown them out this month as she was somewhat preoccupied with the imminent arrival of baby Daisy, and all the prep that that entailed. She was sad to miss out on their girly catch up, especially as it was likely to be the last one in a while for her, but happy events had spiralled, time seemed to have sped up, and there was still so much she had to do.

It had only been eight weeks since Becky had received the phone call from the adoption agency, but it was as if her world had flipped upside down and back again in that time. After the initial meeting with Sandra and Heidi there had been radio silence for what had felt like an eternity, during which they couldn't even talk about what was potentially in the pipeline with anyone, for fear of confidentiality breaches.

And then suddenly everything had happened at once – the panel approved the match in principle, and Sandra sent a load of photos and videos to Becky and Rupert, showing Daisy in her foster parent's home. She was by all accounts thriving, but was still in need of a permanent home and a new mummy and daddy.

Before they knew it, Becky and Rupert were on their way to see Daisy in real life, an arranged meeting on neutral ground with her foster parents and the adoption agency. As Daisy was gently placed in her arms for the very first time, Becky felt a rush of love so strong that it was visceral.

"Hello baby," she said softly, looking down into Daisy's huge eyes. Her own eyes filled with tears as the little girl gazed back at the stranger above her, a tiny smile quivering through her rosebud pink lips. Any fears that Becky had had about not bonding with her instantly evaporated, and she barely felt Rupert's arm slip around her shoulder as he joined the tender scene.

Leaving her there an hour later was harder than anything they'd been through so far. If Becky had had her way, she would've bundled Daisy into the car and driven her home there and then, but they still had to have a meeting with Delilah present too, and all the rest of the placement plan stages needed to be signed off before that could happen.

But happen it did – all the ticks were in the right

boxes and the paperwork had been signed, and now Becky was up to her eyeballs with shopping and decorating before Daisy finally came to live with them permaunently.

JEMIMA, DESPITE BEING much less of a drinker than she had been previously, was adamant that she and Tilly should still get together, even if Becky couldn't make it.

"Absolutely babes, we need our catch up! Plus I have some news…" she'd teased.

So after switching off her computer for the last time that week, Tilly headed to one of their favourite haunts, ordered a lovely bottle of Malbec, and secured a plush velvet booth for them both, whilst she waited for Jemima to arrive. Pulling her phone from her bag, she popped a quick text to Tariq, who was working late on an important legal case. If their evenings finished at similar times they could get the train home together, which Tilly loved. Chatting to your gorgeous boyfriend on the way home was way better than staring out of the window or aimlessly scrolling through Facebook staring at other people's pointless posts.

The door opened and several heads turned as Jemima made her grand entrance. Tilly smiled to herself. Jems could never just enter a building. There was always a gush of wind, a flurry of excitement, or a crash of a door when Jemima walked into any room. She just seemed to announce herself without even trying.

"Darling, I'm so sorry I'm late, I had a huge delivery of the most divine Pooky lamps, and they kept me waiting, bloody London traffic, you know how it is!"

She shimmied her way into the booth and Tilly poured her a glass of wine.

"Oooh lovely, thank you darling. The weekend starts here, right?"

They chinked glasses and Jemima took a sip of her wine before waving at the waiter to attract his attention. "I'm starving babes, no time for lunch, do you want something to eat?"

"No, I'm OK at the moment, but you go ahead."

"Oh help me with a camembert will you? I don't want to eat a whole one myself."

"Oh, go on then," she laughed, smiling at the waiter. "One camembert please."

"And extra bread as well please, and some of that lovely plummy dip you do, thank you." Jemima fluttered her eyelashes at him before he walked away, even though she was probably almost twice his age.

"So, come on then, I'm dying to know, what's your news?" Tilly asked once he'd gone.

Jemima looked at her friend, a grin spreading

across her face.

"I'm keeping the house!"

"What? How come? I didn't even think that was an option!"

"I know! Hugo has agreed – offered – to let me keep the house if I can take on the mortgage myself."

"Wow, that's amazing! Can you afford it?"

"Just about yeah, I'll have to work bloody hard but it's do-able."

"And what about Hugo? Where will he live?"

"Well, he's going to rent somewhere initially, with a view to buying something at some point. Obviously we both put money down as a deposit on our house, so I'm raiding the last of my savings and giving him some cash so that he has something to go towards whatever he buys."

"Oh Jems, I'm so pleased for you, that's brilliant. Well done, honey."

"I know, I'm so relieved. I was trying to convince myself that I'd be OK, but I love my house, and it would've been so much hassle moving. I think he feels a bit guilty to be honest, but… whatever."

By the time they'd finished the wine, and devoured every morsel of camembert, it was nearly eight o'clock, and even without Becky being there, they'd managed to put the world to rights. Tilly pinged a text to Tariq to see how he was getting on, in the hope that he'd be nearly finished, and to her delight he replied straight away to let her know that he was just packing up.

The girls walked to the tube station together and said their farewells. Tilly hugged her friend close.

"I'm so glad things are working out for you, you deserve to be happy after everything that's happened."

"Thanks babe, you too. Give that gorgeous Tariq a kiss from me and tell him I'll see you both very soon. Come for supper one evening, I'd love that."

As they went their own separate ways, Tilly thought about how lucky she was to have such a lovely friend. They'd known each other for so long, been through thick and thin together, and Bex too, and never in all of those years had any of them had a single argument.

When she arrived at Charing Cross, Tariq was waiting for her at the top of the tube station stairs. As he greeted her with a kiss, a warm glow spread throughout her chest. Here she was, her working week done, having had a lovely evening with one of her best friends (and some very fine cheese), and was now being greeted by her extremely handsome boyfriend to join her on their journey home. What a difference a year made. She thought back to last April, when Ethan had come back into her life. The two men could not be more different, and she silently thanked her lucky stars that things had worked out the way that they had.

Tariq switched his briefcase to the other side and took Tilly's hand in his. He smiled as he led her through the Friday night throng, glad it was the weekend and that he'd managed to get everything finished in time to take the train home with Tilly. He'd been psyching himself up all week to ask if she'd like to meet his mum, and thought it might seem less of a big deal if he happened to drop it into conversation somewhere casual. Like on a train. It was about time Tilly met his family – there were lots of big family events looming over the coming months, and he wanted his beautiful, kind, and clever girlfriend to accompany him to every single one.

Chapter 31

Three months later

Tilly stood back from the mirror and gave herself a once over. The dress was perfect, pretty yet sensible, exactly what she'd wanted for the day's ceremony. Slipping into her heels, she gathered the last few items together and pushed them into her overnight bag. Make up, change of clothes, toiletries. The flowers were downstairs in the kitchen keeping fresh in a large bucket of water. Holding onto the handrail as she made her way slowly downstairs, she felt a shiver of anticipation. Today had been a long time coming.

She left her bag in the hallway and picked up her mobile to text the girls.

Can't wait to see you! Such an exciting day!

The sun was shining already, and the weather forecast was glorious. July had been such a good month so far that Tilly had feared every day that the weather would break and today would be a washout. But no, this time the Gods were smiling on them. Glancing at her watch, she realised that she was ready way too early, which was not really surprising considering how important it was to be on time today. A frisson of excitement made her shudder, and she thought back to the last time they'd had such a momentous gathering. Her party, seven months ago. It had been brilliant. Nothing like what she'd imagined, but brilliant nonetheless. For a start she probably wouldn't even have Tariq in her life if she hadn't bitten the bullet and sent that initial Facebook message to all 289 of her "friends." She often thought that getting together with Tariq was the best thing that had come out of her crazy party idea. And the friendships she'd had a year ago had deepened and stretched to accompany each other. She smiled at the thought of how Karen and Alan had become such a regular part of her day to day life, and integrated with her oldest friends. Since they'd moved to Oxted they had all seen so much more of each other, so much so that Karen and Alan would be part of the congregation today. In fact every single person who'd been at Tilly's party would be there today, in somewhat warmer, brighter, and more celebratory circumstances.

Her phone pinged, and she picked it up to see a message from her sister.

Sorry, traffic rubbish, be with you in 10 mins x

Mimi and Andrew were coming to her house first, so that they could all go to the church together. Oscar and Rosie had insisted on going in the same car as Auntie Tilly, which Tilly had thought was really rather adorable.

Since Andrew had changed jobs, things had resolved themselves so far as her sister's life was concerned, much to Mimi – and Tilly's – relief. It was almost as if they'd needed a crisis in order to put themselves back together as a couple again. And since Mimi had started working part time at the bookshop, she seemed to have attained another level of contentedness. It didn't pay her anywhere near as much as she'd been earning before she'd had children, but the job satisfaction she got from the few hours a week that she worked there was immense. She'd got to know the store's regular customers, received a fabulous discount on books, and took great pride in recommending novels to people who asked for her advice.

There was a knock on the door and Tilly opened it to a sea of smiling faces.

"Oh my gosh, you look amazing!" cried Mimi.

Tilly smiled back gratefully and looked down at her niece and nephew, who were wearing their finest clothes and had very neat hair indeed.

"And look at you two, in fact look at all of you, what a gorgeous family! Come in, come in!"

The house was instantly filled with laughter and

love, and as they all admired each other's outfits, excitement for the day ahead practically bubbled out of them. Rosie was wearing a beautiful new dress with several layers of pink tulle in the skirt, and was spinning round and round in the kitchen until Mimi stopped her before she either fell over or threw up.

A knock on the door heralded the arrival of the last member of the group. Tilly went to answer it and grinned broadly when she saw Tariq, who was looking even more handsome than ever in his smart suit, standing on the doorstep.

"Good morning, Miss Jenkins," he smiled. "Are you ready for your big day?!"

FORTY FIVE MINUTES later they arrived at the church of St Peter and St Paul for the christening of Daisy Tabitha Rose. Becky and Rupert looked resplendent in their parental finery, and Tilly felt every inch the proud godmother that she was about to become.

As she and Jemima made their promises to God to pray for Daisy, to lead by example, and walk with her in the way of Christ, Tilly glanced at Tariq, who was smiling at her from his front row pew. She'd never been in a church with him before and for some reason it made her blush whenever she looked at him. Luckily the vicar leant forward at that exact moment to take Daisy from her mother's arms, to bless her and welcome the little girl into the house of God, so only Tilly noticed her cheeks flushing.

After the ceremony they all made their way back to Becky and Rupert's house, where a wonderful post Christening afternoon tea was waiting for them. Delilah was in serious big sister mode, making sure that little Daisy was OK and ensuring that she was also in every single photograph that was taken of the latest addition to the family. Becky was radiant and seemingly unphased by how many people were in her house, whilst Rupert was the perfect host, topping up glasses and entertaining the kids whenever necessary. It was a glorious day, and one which, just a few months ago, they would not even have imagined possible.

"You OK?" asked Tilly, when she finally got Becky on her own for a minute. "You literally haven't stopped all day."

Becky smiled.

"I'm fine, in fact, I've never been better, this is what I've always dreamt of! I can't believe my little family is complete," she said, her eyes welling up.

Tilly gave her friend a hug.

"I'm so happy for you hun, and thank you again for asking me to be her Godmother, I'm honoured. I'll try to be a good example, I promise."

"Oh, you'll always be a good example," said Becky. "It's the other one I'm worried about!" She winked over her shoulder as Jemima walked towards them.

"Alright you two, stop having a gossip without me present," she laughed, waggling her fingers at them. "What are you talking about?"

"You, of course, as always," laughed Tilly. "What have you done with Hugo, is he OK?"

"Yeah, he's alright, he and Alan are debating the merits of some new electric car or something, I don't know, sounded very boring to me!"

Tilly looked over to where the two men were standing, wondering if Karen needed rescuing, before noticing that she was helping Mimi supervise some colouring in with the children. She looked very content, and Tilly wondered how long it would be before Karen and Alan had a baby of their own. Not long if the smile on Karen's face when she'd held Daisy earlier was anything to go by.

Tilly loved that her nearest and dearest had all become part of each other's lives. As she looked around her she realised again that her crazy idea had not been so crazy after all. Her party had cemented the friendships that were so special to her, and created new ones too. The secrets that had come out that night had all done so for a reason, and an evening without electricity, technology, light and heat, had in fact been one of the best evenings of her life. They may not have captured it to post pictures online, but the reality was that it had been so much more fun than anything she'd ever posted on Facebook.

It just went to prove that what you see online isn't always what it appears to be. Real life was so much better than the picture painted. Tilly made a mental note to at least contemplate deleting her social media apps from her phone, realising that she didn't need them to be so accessible. She wanted to live her life in real time, not look at a version of it from a jaunty angle. Everything she needed was here, in her best friend's garden, in her day to day life, no online boasting required.

She thought back to the To Do list that she'd made at the start of last year, the list of things she'd desperately wanted in her life. The golf lessons and sailing club hadn't happened, but she'd been bold, and had held her party despite people's reservations. And so yes, she had sort of had a house full of people, because she now knew that it was quality over quantity every time. And the one time she wasn't actively looking for a boyfriend, he had just appeared, right under her nose. Those wasted hours spent on dating apps had been pointless. Tariq had been there all along, and if she'd looked around her as she walked along the street rather than staring down at her phone, she might well have noticed him properly before.

She'd also put her demons to bed by finally seeing that Ethan wasn't the one for her, and had been able to move on with her life. Being with a man who loved her exactly as she was had made her realise how wrong her relationship with Ethan had been.

Although she hated to admit it, her mum had sort of been right all along about certain areas of her life. And Tilly may have wondered in the past why her parents had disappeared off to Florida, but now she could see exactly why they did. They had a wonderful life out there, with their rounds of golf and their many friends, and since the stroke those friends had rallied round and been there for Gloria and Bob on a daily basis. Luckily her mum had completely recovered from the stroke, aided no doubt by the wonderful Florida sunshine. Good for them, Tilly thought, they really were living their best lives.

That's all they needed, all anybody needed. To live life to the full, to grab it with both hands, and to see things for what they really were. To enjoy the moment, to be in the present, and to live it in real time, not through a phone screen or a social media account.

And standing in her best friend's garden on a sunny summer's day, Tilly Jenkins realised that she was finally doing exactly that.

Living her best life, in real life, with the people who mattered the most.

Her true friends.

THE END.

ACKNOWLEDGEMENTS

I would like to thank a few inspiring women who have taught me the joy of writing over the years; Hélène Cohen, Adrienne Dines, and my fellow writers at Brooklands and Curtis Brown Creative.

Thank you to my dear family and friends who have always believed in my dream to publish a book. To my amazing parents – Mum for being my first reader, and Dad for helping to fill my library shelves! To my lovely sister Tash for never failing to envisage my novels out there in the big wide world. To Milly O'Ryan-Bristow, who never ever doubted that this would happen. Thank you to Zoë Folbigg for sharing the snowflake method and for giving me the motivation to keep going! Enormous thanks to Gabi Mills, Julia Richardson and Phil Hall for all your advice. Thank you to Sarah Mudd for Alan. And apologies to my very dear friends Mark Bryant, Sarah Lewis, Sarah HA and Gaynor Mullen for having to listen to me harp on about "my book" for so many years. Thank you for always being there for me!

And finally to my incredible son Charlie, for believing in me from day one, and for being so patient and understanding every time I said, "Not now darling, Mummy's writing." Charlie, you never stop amazing me – I am so proud of you, and I love you to the moon and back.

www.joclynes.com
www.289friends.com

Printed in Great Britain
by Amazon